ROYAL
DATE

ALSO BY SARIAH WILSON

The Ugly Stepsister Strikes Back

The Royals of Monterra Series

Royal Chase

Royal Games

ROYAL DATE

SARIAH WILSON

FIRE & ICE BOOKS

For Charity, because she loves Nico and Kat as much as I do, and because she's the mom of my favorite real-life twins.

Chapter 1

"A little light reading?" His accent was faint, and I couldn't quite place it. Italian-ish. But I didn't care enough to ask. I felt him standing next to my stuffed armchair, hovering, and sighed. What was it with European men? American guys didn't give me the time of day. But over here I was like some kind of dude catnip.

I didn't take my eyes off of my book. "Sorry, not interested."

He moved away from me, sitting in an armchair next to mine. Well, I suppose this was what I got for hanging out in the lodge's lobby. I should have stayed in my room until my best friend, Lemon, was ready to leave.

"You're not interested in Shakespeare?" he asked. I could hear the amusement in his voice.

"I'm not interested in you."

"Why not?" This guy just could not take a hint. I turned to look at him, ready to tell him off, and nearly choked.

Gorgeous was an understatement. Tall, athletic, high cheekbones, black hair, and blue eyes. Like Superman's hotter Italian cousin. He was dressed for a day of skiing—a black turtleneck with an unzipped royal-blue winter coat. And he topped it off with a smile, a blinding, unbelievable smile that nearly did me in.

He leaned in conspiratorially, and I got a whiff of his cologne. He smelled as good as he looked. His glacier-blue eyes were full of intensity and fun, and I wanted to sit and stare into them all day. "I've been told I'm very charming."

I didn't doubt it. I would never have admitted it out loud, but I was very charmed. Like I was the snake and he was playing a hypnotizing tune that only I could hear.

And I didn't like the way that made me feel.

Plus, I had to consider reality in this situation. No way could this guy really be hitting on me. He probably dated supermodels and I . . . didn't date at all. Like, ever. He was so out of my league.

I'd never been so tongue-tied before. I was typically handy with the quips and comebacks. But I couldn't respond. I had to look away from him and back at my book. The words on the page swam around in front of me, and I was unable to focus on a single one. I needed him to leave so I could regain my equilibrium. "Nothing personal. Italian men don't do it for me."

I was the lyingest liar who ever lied.

"How fortunate for me then that I am Monterran." He had a deep, rumbly, smooth voice that felt like honey and laughter mixed together. I wasn't immune, and he hadn't been kidding. He really was disgustingly charming.

My mouth twitched, wanting to smile. I turned a page, pretending to be entranced. I was on Christmas break, I reminded myself. I was here in Monterra to ski with Lemon. It was the last time we would be together before getting our master's degrees in a few months. I had priorities and plans, and SuperHottie was not on the list.

And if I were being truly honest—he kind of scared me. A guy like that would have expectations, and I wasn't like other girls.

"I'm Nico, by the way."

"That's nice for you."

But he again failed to parse out the subtext here (and I wasn't being very subtextual). Short of blatantly telling him to get lost, what else could I do? Would I have to be rude? Because instead of realizing that I was a lost cause, he laughed. He laughed and it did funny things to my insides. I wanted to laugh with him. And crawl into his lap and beg him to be mine.

"And you are?" he prompted.

"Still not interested." It was becoming a bigger lie as time passed. If some other guy had pursued me this way, I would have thought it was creepy and called for security to have him escorted off the mountain. Instead, I secretly hoped he would keep talking to me.

I thought he'd finally gotten the message as an entire minute of silence passed between us before he reached over to look at my book's spine to see the title. I gulped in response—his hands were large and masculine, and I wondered how his long fingers would feel interlaced with mine.

I shook my head and let out a shaky breath. I had gone seriously crazy. Like jumping-on-Oprah's-couch crazy.

"*Macbeth*? I would have guessed *Romeo and Juliet*."

I couldn't help myself. I had to look at him. "Two fifteen-year-olds who kill themselves in the name of love after only knowing each other for three days? No thanks."

That smile. He was killing me. "You don't find it romantic?"

"I don't find anything romantic about suicide."

"You don't think love at first sight is romantic?" he persisted.

I'd never believed such a thing possible before this moment, but now I was sort of getting where Romeo had been coming from. Nico was literally the most handsome man I'd ever met in real life. If anyone could convince me to believe in love at first sight, he was the guy.

"Nope," I finally managed. He smiled like he didn't believe me.

"*Nico! Andiamo!*"

Nico looked over his shoulder at a group of guys who were waving and calling out to him. He shouted something back to them, and they headed out the door, hooting and hollering as they went.

He stood up. He was taller than I'd first thought. Yummy tall. Way taller than me tall, and that wasn't easy to find. "How long will you be in Monterra?"

It was such a personal question my gut reaction was to tell him to mind his own business, but to my surprise, I found myself saying, "For the next couple of weeks."

"May I see your phone?"

I didn't actually own a cell phone. I could barely afford food.

"No phone, and I'm not phone adjacent."

Nico smiled again, and I wanted to melt into my chair. He reached inside his coat, pulled out a small white business card, and handed it to me. "If you do ever find yourself adjacent to a phone while you're here, please call. I would love to take you to dinner before you leave."

When I reached out he took my hand and turned it over, leaning down to kiss my knuckles. A lightning arc exploded inside my hand and zoomed around my entire body, all the way down to my toenails. I might have gasped, but I decided to pretend that I would never do something so lame.

He straightened back up to put the card in my shaking hand, closing my fingers around it. "I look forward to your call," he said as he walked backward toward the exit. "*Ciao, bella.*"

He left and it took my eyes a second to adjust. Like I'd been staring at the sun and now had third-degree burns on my retinas. Who did that? Who just kissed people's hands like that? This wasn't the fifteenth century. So weird. And exciting. But weird.

The business card was white and thick. Obviously expensive. There was only a series of numbers, presumably his telephone number. I flipped the card over. Blank. Who had a card without a name on it? Just their phone number?

I'd tell you who. A guy who kissed your hand.

I closed my book and put it on the coffee table in front of me. I looked at the card again, turning it over a couple of times as I considered my decision.

I didn't need this while I was here. And I couldn't let Lemon see it or she'd hogtie me and force me to call him. I was here to relax, forget about my school troubles, and enjoy time with my best friend. Boys were not part of the equation.

A massive fire burned in the fireplace across the room. Decision made, I walked over and before I could change my mind, threw the card into the fire.

And informed myself that I absolutely, totally and completely did *not* regret it.

Lemon's "five more minutes" turned out to be "more than an hour." She came down, all smiles and sorries, in her bright pink snowsuit. "Come on, Kat, darlin'! Let's go!" she said in her sweet Southern twang.

I smiled back. She'd been my best friend since our freshman year when we were assigned to be roommates in our dorm. The computer couldn't have matched up a more polar opposite pair than us. Lemon Beauchamp was from a premiere (read: way wealthy) family in Atlanta, Georgia. She was like a tiny, modern-day Marilyn Monroe—platinum blonde, bright red lips, curves for miles.

I was from a not-so-great family in a trailer park in Colorado (read: way poor) and was tall, usually wore no makeup, and had dark brown hair. Lemon kept encouraging me to call it auburn, but it was definitely brown (with maybe a little hint of red when I went out into the sun).

She kept up a giddy, totally one-sided conversation as we gathered up our skis (hers: top-of-the-line; mine: rented), helmets, and poles. We stepped outside and the light nearly blinded me. I put my sunglasses on and shaded my eyes with my hand to look straight up at the Alps. I thought the Rocky Mountains back home were huge, but these were massive. Impressive. Majestic.

"I am so excited!" Lemon kept saying throughout her monologue. I didn't know if anyone else on the planet loved to ski as much as she did. Lemon had come to Brighton University, our small liberal arts college, solely because of the skiing. She spent every winter weekend on the mountain. In fact, after freshman year Lemon continued living with me in a small apartment off campus instead of the condo her parents thought she rented. She used the extra money to fund her skiing habit.

I, on the other hand, had only gone skiing once about twelve years ago for a class trip in sixth grade. I remembered our group lesson, and it turned out I had exceptional balancing skills, as I was the only one to not fall forty times in the first ten minutes.

So when Lemon begged me to spend Christmas with her, offering to foot the entire bill for us to ski in some foreign country I'd never even heard of, I had to say yes. I hated that she had to pay for it, and when I offered to reimburse her, she got offended and said it was her Christmas gift to me. Her parents were off celebrating their thirtieth wedding anniversary on a cruise in the Caribbean, and Lemon did not want to be alone. How could I say no?

I really had tried to refuse at first, but then Lemon went and got her mother involved. Sue Ellen Beauchamp wasn't the discussion type. She was the sending-down-tablets-of-stone type. Which quickly settled everything. Lemon and I were going to Monterra, and neither Beauchamp woman would hear another word about it.

Since it had been a while since I'd last skied, Lemon suggested another class. I wasn't interested. It was just like riding a bike, right? I would remember. Besides, I had planned on spending most of my time reading and hanging out at the spa. But I'd promised Lemon I would spend at least one day skiing with her, and today was the day.

I saw Nico and his friends standing in line at a ski lift for an intermediate run. He didn't notice me, and a small part of me was glad for the chance to watch him one last time as he joked around with his five friends. My heart did a funny little flip as he moved into position to take the lift. I felt a tinge of sadness that I would never see him again.

We got to our ski lift and the operators stopped me. Turned out I had forgotten to attach my lift ticket to my zipper.

Lemon looked thoroughly disappointed, watching the lift climb up the mountain. "You go on ahead, I'll catch up."

"Are you sure?"

"I'm sure. I'll just find you up at the top." Most ski resorts had their bunny slopes next to the lodge at the bottom of the mountain. Lemon had explained that some, like this one, had the easier slopes up higher.

I trudged back to our room in my puffy red rented ski outfit, located my ticket, and got back to the lift as quickly as I could. Which wasn't very fast, as my coat and pants made me waddle like a stuffed, drunk duck. When I got back outside I snapped my helmet on and struggled with getting my shoes into the ski bindings, but I finally managed it.

Standing in front of the lift, I said a quick prayer that it wouldn't knock me over. It stole my breath away as it came up behind me, scooping me up and forcing me to sit down. But I enjoyed the slow trip up the mountain. The sun was high and bright, the air clean and crisp. So much beautiful white snow, sparkling all over like a field of scattered diamonds. I inhaled the cold air deeply and grinned. I had always loved winter, the way ugly things became beautiful when they were covered in white.

Thankfully, I didn't fall when I jumped off the lift. I used my poles to propel myself forward, walking at the top of the run to see if I could spot Lemon. The slope was covered with people enjoying the day—mostly families.

Farther down I saw Lemon's bright pink outfit. I tried calling out to her and waving, but she was too far away to hear me. I pushed out onto the slope after her.

It was a gentle downgrade, and I watched the delighted children who giggled and yelled as they played, skiing circles around me. It made me smile. I was right. Super easy. I didn't need a class. Up ahead, Lemon headed to her left and I tried to follow.

She disappeared from sight behind a line of trees, so I continued going left. I came down to a wide passageway between a group of trees. I figured she had gone this way. I skied on the path until I merged into the new area. After a few moments I noticed that there were no kids here and the ground felt funny. I also felt like I was going faster. I looked down and realized I was no longer on the smooth, machine-flattened snow on the bunny slope. This looked like ice. It was steeper. I must have accidentally skied onto a more difficult slope.

I went flying forward, scarily fast. I started breathing hard and my heartbeat raced as I realized the danger I was in. I went numb. I had to stop. How did I stop? My brain wouldn't function. *Think, think!*

I turned my skis to the side, to cut into the snow. But that made me go faster. Not good. I straightened back out. What was I supposed to do again?

In a panic, I let go of my poles. I immediately realized my mistake. But it was too late as I kept going faster and faster.

If knew that if I hit a tree, I would be dead. I came around a bend to see a huge forest of trees on my left. I tried to lean away from them, praying that I could stay upright.

Maybe I could drag my hand like an anchor and slow myself down. I crouched down, which made my momentum pick up. I put my gloved hand behind me into the snow, but hit something hard. I let out a loud yell of pain and pulled my left hand up to my chest, cradling it. The tears sprang to my eyes. I had broken it.

What now? The white-hot pain was interfering with my ability to think. My eyes watered more, making it hard to see. I had a moment where I thought, *This is it. This is how I die.*

"Fall down!" I heard a voice on the wind and turned my head slightly to look. It was Nico and his buddies, skiing fast until they were alongside me. It filled me with relief. They would help me. Save me. Until I processed what he had said.

"What?" I yelled back.

"You have to fall down!"

I shook my head. No way. Panic and fear threatened to overwhelm me. I had never been this scared.

"Fall backward, on your side!" he instructed me. "You have to. Now!"

What choice did I have? If I tried to stop on my own, I would fall. If I ran into something, I'd be dead. I needed this to be over. I needed to get to a hospital. I had to do what he said. Before I could talk myself out of it, I closed my eyes and took a deep breath, falling back toward the mountain on my right side. I hit the ground hard. I had my breath knocked out of me as I began tumbling over and over through the snow. I felt something twist in my left ankle, but I couldn't cry out as I rolled and rolled until I finally stopped and everything went black.

Shouts and voices crept into my consciousness, and I became aware of the fact that I was dizzy and flat on my back, in the snow, looking up at the sun. Nico leaned over me, blocking the sun in a way that made him look like he had a halo. Maybe he was an angel and I was dead.

"Stay still, don't move," he told me. I noticed that his forehead was bleeding. I wanted to ask if I was alive, but I couldn't catch my breath. And every single part of me throbbed in pain.

I didn't know how much time had passed, but Nico kept talking to me, telling me I had to stay awake. I didn't want to stay awake because the pain was excruciating. I tried pushing him away but could barely lift my arm. I saw my sunglasses in the snow, broken into tiny black shards.

Someone put a neck brace on me, and the men moved me to what felt like a long board. They buckled me in, and I was aware of being pulled down the mountain, surrounded by people in bright orange outfits.

The whole time Nico skied next to me, talking to me. I didn't know what he was saying. I hoped he was speaking Monterran or something and that I hadn't lost my ability to understand English. I closed my eyes just for a minute. I so wanted to rest. But mostly I wanted the pain to stop.

The farther we went down the mountain, the more I heard voices and yelling. One pierced my haze.

"Kat? Kat? Are you okay? What happened? Let me through, I'm her friend. Kat!" Lemon looked totally freaked out as she reached for me. I tried to answer her, but my voice was so weak. They stopped her, and one of Nico's friends was hugging her as she sobbed into his shoulder.

I heard the helicopter before I saw it, and I felt the strong rush of wind from the blades as they loaded me into the waiting chopper. The paramedics started checking me, and I yelped when they touched my wrist. Lemon was on my right, holding my hand and crying. "You're going to be okay!" she yelled at me. I squeezed her hand back. Strong breezes swirled around us as the helicopter lifted up. I felt a poke in my arm as someone inserted an IV. I realized that Nico was sitting on my left side. He gave me a sad smile while a paramedic cleaned Nico's forehead.

"I'm sorry," I said. He shook his head, to indicate that he couldn't hear me. He handed the gauze back to the paramedic and shooed the man away. He leaned in, putting his ear close to my mouth. "Sorry," I repeated.

"For what?" he asked as he pulled back to look at me.

I turned my head and puked all over him.

Chapter 2

I awoke to the sound of a little girl singing "Let It Go." I opened my eyes slowly, taking in my surroundings. I was in a massive bed, covered by a thick, white comforter. There was a sheer white canopy hanging across the top of the bed and down the sides. I sat up and pushed it aside to look at the room. The ceilings were easily twenty feet high, and the room was full of antique-looking furniture and expensive rugs. A small fire snapped and crackled in a fireplace nearby.

I didn't recognize any of this. Definitely not our room at the resort. My heart started to race. Where was I?

The singing stopped. "*Buonasera. Come stai?*"

A girl lay on her stomach at the foot of my bed where she had been coloring in a book but was now staring at me. She had black hair and light brown eyes and seemed familiar, somehow.

"What?" My head felt thick, like I couldn't focus or process what was happening.

She gave me a jack-o'-lantern grin. "I forgot you were an American. Hello."

"Hi. You, uh, speak English really well."

She shrugged. "I work on it every day with my tutor. And I watch a lot of Disney movies."

"Yeah, I heard you singing." I held my head in both of my hands. What had happened to me?

"*Frozen* is my favorite movie."

I let go of my aching head and pulled the comforter up to my chest, holding on to it tightly. "Mine too."

Her eyes got big, and she crawled across the bed to me. "What is your favorite color?" She asked this like my answer to it was the most important thing in the whole world.

I wanted to ask her what was going on, but instead said, "Purple?"

"Mine too!" she said reverently, clasping her hands together on her chest. "I'm Serafina. I'm seven and a half, and you are my new best friend."

"Oh. Thanks?"

"You're welcome." She nodded seriously. "Have you lost all your baby teeth?"

I was starting to feel like I was in some kind of strange Wonderland conversation where I wasn't quite sure what was happening or who anyone was. "I have."

"I've only lost four. See?" She came in super close, holding her mouth open so that I could see her front four teeth were gone. "My two big teeth are coming in on the bottom, but not on the top yet."

"Awesome."

"The *Topolino* brought me some gold coins that have my grandfather's picture on them."

I must have looked confused because she continued on. "*Topolino? Il Topolino dei denti da latte?*" I shook my head. "The tooth mouse?" she translated slowly.

Tooth mouse? What the frak was a tooth mouse? It sounded creepy. She sighed impatiently at my obvious slowness. "The mouse that brings you money when you put your tooth under your pillow?"

This just kept getting weirder. I nodded, and that finally seemed to satisfy her. "I'm not supposed to bother you. Am I bothering you?"

Other than my slight panic and total bewilderment at this conversation? "Not too much."

"Good."

She went back over to her coloring and pulled a cell phone out from under the book. "Serafina, where am I?"

"At my home."

"Why?"

"My brother brought you here." She started dialing numbers.

"Who is your brother?"

She again looked at me like I was very stupid. "Nico."

"Who?" I tried to place the name, and the memories came flooding back to me. Oh crap, Nico. Tall, dark, and charming. The guy who rescued me after my skiing accident. I had brief flashes of the helicopter and the hospital, but I didn't remember coming here. However, I did remember throwing up on him, and my face flushed a bright red.

"You look like a tomato," Serafina informed me. "Chiara, she's awake." She paused. "No, I did not steal this phone. Violetta left it in her room for me. I am only borrowing it!" Then she started to yell in a foreign language at this Chiara, and abruptly turned the phone off.

"Who is Chiara?"

"My sister."

"How many brothers and sisters do you have?"

"Three brothers, two sisters. I had another brother, but he died before I was born." Serafina said this as she sat right next to me, putting her head against mine. She held up the phone and took three pictures of us together.

"Why were you fighting with your sister?" I asked when she finished.

Serafina flicked through the pictures, altering them with some app. "She accused me of stealing my other sister Violetta's phone."

"Did you?"

"Yes, but she's not allowed to tell me what to do. Mamma says I'm not responsible enough yet to have my own phone, and I *needed* to take a picture of us together."

"Know what might help you get your own phone? Not stealing other people's."

I heard running footsteps out in the hallway, and a teenage girl threw the bedroom door open. She looked like an older version of Serafina.

13

"I'm Chiara. Nice to meet you. Nico's never brought a girl home before. Especially not one who was injured." She said everything quickly, run together, without a pause to breathe.

Injured? I became aware of an ACE bandage on my left wrist, which I hadn't noticed before. A dull ache started in that wrist, my chest tightened every time I needed to breathe, and it hurt to move my left leg. I remembered how much pain I was in right after the accident, and I was grateful for how much better it was now.

"Do you need some medication?" Chiara asked me with a worried look on her delicate features. "You have some on the table next to your bed." I turned to see unopened bottles of water and prescription pill bottles. I picked up one and it had my name right there on the bottle. Kat MacTaggart. Vicodin.

"I'm okay," I said as I put the bottle back down. I didn't need to explain to children why I had no intention of taking even a single pill.

Instead I pulled my covers off to investigate my leg. I had another bandage there, with bright purple, yellow, and brown bruises all over both legs. Serafina took more pictures.

"At least your toes look pretty!" Chiara said brightly. "I painted them for you." My toenails were hot pink with sparkles.

"When did you do that?" I asked, alarmed.

Chiara crawled up onto the bed next to her picture-taking sister. "While you were sleeping. Nico said I wasn't supposed to bother you. I'm not bothering you, am I?"

This whole surreal situation was bothering me.

"Let's watch *Frozen*!" Serafina said after she put the phone down. She ran over to a dresser and picked up a remote. She pushed a button, and a massive flat-screen TV rose up out of the dresser while she climbed back onto the bed, making her way over to me. With a few more clicks, she had queued up the movie. She cuddled up on my side, laying her head against my shoulder. I adored children, but this kid had no personal boundaries at all.

The opening credits started, and I asked Chiara, "Is my friend here?"

14

"She's talking about the fruit one," Serafina said, without taking her eyes off the screen. "She's next door."

"Let me go get her for you," Chiara said, jumping off the bed and running out into the hallway. I heard a rapid knocking, a door open, and then to my great relief, Lemon's voice.

Anna had just started singing about building a snowman with Elsa when Lemon came in, a look of worry on her face. I noticed she was wearing what she called her "work clothes." They were the white button-up long-sleeved shirts and crisp dark slacks she wore when she wanted to be taken seriously. I had teased her about packing them, but it looked like she'd found some use for them. She rushed over to me and enveloped me in a giant hug. "Kat, darlin', I am so, so glad that you are okay."

She held me for longer than we might normally hug, finally letting go and standing back at arm's length to look at me. "How are you feeling?"

"Sore and a bit weirded out," I said, nodding my head toward an oblivious Serafina.

Lemon looked over at the fireplace to where there were two comfortable-looking chairs. "Can you walk?"

I didn't know, but I wanted to try. I felt stiff, like I hadn't moved in a week. Serafina moved away as I swung my legs over to the side of the bed. I flexed at the ankle, which hurt, and at my knees, which didn't. Lemon offered me her hand and helped me to stand. My ankle was a bit painful, but I could manage it. I let out a shaky breath, and I saw Lemon's eyes dart to my nightstand. Fortunately, she knew better than to offer me any of the pills.

We walked slowly over to the chairs and sat down in front of the fire. "What happened? Where are we?"

Lemon looked like the cat who ate an entire flock of canaries. "We are at the Monterran royal palace. Home of King Dominic, Queen Aria, and the crown prince, Dominic II." She seemed to enjoy my look of confusion. "You know him as Nico."

"Say what now?" A prince? A crown prince? And how was that different from a regular prince? I looked over my bed. That made little Serafina and Chiara princesses.

"You remember the man who saved you on the slopes, right?"

The one who looked like a fallen god turned human? Vague recollection. "Yeah."

"He brought you here to his *palace*," she emphasized, her eyes gleaming. "Can you believe he's an actual prince?"

I didn't think I had sustained any brain damage. She didn't need to keep repeating herself. "Yeah, you mentioned that. But how did we get here?"

Lemon explained that the helicopter had taken me to a hospital, where it was determined I had sustained bruised ribs, a minor sprain in my ankle, a major sprain in my wrist, a mild concussion, and bruising everywhere else. I was very lucky. I knew it could have been much worse. But when she started talking about the tests they ran and how worried she had been, I put my hand on her arm to keep her from continuing.

"CT scans and X-rays? How much was that?" Visions of bankruptcy danced in my head. I willed myself to not have a full-blown panic attack. No way could I afford all that. My student health insurance only worked on campus.

"Stop worrying about money," she replied. Such an easy thing for someone with a lot of money to say. "The only thing that matters is that you're all right. Prince Nico paid for all of your expenses and brought you here to recover. Apparently his father is ill and they have a small army of doctors and nurses to look after him, and they've been watching over you, too. He wanted you to be close by so he could make sure you were all right."

Lemon looked way too happy about that. It had been her life's mission since freshman year to get me to hook up with someone. She couldn't understand my aversion to men. She used to ask me if I wasn't, um, interested in men, that she would understand, but that wasn't the situation. I was definitely attracted to guys, but I just couldn't with any of them.

"And he feels responsible."

16

"Why?"

"His family owns the resort. One of many." She practically bounced in her chair. "So not only is he gorgeous and royal, but rich to boot. Well done, darlin'."

Lemon had more energy than someone without a crystal meth addiction should have. I gave her a look of disdain. She should know me better than that. "When are we leaving?"

"Here's the thing about that. I think we should stay here for a little while."

"Why? I'm awake. I feel better. We can go back to the resort or back home . . . wait. How many days has it been since the accident?"

"Three."

"Three days?" I tried to keep the hysterics out of my voice. "I've been sleeping for three days?"

"You needed time to recover. But listen, Kat, I've been talking with the prince. And funnily enough, he's in dire need of someone with modern marketing skills."

Lemon was about to finish up her master's degree in marketing and branding; I was getting mine in social work. Or, at least, that had been the plan before my scholarship had been defunded. But I didn't want to think about that right then. One problem at a time.

"And?"

"And his family uses this old stuffy British firm that's never even heard of Facebook. He really wants to increase tourism to his country, so I started laying out strategies for him and his press secretaries. I can use this as my thesis. You know how I've been stressing about this, and it's like an answer to my prayers. A thesis dropped right in my lap! Who else gets to write their master's thesis on the effect of social media on an obscure royal family?"

She had been struggling. I remembered her spouting off ideas to me back in our apartment last semester about overt international pricing strategies

17

and brand image. She hadn't seemed too thrilled about it. But this—I could see her giddy excitement.

"I'm getting real-life work experience here, and they seem to love my ideas."

"Like what?" The aching was starting to get worse. I shifted in my seat, hoping to relieve it.

"I was thinking of getting the prince on that TV show with the single guy and all the women who compete to marry him. I have a sorority sister who works as an assistant director on it, and I made a phone call. It's a done deal. But we need to build up his brand, get the whole world talking about him. Pour some chum in the water to get the sharks feeding. And that's where you come in."

"Me?" I asked in surprise.

She avoided looking me in the eyes, picking nonexistent lint off of her slacks. "You and he are going to spend some time together. Go on some pretend 'royal' dates. Then you're going to write about it. With your words and that man's face on the new website I'm having designed, this thing will go viral faster than a hare with a hot foot." She sounded very proud of herself.

But there was no way I was doing that. Just the thought of it was enough to give me a coronary.

"Nope."

"Kat, please, it's already been agreed to. Just say you'll do it."

"When was this agreed to?"

"While you were sleeping."

"So you've just been arranging my whole life while I was in a coma?"

"Oh, calm down. You weren't in a coma. Just knocked out." Lemon never sugarcoated anything. She was sweet and kind, even with her passive-aggressive "bless your hearts," but she did not pull her punches. Flying here to Monterra was my first time ever on a plane, and I had been a tad freaked out. When I asked Lemon for any last-minute advice, what was her loving response? "Don't touch any red buttons."

"How are those two things different?"

18

"In both length and seriousness." Lemon was one of those all-is-fair-in-love-and-war-and-getting-me-a-boyfriend people. Anything went, and when it came to her mission, she had no boundaries or filters. It made me very uneasy that they'd spent three days together. Talking about me.

Who knew what she had told him? I couldn't date him. Not even fake date him. I had thrown up on him. I nearly died on his family's mountain. I had been rude to him. Dismissive. Cold. He probably thought I was the world's biggest hag. Why would he agree to it?

"I think I need to lie down."

Lemon got up to help me back over to the bed. "He'll pay you to write the article, and he's so nice. It's really no big deal. You'll have a good time."

I eased myself back into the bed, realizing it was probably the most comfortable one I'd ever slept in. The pillows were like fluffs of heaven, the comforter soft and downy and perfect. It was hard to stay mad while lying in this bed.

"Please," she said, looking down at me. "I know this is huge. But I've never asked you for anything like this before."

I sighed. She was right. Lemon was a nurturer, and she lived to take care of others. Including me. She had always been generous, even when I didn't want her to be, and so supportive. At times I had felt like our friendship was somehow unequal because of our financial situations. This was my chance to pay her back.

I could do this for her. I closed my eyes. "Okay. Fine. I'll do it."

"Fantastic! The prince said he wanted to discuss the details with you himself." My heart skipped a beat before settling back down. Despite my denials, I actually wanted to see Nico again. Some part of me was excited about it. I opened my eyes because I realized there was something she wasn't telling me. I could hear in her voice that she'd left something out.

"What else?"

She perched on the side of my bed with one of her "I found a new man" smiles. "His name is Salvatore, the Duca di Brista. That's a duke. He's one of

Nico's friends. And I think he's interested. I've been trying your game. The virgin ploy."

I glanced over at Serafina, who had moved back to the foot of the bed during our conversation. She was totally engrossed in the movie. "It's not a game or a ploy. It's an actual thing. Waiting until marriage."

Waving her hand she said, "Of course. Whatever. But why didn't you ever tell me how well this works? It makes them want you more."

Because I had absolutely zero experience in that department. Since my freshman year in high school, no guy had ever been interested in my virginity or relieving me of it. It was a nonissue.

It didn't surprise me though that Lemon had already found a guy to crush on. She'd always had a thing for foreign men. Those same foreign men had a thing for cheating on her constantly. Which I didn't understand, because her dad was as loyal as one of his hound dogs. Unlike me, she'd grown up with a great father. But she only liked jerks, which I would never understand. I knew this would have to play out until this Salvatore messed up, which he inevitably would, and Lemon could move on to the next lowlife.

"Momma always told me to play hard to get; I just never realized how well it works or how much fun it could be. And that Salvatore may be three pickles short of a quart, but I am going to get him to propose to me. And someday I will tell my grandchildren about the time a duke from Monterra proposed to me. Just like you'll be telling your grandchildren about your fling with an almost king."

Fling? "I'm not having a fling. You fling him."

She gave me her knowing smile. "He's not interested in me, and I already have my man all picked out. If you had the sense that God gave a tick, you'd be all over that man. If I'm not allowed to get him in your bed, then I'm at least gonna get you kissed."

I heard a knock on my open door, and I looked over Lemon's shoulder to see Nico standing in the doorway, sheer godlike perfection in a designer suit.

I had three-day-old bed head and morning breath and what felt suspiciously like a new zit forming on my chin.

I fervently hoped he hadn't heard anything Lemon had just said.

"Am I interrupting?"

Chapter 3

Lemon shot me a wink before she said, "Not at all. Serafina and I were just leaving to watch her movie in my room, right?"

Uncomprehending, Serafina started to protest when Lemon shut off the television. Despite her complaining, Lemon had her by the hand and out of the room before I could tell them not to go.

She'd left us alone. Me and the guy who should be *People* magazine's sexiest man alive.

Holy crap.

"May I come in?"

"Oh, uh, yeah." I pulled the comforter up to my neck, wishing I could disappear underneath it.

He crossed over to grab a chair, bringing it back to sit next to the bed. He seated himself, undoing the buttons on his coat, settling in. I was nervous. So over-the-top nervous that I was actually shaking. And he looked like the picture of ease and comfort.

Nico was every bit as handsome as I'd remembered. Better. He made my ovaries stand up and cheer. I told them to be quiet.

"It is a pleasure to see you looking so much better, Kat MacTaggart." I heard the subtle dig in his voice. He did look pleased that he knew my name when I wouldn't give it to him.

I should say something.

But what? He sort of made me speechless.

"Did your parents have a particular fondness for felines?"

"What? No. My, uh, mother named me after her favorite soap character on *Days of Our Lives*. Her name was Katerina."

He had a blank look on his face.

"*Days of Our Lives*? It's a soap opera. An American TV show."

"Katerina," he repeated, rolling the *r* slightly, which made my stomach do flips.

"But everyone calls me Kat." If he kept calling me Katerina like that, with those amazing twinkling blue eyes of his, there was no telling what I might do.

"Does anyone ever call you Kitty-Kat?"

"Not twice they don't."

He laughed and I remembered how much I liked it. How it made me want to act like a totally different person.

I noticed a bright red scar on his forehead near his hairline and flashed back to him bleeding at the accident in the same spot. I pointed to it. "What happened? Did I do that?"

For the first time since I'd met him, he seemed less than happy. "The binding on your ski was done improperly. Your ski should have automatically come off when you fell, but I caught the tip of one with my head. My employees should know better." He sounded mad. I decided to not tell the very hot and very angry man that I was the one who had done the bindings.

"I'm so sorry."

He was all smiles again. "*Lascia perdere*. It doesn't matter. It should be me apologizing to you. It wasn't your fault. Besides, I've been told that women like scars. That it would make me look sexier. What do you think?"

I thought he did not need one single iota of help in that department.

Which I obviously couldn't say, so instead I sat there stupidly with my mouth hanging open.

"Speaking of which, I was impressed with your ability to stay upright for so long on your skis. Lemon mentioned that you were a novice."

"I do a lot of yoga."

"Really?"

"No, not even a little." Why was I saying stupid things to him? "I just have good balance." We sat in silence for a moment, me looking everywhere around the room except at him. "So, uh, you went up the mountain before I did.

How did you get behind me? And how did you know I needed help? Do you just ski around up there waiting to rescue damsels in distress?"

Nico glanced toward the window. "The intermediate slope begins much farther up the mountain than the nursery slope. We were also, as you Americans say, taking our time. But I noticed you immediately, because I remembered your red outfit. And you just looked like you were in trouble and out of control. I did what I could to help. Fortunately my security detail was able to immediately call the rescue patrol to get you off the mountain. I'm glad that things turned out as well as they did."

I thought about the famous actress a few years back who had hit her head while skiing and died three days later. I was also glad that things had turned out as well as they did.

"Wait—security detail?"

"A necessity in my position, I'm afraid."

"Right. The prince thing." He had bodyguards. That was kind of cool. I wondered if I could volunteer for the position. *I would guard his body real well.*

Where the frak had that come from? What was wrong with me? Maybe I needed to hit my head again to bring back my actual self.

"Not to change the subject, but I'm assuming your friend Lemon explained to you our current plans."

The dates. The article. My heart thudded loudly and slowly in my throat. I hoped he couldn't hear it. "Sort of."

"In short, I would like to take you to several social events as my date. I will take you out to explore interesting local Monterran spots. We have Christmas parties coming up, balls, a winter carnival, New Year's Eve. I think you will enjoy it, and then you can write about everything for the website."

He must have seen the concern on my face. I was trying to figure out how I was going to get through this. Normal girls would have cut off their right foot to be with Nico. But he scared me to death, and I couldn't explain why without sounding totally pathetic.

"Don't look so concerned, *bella*. I promise I don't bite." His voice rumbled softly, subtle seduction emanating from every syllable. He reached out and took my right hand from where it sat on top of the comforter. I hysterically wondered whether he was going to kiss it again, but he just ran his thumb over my knuckles absentmindedly, like he didn't even realize that he was making my skin tingle in response.

Which only made it worse. I wanted to run away from him, my arms flailing in the air like a Muppet. Only I probably wouldn't make it very far on this stupid ankle. I saw a look of confusion in his eyes as he studied me for a second. He released my hand and I put it under the covers, ignoring my short and shallow breaths. He leaned back, crossing his arms and smiling like he knew something I didn't.

"I don't know what rates are appropriate, but I thought perhaps one US dollar for each word in the article?"

Turned out all it took to drive back abject fear was the mention of a possibly obscene amount of money. That was fantastic. I wondered if I could write fifty thousand words in the next week. Even a few thousand words could really help with my tuition problem. Now I would definitely have to do it. Especially since I promised Lemon. But I didn't want to seem like I could be so easily swayed. Even though I totally had been.

"Why do you want me to write it? Shouldn't you have Lemon hire a professional writer? I'm just a grad student."

"Lemon showed me your books. You are an excellent writer, and I think a perfect fit for this article."

It took a second before my brain properly translated what he had said. Lemon had showed him my stories.

I had always loved romances, and had started writing them as an escape when I was in high school. I'd just kept them on my ancient laptop, intending them to be for my eyes only. They were sweet little things, riffs on fairy tales. Novellas, really.

25

A few years ago I'd briefly flirted with the idea of becoming an actual author, and I had joined a local writers' group where I'd learned about self-publishing. Thinking this might be a road to success, I got stock covers, traded services with an English major at school for editing, and put my stories up on Amazon under a pseudonym. Where I totally languished in obscurity. I only sold a copy or two a month. Which was when I realized that, for me, it wasn't a valid career path.

But the only person in the whole entire world who knew about my little hobby was Lemon. She'd told Nico. Hot and terrible anger exploded inside me. I was going to absolutely kill her. Then I'd find a voodoo shaman to resurrect her as a zombie just so that I could kill her again. She was so dead.

"Did I say something wrong?"

I'd never been very good at hiding my emotions. "I'm just, uh, surprised that Lemon told you about that."

"Do you plan to become a writer?"

"No, the writing's just for me. I'm going to be a social worker." He looked at me like I was the most interesting person on the whole planet, and he couldn't wait to hear what I said next. So I started babbling like an idiot. "I like food and I'm kind of over the poverty thing. I mean, social workers don't make much money either, but I'll make enough to at least have proteins and vegetables on a daily basis. So that's good because I'm very done with ramen noodles. But I'm obviously not going into social work for the money. I love kids. And I want to help every kid I can find that needs help."

I finally ran out of breath and we both sat, him smiling at me, me still freaking out. "Regardless, I think this could work. Will you at least consider it?"

"Sure. I'll consider it and, uh, let you know. My people will call your people."

He didn't get the joke. Probably because he actually had people. He stood up, buttoning up his suit jacket and returning the chair to where he had taken it from. "My mother would like for you and Lemon to join us for dinner this evening in our private dining room, if you're amenable."

"Okay." Were you allowed to say no to a queen? I eyed his suit. "Am I supposed to wear a dress? I don't have one with me."

"I'm certain everyone will be understanding given your situation. My mother has assigned one of her assistant secretaries, Giacomo, to assist you while you're here. He's an expert in protocol and an excellent stylist. He will see that all your needs are met. Please let him know what you need and he will take care of it."

"Okay."

He stood there expectantly, looking down at me. "I don't want to rush you, but we're scheduled to have dinner in a few minutes."

"Oh, okay. So I should probably shower and get ready. But I didn't bring any soap or shampoo with me."

Nico gestured toward a closed door on the other side of the bed with an amused half smile. "The bathroom is through there. I believe Giacomo purchased some apple-scented shampoo and soap for you."

I must have given him a weird look because he suddenly looked sheepish. "I told him you smelled like apples."

Before I could examine that statement too closely, I told him, "I don't know where the 'private dining room' is."

"I could stay here and escort you down. Give you a tour of the palace after dinner?" He looked so hopeful that I didn't have it in me to say no. I just nodded.

A grin broke out on his face, like the sun emerging from behind a cloud. "Excellent."

"Okay, so, I'll go do that."

I took the covers off, acutely aware of my bare, bruised, and slightly hairy legs. I didn't look at him, so I didn't know if they were grossing him out or not. I started to stand up, and he walked over as if he wanted to help, but stopped short. He clasped his hands together behind his back. "May I assist you?"

"I can do it. Thanks, though." I hated feeling this weak. I bet eating dinner would help me start to feel better. My stomach growled in response to this thought, and I caught him suppressing a smile at the noise. I felt the flush starting on my cheeks. I wanted to die from embarrassment.

"Is there anything that I can get for you?"

My normal heartbeat back? Right now I would settle for that. He was standing so close that it made me feel faint. The weakness in my ankles was from the accident. The weakness in my knees was all him. Nico practically radiated warmth and charm, and I felt an actual physical attraction to him. Not in a he was gorgeous and as a woman in possession of functioning eyes I appreciated his hotness kind of way, but in the sense that all I wanted was to get closer and closer to him. "No, I'm fine. Should I meet you somewhere?"

"If you don't mind, I can wait for you in the hallway. My mother doesn't like for people to be late."

No pressure there. "I'm sure you're busy, I don't want to . . ."

He walked over to my door and put his hand on the knob to pull it shut behind him. "I am happy to wait for you."

I headed off to my shower, trying not to think too hard about what that meant.

Chapter 4

I went on total autopilot. I quickly undressed, figured out how to get the shower to scalding, and took off my bandages. I only clenched my teeth in pain twice while doing it.

Sure enough, the shampoo was apple-scented. It was a much more expensive brand than I normally used, but oddly enough, it gave me a small bit of comfort and familiarity. Once I'd rinsed and dried off with the softest towel in all of human existence, I did my best to rewrap my aching limbs.

Next to the bathroom stood a huge walk-in closet. It was bigger than my bedroom back home. My suitcase was there on the floor. I lifted the lid. Empty. All of my belongings had been put away in the built-in drawers. I had a momentary pang of embarrassment as I imagined someone putting my underwear away.

I threw on a black shirt and the darkest jeans I owned. I wished I could borrow something from Lemon, but all her clothes were too tiny. It was like having Barbie as your roommate.

I came back into the bathroom and twisted my hair into a bun. There was no time to blow-dry it. I didn't want to examine too closely why it was suddenly important to me to spend some time on my appearance. I wanted to say it was because I was about to meet Nico's family, but the honest truth would have been that it was for Nico himself.

Grabbing my flats, I did a skipping/running thing putting them on as I went to my bedroom door, ignoring the twinge in my ankle. I stopped in front of the door, trying to calm down. I could do this.

True to his word, Nico stood right across the hallway. He leaned against the wall, texting on his phone, but slid it into his pants pocket when I walked out. He gave me an appraising look and smiled. "You look lovely, *bella*."

"Thank you?"

I couldn't even take a compliment like a normal person. I fervently hoped I wasn't blushing. Nico put his elbow out, looking at me. What now?

After a moment he took my hand and wrapped it around the inside of his elbow and started walking. What was this supposed to be? Why couldn't we just walk? I contemplated taking my hand off of his arm, but instead held on tighter and hurried to keep up.

I blamed my rising heartbeat and shortness of breath on anxiety over meeting an actual queen. Not on the addictive smell coming from Nico that made me want to bury my nose in his neck to get a better whiff. Not on the large, hard muscles that I didn't see but could feel flexing against my upper arm. Not on the sexy five o'clock shadow that had just started to form on his strong jaw.

Exhaling a loud breath, I forced myself to pay attention to our surroundings. Nico explained that we were in the family's private apartments, and they were all connected by drawing rooms and hallways. Everyone had their privacy, but had easy access to one another. He indicated that the guest rooms were in another part of the castle.

"But Lemon and I are staying here."

I saw his eyes flicker toward me briefly, but he didn't respond. Instead he kept talking about how things were laid out.

Why weren't we in the guest wing? Why were we in the family's personal area? Was that supposed to mean something? I tried to distract myself by making a mental map so that I wouldn't ever need him to escort me again. This hallway was decorated in different shades of ivory and blue, with artwork that I knew was very expensive from the two weeks I'd been enrolled in Art Appreciation 101.

We came upon a couple of men in dark suits, and they both wore white earpieces. The security that Nico had mentioned. He greeted each man by name as we passed.

Then he pointed out the family's private kitchen, telling me I could help myself anytime that I wanted as it was always well stocked with their favorite treats and snacks.

"Do you ever cook in there yourself?"

He gave a slight shrug. "If the mood strikes me."

"Does it ever strike you?"

His eyes met mine, and it was like sitting too close to a fire that suddenly roared to life. I stumbled over my own feet, but he righted me quickly.

"On occasion I have been known to cook."

He cooked too? Could he at least try to not be like the totally perfect man? "Please don't tell me you wash your own dishes." I wasn't sure my heart could handle it.

Nico looked completely amused. "I am saddened to say that I leave them for someone else. Have I lessened your opinion of me?"

"It's actually sort of a relief. I was worried you were too perfect. No one would believe anything I said when I wrote about you."

"Did you hear that?"

"What?"

He looked smug. "That was almost a compliment."

"Only almost."

"I am going to consider that progress."

I couldn't help smiling back. Nico went on to explain that if I didn't want to get something myself, I could ring for a servant to bring it for me. Ring for a servant? I pressed my lips together with a suppressed glee. Holy crap, it was like being in a real-life *Downton Abbey*.

But before I could ask him if he had an evil under-butler, he was opening two large doors into another high-ceilinged room that stunned me with its expensive elegance. I saw chandeliers, ivory and silver wallpapered walls, and an enormous, beautifully decorated dark wooden table that had Nico's whole family sitting at it.

Two men stood when we walked in, and I realized they were identical twins. Lemon was seated between them. Chiara waved at me, and I waved back while Serafina stood in her chair and yelled, "Hello, Kat! Come sit by me!"

"Introductions first," an older woman said. She sat at the end of the table. "Please sit down, Serafina. Remember your manners."

Serafina rolled her eyes and slunk back down in her chair.

Nico walked me across the room to the woman who had to be his mother. For reasons I didn't understand, I really wanted her to like me.

"What am I supposed to do here? Bow? Curtsy? Kneel?" I whispered to him as we got closer to the queen.

He leaned down slightly to whisper back, his breath hot against my neck. It almost felt like a caress. "You're an American. You don't have to do anything. She's not your queen. Just follow her lead."

We stopped in front of her, and my body tensed. I did not want to mess this up. It struck me how beautiful she was. I could see where Nico had gotten his looks from. There was a regal elegance to her, but also a kindness in her bright blue eyes that made me relax.

"Mother, may I present Miss Katerina MacTaggart? Katerina, this is my mother, Her Royal Highness, Queen Aria of Monterra."

The queen nodded at me. "It is very nice to meet you, Miss MacTaggart."

"Kat, please. Your, uh, Majesty."

That seemed to please her for some reason. She reached out for my hand, and I gave it to her. She squeezed it. "Then you must call me Aria." Yeah, I couldn't see that ever happening. She let go of me to gesture toward the table. "I hear that you are already acquainted with Chiara and Serafina."

"She's my best friend, Mamma!" Serafina called from her end of the table.

"This is my eldest daughter, Violetta." A sullen teenage girl who also had Nico's blue eyes glanced up at me with a withering look. I saw the earbuds attached to the phone she held under the table. "No technology at the table,

32

please." Violetta let out a loud sigh as she yanked the buds out and turned her phone off.

The two men were still standing as Nico walked me over to them. "These are my brothers, Dante and Raphael." They had the same black hair as the rest of their family, but their brown eyes were a lighter shade than the rest. The one called Raphael wore a pair of silver-rimmed glasses.

It shouldn't have surprised me when Dante leaned in to kiss me on my right cheek, then my left. I didn't think that I would ever get used to that particular European greeting. "Welcome," he said with a mischievous grin.

"Thanks."

His twin leaned in to greet me in the same fashion, but added before he pulled back, "Anyone who puts that kind of smile on my oldest brother's face can call me Rafe."

Lemon just smiled at me knowingly before Nico led me over to the only empty spot remaining at the table. It was situated near the end of the table with Serafina on my left, who bounced up and down with excitement, and Nico on my right, who sat at the foot of the table. The twins and Lemon sat across from me. I was glad she was in my eye line.

Nico stood behind my chair, waiting. Another situation where I had no idea what, exactly, I was supposed to do. Everyone stared at me as I sat down and started scooting myself in, with Nico assisting behind me. Once I was settled, he walked back to his chair.

In front of me sat several china plates, all rimmed in what I suspected was real gold, with an embroidered ivory linen napkin laid across them. There was a row of crystal glasses in front of me, and next to my plate there were more forks than the Colorado River. I found myself feeling overwhelmed again. Not to mention the fact that I was totally underdressed. The men were all in suits, the women in dresses.

And I was in jeans.

Please, please, don't let me screw this up any more than I already have.

Somehow I made it through without doing anything too embarrassing. The only time I seemed to step in it was when I asked about the king joining us. That brought a lot of exchanged glances and a physical, awkward charge in the atmosphere. The queen looked at me for a moment before she said, "He is not feeling well this evening," and the subject was quickly changed and forgotten.

The food was, literally, the best I had ever tasted. For our main course (yes, main course—we had several courses, including an incredible tiramisu for dessert) we had steak and some kind of roasted potato, which surprised me. The few meals we'd had at the resort before the accident had consisted of one variety or another of pasta. When I pointed that out to Nico, he gave me a boyish grin that warmed my insides. "Lemon said it was your favorite."

My heart sank. I should have been touched, but I was just sad. He needed to stop being so nice to me. I was not someone who was capable of being nice back to him. This would all end badly.

No matter how attractive I found him.

When we were finished with our dessert and I considered the real possibility that I might never eat again because I was so stuffed, I asked, "Can I help clear the dishes?" It seemed like the polite thing to do.

The queen gave me a sweet smile. "No, dear, but thank you. That is very kind of you to offer."

The men in matching uniforms who had been bringing in our food all night came in to clear away the dessert plates. I noticed Violetta hadn't touched her tiramisu at all while I'd had to refrain from licking my plate.

"I understand that Nico plans to give you a tour this evening," his mother said to me. I felt a little like I'd been on display all night, with just a touch of third-degree interrogating going on by his brothers. All very kindly and nicely done, but there had been a lot of questions. This was a statement more than a question, but it still felt like I was under scrutiny.

"Yeah, he mentioned that."

"But only if you're feeling up to it," Nico said, and I wanted to melt at the look of concern on his face.

"I'll be fine." I wanted to reassure him when it probably should have been the other way around. I couldn't help it. Besides, it was true. I barely even felt the pain any longer, which was probably due in part to the fact that I no longer felt like I was going to die of starvation. The food had helped, as I'd hoped it would.

"Then shall we?"

I went to stand up, and Nico practically knocked his own chair over rushing over to help me out of mine. The twins again got to their feet. Serafina jumped up and threw her arms around my waist, and I put my arm around her shoulders. "Goodbye. I wanted to come with you, but Mamma said I can't because you and Nico are going to be alone," she announced in a stage whisper voice. Everyone around the table hid their smiles, and I willed myself not to blush. Had Lemon recruited all of them into her plan to find me a boyfriend?

"Maybe next time," I said to her. I wished she could come. I was worried I might find myself in need of a chaperone.

"Make sure you show her the moonlight gardens," the queen said as Nico and I walked to the door. "They're my pride and joy. After my children, of course." They all laughed, but I could barely muster a smile as my stomach screwed itself into tiny little knots.

"Shall we?" Nico asked as he opened the door.

I was about to walk around with a too-attractive-for-his-own-good prince in a romantic, darkened castle and go someplace called a moonlight garden. I should have said no. I should have said I was in pain and needed to go back to my room. I should have let Serafina come with us.

But I didn't do any of those things.

Chapter 5

Nico did not take my arm this time, but kept his hands clasped behind his back. I didn't know if that was his natural stance, or if he was avoiding touching me.

He took me down to the main part of the castle, showing me the Great Hall, the ballroom, a banquet hall. There was the White Drawing Room and the Green Drawing Room and the Blue Drawing Room. Each room was more luxurious and bigger than the last. Nico kept up a steady stream of information about everything he showed me. But I'd seen one drawing room. I didn't really need to see all of them.

"How many rooms does the palace have?"

"Including bathrooms and staterooms, over eight hundred."

Eight hundred rooms? I stopped. He realized I was no longer standing next to him and turned to see what I was doing. "We're not going to look at all eight hundred rooms, are we?"

He smiled. "I'll show you one last place that I like, and then I'll take you to the garden."

On our way, Nico continued to point out rooms and their names, like some kind of hot, determined tour guide. He nodded toward the library. I was torn between asking him to stop so that I could see it and wanting to hurry this up so the evening could end. I decided to go back and check out the library when I had a chance. Alone. We passed by a conservatory and a lounge.

"I feel like I'm in a real-life version of Clue."

"Don't worry. Nobody's been killed here in decades." I heard the teasing in his voice, but I immediately wanted to know who had been killed in the palace and why. Before I could ask, he held open another door and led me into a quiet, long room that had floor-to-ceiling paintings.

"This is the gallery. Every member of the royal family has a portrait here." Some of the portraits looked newer, but many of them looked really old.

"Every time that I am feeling unsure of myself, I come here. All of this history, all of these people, my ancestors, remind me that I can do what needs to be done." Nico looked lost in his own thoughts, as he moved down the room's length.

It was the most personal thing he had ever said to me. He seemed so polished, so perfect. Like nothing bothered him. And here he was announcing that he had self-doubts. Actual chinks in his armor. And he had sounded . . . lonely. The wall around my heart lost a few bricks.

"I can't even imagine what it must be like to be in a room full of pictures of your family," I told him as we came to stop in front of a massive tapestry that contained his family tree. I saw the latest embroidered entry of Serafina Maria Theresa Aria and ran my fingers over her name. "To have your whole family tree laid out like this. To know who you are and where you come from."

"You don't?" He stopped to look at me.

"What little I do know is not fun. Not all of us come from a long line of kings and queens." I waved my hand up at the wall. "I personally am the proud offspring of a bunch of addicts and alcoholics."

Nico didn't say anything, just cocked his head to the side.

I let out a little laugh. "Pretty sure if you put my family tree up on your wall there would be a car wrapped around the trunk."

"These are not all nice people, *bella*," he said. "You think we're without our share of addicts and alcoholics? I assure you, we are not. There would be too many here to count. And we have worse. Here, look at this one."

He took me by the hand, and I loved the way our hands fit together, how it felt . . . natural. Right. So right that I forgot to freak out. We stopped in front of an old painting of a woman with black hair and an evil-looking smirk.

"This is Queen Isabella. She was a Spanish princess who married the Monterran king. She decided she would make a better monarch, so she poisoned her husband and her four oldest sons. The nobles had to band together to kidnap her youngest son to protect him from her. That prince grew up to overthrow his mother. And here."

We moved farther down the line. "This is King Stefan. He used to accuse his wives of witchcraft so that he could put them to death and obtain newer and younger models. My family comes from his fourth wife, who managed to have one son before he had her killed."

He sighed. "Assassinations, murders, coups, we have them all." He flashed me a grin. "But look at how well the final product turned out."

I wanted to roll my eyes. Yes, we all got it. He was gorgeous. I settled for shaking my head.

He tugged on my hand. "The garden is this way."

He didn't let go of my hand, and to my surprise, I didn't let go of his. We walked in silence, only for the first time it wasn't an awkward one. It was strange to feel this way. To feel comfortable with a man who seemed like he was attracted to me. To think that I might even let him . . . I mean if he tried . . . obviously, I was being presumptuous because he might not have even thought of me that way . . . but if he did . . . would I?

"Here we are." He led me into an extremely large greenhouse that had completely clear paneling so that you could see everything outside. The palace must have sat high on a hill as I could see nothing but snow and twinkling lights from valley floors in every direction.

"Beautiful," I sighed.

Nico looked at me and said, "I was thinking the same thing."

My heart beat painfully, but I ignored his implication and instead looked at the full moon that hung high in the sky above us, lighting up the entire garden. I heard running water, and Nico led me down a cobblestone path that was highlighted by little paper lanterns with tea candles burning inside them. We went to a sheltered, padded bench that sat situated on a little island in the middle of a large pond where koi fish swam, darting in and out of crimson-colored water lilies. We sat down and I tried to take it all in. In addition to the fantastic view outside, everything here was lush and green and warm. Bright yellow, white, pink, and purple flowers surrounded us. "What is that scent?"

"Casablanca lilies. Did you know that every flower in here only blooms at night?"

"Really?"

He looked up and reached for a white flower above us. "It's a moonflower. It actually closes up whenever sunlight touches the petals."

"Cool."

He reached over, tucking the flower into my hair, just above my ear. I didn't realize that I was holding my breath until he moved his hand away. He rested his arm across the top of the bench behind me. "My mother has always loved gardens. She created this one not long after . . ." He trailed off, taking a deep breath. "She made it because she wanted us to remember that even beautiful things could grow in darkness."

I wondered if that could be true for me as well. Could something beautiful grow here and now despite my darkness? I wanted to believe.

Nico stood up, removing his suit jacket. He put it on the bench's arm, and as he sat back down he was undoing the cuffs of his sleeves and rolling them back. He loosened his tie and undid his top button. He let out a sigh of relaxation.

I wondered briefly what he'd look like in regular clothes. The closest thing to normal I'd seen him in was back at the ski lodge. That memory sparked a question that escaped my mouth before I could stop it. "Why did you come up to me at the lodge?"

Did everything I say amuse him? "Do you mean besides the fact that you are a beautiful woman?"

I made a face at him. We both knew that wasn't true. "Yeah, besides that."

"You were reading Shakespeare." Had he moved closer to me, or was that my imagination? "Every other woman in the lobby was preening and made up with fake hair and fake"—he stopped and looked at me before continuing—

"other body parts and there you sat, uncaring if anyone even noticed you. You were fresh, natural, and obviously intelligent, and I wanted to talk to you."

"Bet you'd never been shot down before, huh?" I could at least take some pride in that.

Not my imagination. He was definitely closer. "But you didn't 'shoot me down.' We're here, aren't we?"

Oh frak, he was right. He had me on a date. He took me to dinner. I'd been tricked. I should have been indignant. Outraged, even. Instead, my lips twitched and I forced myself not to smile. Because it was funny to have gone from that to this.

Now his fingers were playing with the few tendrils that had escaped my bun. I went still and forgot to breathe. "There is something I've wondered since the moment I met you."

"What?" My voice sounded breathy and weird.

"What this would be like."

He was going to kiss me, and I was going to let him. My heart started trying to pound its way out of my chest.

I should have stopped him. I should have been afraid. But I wasn't.

His kiss was feathery light, barely touching me. His lips were warm, soft, and strong. If I'd realized earlier they'd feel like this against my own, I probably would have spent a lot more time studying them. My eyes drifted shut as my stomach went completely hollow, and a warm thickness started spreading through all of my limbs. He kissed me again, gentle and persuasive.

"Relax, *bella*," he murmured against my lips, running his fingers along my jawbone. I realized that I was clenching his shirtfront with my fists. I loosened my grip. He continued to plant sweet and soft kisses on my lips. "This works better if you kiss me back," he said with a smile as he leaned back slightly to look at me, his eyes glittery and intense. He ran his thumb along my lower lip, which made all sorts of unmentionable things happen to my insides.

Leave it to me to mess something up as basic as kissing. Fortunately, I wasn't a total idiot. I could do what he was doing. Scared as I was, I managed to give myself a pep talk. I was twenty-four years old. I was the oldest person on the planet who had never been kissed. I couldn't have asked for a more perfect setting, or a more perfect man. So gathering up every bit of courage I possessed, I leaned in to kiss him. Just a small peck. A little smooch. It was all I could manage.

I pulled back to see a delighted and appreciative look in his eyes.

"That wasn't as bad as I expected."

"Not as bad as you expected? Katerina, I can do much better than 'not as bad as you expected.'"

I hadn't meant to issue a challenge, but he accepted it anyway. I thought I heard him growl before he pressed our lips together more firmly, his hands framing and holding my head in place as he kissed me over and over. It was all I could do to keep up. Electricity exploded everywhere he touched and kissed me.

Was it possible to die from a kiss?

My hands moved from his shirt to his wrists, and I felt like I was clinging on for dear life. His kisses started to escalate in intensity until he suddenly stopped. He leaned his forehead against mine, and we were both breathing fast.

"I think . . . I think it's time for me to return you to your room."

I nodded, unable to think.

He could have said, "I think it's time for us to get on a spaceship and fly to the moon," and I would have agreed to that, too.

He pulled me up with one hand, and as we rushed from the moonlight garden, I realized that he had left his coat behind. I was going to mention it, but when I looked back all I could think of was us on that bench and that kiss. I touched my lips with my fingers, still able to feel the phantom pressure there.

Lemon was going to pee her pants with excitement.

I must have been in some kind of Nico-induced trance, because next thing I knew we were standing in front of my room. I had been so caught up in my own head that I hadn't paid any attention to where we had been going. I opened my door and saw that my bed had been made.

I turned back to Nico, suddenly very nervous and unsure of what to say. I didn't think, "Hey, thanks for my first kiss! That was awesome!" would be appropriate. Should I high-five him or something?

He held both of my hands in his, and released them to run his hands up my arms, onto my shoulders, settling one on the side of my neck, the other at the back of my head. He was going to kiss me again.

He kissed me once, softly and briefly. He murmured, "Good night, *bella*," against my cheek. He let go and began to walk away.

Wait. What? "Good night?"

He turned to face me. "Unless you'd like to invite me into your room?"

It was like he'd poured a bucket of ice water on top of me. Reality came crashing down, hard. "Uh, no."

He smiled like he knew something I didn't. "Then, good night."

I hurried inside my room and slammed the door shut before he changed his mind. Because if he pushed, I didn't think I was currently strong enough to resist.

Chapter 6

I stuck my head out of the door to make certain that Nico had left. The hallway was empty. I ran next door to Lemon's room and knocked frantically. No response. No way was she asleep already. I opened the door and switched on the light. "Lemon?" I looked around for a minute, but it was obvious she wasn't there. Had she gone off with her duke somewhere?

Closing her door, I headed back to my own room. I didn't want to be my only company right now, but I didn't have much of a choice.

I changed into my pajamas and absentmindedly brushed my teeth. I climbed into the world's best bed and turned on my side, curled up in a fetal position.

Now I had to face what I had done. I had kissed Nico. Kissed him. Really, really kissed him. A flush started on my cheeks, filled my whole face, and worked its way down my neck. I had done nothing the last ten years but avoid this very situation. And I had walked into it willingly. It was so unlike me that it almost felt like it had happened to someone else.

But I only had to close my eyes to be back in that garden with him, kissing him and liking it. The memory of his lips against mine was intense.

I should have freaked out at the time, but there was something about it that made me unafraid. Something about him. Curiosity? Attraction? I had no explanation for it, and that bothered me more than anything. I had been so careful to always keep to myself, so afraid that any step I might take would lead me right back to that same situation I'd barely escaped the first time.

Nothing had happened tonight that made me think of that other night.

It didn't mean that I didn't feel a full-blown panic right now, though. The feelings threatened to overwhelm and drown me. He would want it to happen again. I would probably want it to happen again. And then things would quickly go further and I couldn't do that. I tried to slow down my breathing, to remain calm.

I reminded myself that this had a shelf life. I didn't need to panic. I would go back to Colorado. He would . . . do whatever it was that princes did. There was no point to any of this.

I wasn't sure I could protect my heart from him. I would have to put down my foot and draw a line. These were supposed to be fake dates, not real ones. I couldn't risk my sanity, the peace and balance I had worked so hard to achieve.

I turned over and felt something soft against my temple. I reached up to pull the moonflower out of my hair. It was already wilting. I put it on my nightstand.

There would be no more kissing. I didn't know how that conversation was going to happen, but I would not be kissing Nico . . . whatever his last name was . . . ever again.

I spent a good two hours arguing with myself that I wasn't hungry. I tried every distraction I could think of. I spent twenty minutes just brushing my hair. I watched television in a language I didn't understand. I wished I had a good book. But I eventually lost the fight.

Lemon still hadn't returned, and I was in desperate need of a snack. So I grabbed some socks, threw a sweater on, and headed for the family kitchen Nico had shown me earlier.

The kitchen was all stainless steel and glossy countertops, with under-cabinet lighting that ran the length of the back wall. I didn't switch on any of the overhead lights. I already felt guilty enough opening cabinets and peering at their contents without a bright glare to expose me.

At first I couldn't find the refrigerator, until I realized it was built in to match the rest of the cabinetry. And true to Nico's promise, everything was well stocked. They had nearly every imaginable variety of ice cream in the freezer. I grabbed a pint of chocolate and searched the drawers until I found a spoon.

I jumped up on the counter on the island in the middle of the room and opened up the container. The first bite was divine. I closed my eyes and let out a sigh of contentment. This was exactly what I needed.

I heard a sound to my right, and turned to face the darkness. It looked like there was a table there, but I couldn't make anything out.

My heart froze. "Who's there?"

I heard a chair scraping across the tile floor. "*Sono io.*"

Not helpful. "I don't know what that means."

"It means 'it's me.' Remember? Your favorite prince." Nico stepped into the faint kitchen light wearing pajama bottoms and nothing else. If I thought I'd been mesmerized before, it was nothing compared to a shirtless Nico. His upper torso was total perfection. Like he wasn't real and somebody had sculpted him out of clay. In an I-was-pretty-sure-he-could-cut-glass-with-those-abs kind of way.

I actually had to stop chocolate-flavored drool escaping from my mouth. "I don't have a favorite real-life prince. The only one I know is cocky and kind of full of himself." Which probably wasn't fair, because he wasn't anywhere near as arrogant as he could be. If I looked like him I'd probably spend all day staring in the mirror, telling myself how gorgeous I was.

He had a plate in his hands and walked over to put it in the sink. He turned and leaned against it, directly across from me. "You have a favorite fictional prince then?"

Nobody had ever asked me that. So many animated cuties to choose from. "Probably Prince Eric. From *The Little Mermaid.*"

"Hmm." He crossed his arms across his chest, which caused his shoulder and chest muscles to flex. I felt my internal temperature rise. "Was he the one with dark hair and blue eyes?"

Darn him. "How would you even know that?"

He looked far too smug. "I have three younger sisters, remember?"

I tried to regulate my breathing. He was just a guy. Prince or not, handsome or not, bare-chested or not, still just a guy. I took another bite of my ice cream. "What are you doing up?"

"I was hungry. And sometimes I deal with bouts of insomnia. Usually when I'm worried. And unfortunately, I'm almost always worried." He shrugged. My heart ached for him, and I resisted the urge to go over and hug him. His words made me sad. I also felt bad that he had so much to worry about. But I think I felt the worst about the no sleep. Of all the things that I loved, sleep was probably my favorite, right after food.

"And you?" He pointed at my ice cream.

"I have this horrible habit of getting up to eat around midnight. Growing up it was the only time in my house when I could be alone and not have to worry about . . ." I sucked in a deep breath. I had almost just told him . . . things I'd never told anyone. I cleared my throat. "I guess it stuck."

He looked thoughtful, but thankfully, he didn't push me the way that Lemon would have. But while we sat in silence, I became aware of a faint drumming sound. At first I wondered if it was my heartbeat, but then I realized it came from somewhere else. "What is that noise?"

He turned his head to the left and listened. "Probably Dante's nightclub."

"Dante's nightclub?"

"He converted part of the old dungeon. He must have it up loud tonight. Usually you can't hear it. The dungeon was well soundproofed because no one wants to listen to people screaming and begging for their lives, apparently."

I took another bite and tried not to smile. That was probably where Lemon had been. "I wonder if Salvatore's down there."

"Why would you care if Salvatore was there?" The tenor of his voice had changed slightly, his facial expression hardened.

Oh my frak, he was *jealous*. Why did that make me giddy? "Because Lemon likes him. Easy there, Mr. Green."

"Are we speaking of board games again?"

"No, the color your face just turned." He was jealous. I saw it. And I had liked it.

I was so in over my head. I took another big bite. He looked uncomfortable. He shifted his feet like he was going to leave. Which gave me a major compulsion to keep talking so that he would stay. "If we were speaking of board games, there would be no conversation. I would destroy you at any game you chose."

"Oh, really?" He raised one eyebrow at me.

"Definitely. I would kill you at Monopoly. I had plans to go professional until I tore my rotator cuffs."

That put a smile on his face. "Both of them?"

"Yes. It was terrible. My sponsors were sorely disappointed."

"Didn't that interfere with your studies? Social work, wasn't it?"

I nodded. "What about you? Where did you go to school? What did you major in?"

"Oxford. International relations."

That sounded sort of useless. "How's that working out for you? Spending a lot of time relating to internationals?"

He grinned. "I've been enjoying it recently, yes." It took me a second before I figured out that he was talking about me, but before I could respond, he continued. "My studies focused mainly on means of building up my country's infrastructure. For too long we've been reliant on mining done in the mountains. We need other ways to help our economy. One of my plans now is to offer lower taxes to technology companies. We have a low cost of living comparatively to other European nations, and the lower taxes will help to bring in companies and jobs and encourage the growth of small businesses, which is vital to our success. Increasing tourism is also essential to bettering the lives of my citizens and keeping our young people here in Monterra." He stopped. "I'm sorry, am I boring you?"

I don't know what he thought he saw on my face, but it wasn't boredom. I should have been bored. I should have been Chairman of the Bored.

But when he talked, I found myself fascinated by him. The way his mouth moved, how his eyes lit up, the deep, smooth quality of his voice. "Not at all. I can tell you're really excited about this stuff. That's so . . ."

Cute. Sexy. Adorable. Hot. Endearing. Rar. "Never mind."

My ice cream was nearly halfway gone and had gotten to that slight melty stage where it tasted even better. "It sounds like some good planning. I am all about a good plan," I told him.

"Oh?"

I licked some chocolate off of my spoon, but I stopped when I noticed him watching me intently. My heart rate kicked up a notch. What were we talking about again? Plans. My plans. Right. "My life is one carefully orchestrated plan. I am a firm believer in creating a plan and sticking to it." I liked the way it made me feel in control of my life, especially when everything else felt out of control.

"And you never deviate from your plans, *bella*?"

Tonight had been one giant exercise in deviating from my master plan. My life up to now had been moving from set point to set point. I would graduate in five months with a master's degree in social work. I had already been offered a full-time position at our county's Department of Family Services once I graduated. I had an apartment picked out; I had put the first and last months' rent down. I knew exactly what my life would look like in six months. In five years. In ten.

And not one of those projections had a prince in it.

"What is this, Twenty Questions?"

He looked puzzled and then said, "Is that one of those games you play at American high school parties?"

I hadn't gone to many parties. "All the kids at parties in my high school just got drunk and then pregnant."

He pushed off from the cabinet and came over. I might have gasped when he jumped up onto the counter next to me, sitting closer than necessary, making our shoulders touch. It made my pulse pound. "Maybe you could show me how some of those games were played."

We were not (NOT) going to play any game that involved kissing. "Twenty Questions is easy."

"So I ask you twenty questions, and you have to answer them truthfully?"

He was wrecking my concentration. "No, you think of something and then I ask you twenty questions that have either a yes or no answer until I guess what it is or I run out of questions and lose."

"I like my version better."

"You can't just change the rules."

"I'm the crown prince of Monterra. I can make whatever rules I want." On someone else that might have sounded conceited, but with his mischievous tone and sparkling eyes, I agreed with him. He could make whatever rules he wanted.

"If I don't agree—what? Off with my head?"

He gave me a sly look. "We have much better ways of getting you to comply, *bella*."

That I could not risk. So we'd be playing the game his way. "You start. Ask away."

"Who is your favorite author? Wait, don't answer. I already know. Jane Austen."

I wanted to be outraged, but just couldn't because he was right. Jane Austen was my favorite author. "How did you . . . ?"

"I've found that most of the women that I have most enjoyed being with list Austen as their favorite author."

What was he saying? That he enjoyed being with me more than he did other people? Was this some kind of admission that was just going over my head? A whole herd of butterflies took to wing in my stomach.

"What about you?" I asked in between bites, watching him out of the corner of my eye.

He looked up at the ceiling for a moment before looking back at me. "F. Scott Fitzgerald."

"I'm so glad you didn't say Hemingway or Faust. I hate those guys."

That made him laugh. "I also like J. R. R. Tolkien."

"You like fantasy?" He nodded. I had to admit it—he surprised me. Then again, he already lived in a fantasy world with castles and kings and huge mountains. Maybe he could relate to it.

"Have you read any of his works?"

"I tried to read the *Lord of the Rings* series but could not get past that Tom Bombadil character. The movies were much better. That Legolas guy was seriously hot." Not Nico hot, but still.

He nudged me with his shoulder. "I thought you preferred dark-haired men."

I gulped and begged my heart to stay inside my chest. "Please don't tell Prince Eric that I've been fictionally unfaithful to him."

He laughed again. "Your turn to ask a question."

"I feel stupid asking this, but what language do you actually speak?"

"English."

Now it was my turn to laugh. "You know what I mean."

He had his chin resting on his shoulder so that all I would have to do is turn my head and our lips would be just a kiss apart. So I kept my attention focused on my ever-dwindling ice cream. "Monterrans speak Italian. We have a lot of different slang terms, some German and French words and phrases thrown in. The accent is what sets us apart. It's like the difference between British English and American English. You can understand one another, but the accents are noticeable."

"That's pretty impressive, being bilingual. I had a couple years of Spanish as an undergrad, but it didn't really stick."

"Not just bilingual. I also speak German, French, and can get by in Spanish." He nudged my shoulder again. "Impressed?"

Obviously. "No." I started scarfing down the rest of my food, needing to be done and leave. Nico was getting to me. Every sense was heightened, every nerve ending painfully excited, and he was making me laugh and like him even more.

As if he could sense my inner turmoil, he jumped off the counter and came to stand right in front of me, pressing his legs against mine and putting his hands on either side of me, trapping me in place.

"I don't know that I've ever seen a woman do that before."

"What?" I refused to meet his eyes.

"Eat."

Now I had to look up to see if he was serious, or if he was teasing me. Serious. "Spend a lot of time watching women eat, do you?"

"You might be surprised. A lot of state dinners and balls, things like that. Most women push the salad around on their plate without ever eating any of it."

That was stupid. "I like to eat."

He reached over and took the spoon and ice cream out of my hands, gently placing them on the counter. "I like that you like to eat."

My breath caught. "That's kind of a weird thing to like. Why would you like that?"

He leaned in. "Because an appetite for one thing indicates appetites for . . . other things."

I felt like I had just run a marathon. (Or a half marathon, because if I were honest, a real marathon wouldn't happen even in my imagination.) I hoped he wouldn't notice my chest heaving, trying to get enough air. I could feel my face going beet red.

"She blushes! Oh, I am going to enjoy spending time with you."

"I haven't said yes yet. To the article or spending time with you."

He reached up to separate out a lock of my hair, twisting it around his finger. "You will."

He was right. I would. But I needed to retain some pride. "If I say yes, it will only be because I need the money."

Nico leaned in, and I could feel his breath against the spot where my neck met my shoulder. I wanted to melt like my ice cream. "Why do you need the money, *bella*?"

I tried to swallow but couldn't. My eyelids drifted shut. "My tuition scholarship was defunded. I've already borrowed as much as I'm allowed, and I can't keep a job because of all the fieldwork I'm required to do. If I don't find some way to get the money, I won't be able to graduate."

"And that will ruin your carefully laid plans."

"Uh-huh." What was he doing with his fingers? Everywhere he touched me he left little pools of flame behind.

He was unfairly using his masculine wiles against me, and I was stupidly giving in. I opened my eyes to see him studying me as he slowly ran his knuckles against my cheek. "So is that a yes?"

"It will be a yes. I will pretend to date you, go where you want me to, write what you want me to write. On one condition."

He waited for me to continue.

"No more kissing."

Chapter 7

His hands stilled. "*Ma che?*" I guessed that was Italian for "What the frak did you just say?"

"If you think about it, you want me to stay objective when I write the story, don't you? So we should take kissing off the table, right?" I didn't know if I was trying to convince him or me.

"So you're worried that my kisses will sway you and harm your objectivity?" He paused, as if considering. "That's probably true." He went back to lightly caressing me, and I worried that I might have to start planning my own funeral because I was *dying*.

But I couldn't let on just how much he affected me. "Full of yourself much?"

He had his face close to mine, and I could feel his smile, hear it in his voice. He moved to put his lips right above mine. "You and I both know that I could prove as much right now."

Of all the things I expected him to do and say, the next thing to come out of his mouth was not one of them. "I can do that. If you don't want me to kiss you, I won't. I will wait until you ask me to."

Usually I would have been like, so not going to happen, but in this case . . . well, I hoped I was strong enough to stick to my guns.

Nico ran his fingers through my hair, and I unconsciously tilted my head to lean into his open hand. "Am I allowed to still touch you? I'm not sure I can promise not to touch you."

"Uh . . ." I meant to say something. I did. He completely disrupted all of my brain waves.

"Because it would seem you like touching me as well." I opened my eyes and looked down. I had both of my hands on his bare chest. When had that happened? I didn't even remember doing it. My hands obviously had minds of their own. I clenched them shut and put them back in my lap.

"Touching is okay, I guess," I said in that same breathy voice that I only had around him, and now felt like my new permanent one. To be fair, and putting aside the fact that I enjoyed it, Monterrans had repeatedly proven themselves to be an affectionate and kind of handsy people. I couldn't exactly say no to him for something that was cultural, could I?

Yes, even in my foggy haze I was aware of my pathetic attempts to justify and rationalize.

"Good. Although I don't know if it's very fair to give a man a taste of heaven and tell him he can't have it again."

My heart barreled against my chest as he did that thing where he ran his thumb gently over my lips, across my jawline, back to my lips. I sort of loved that. I would probably give up my firstborn child if we could just stay in this spot all night doing that.

I was going to lose every last bit of resolve I had. I blinked a few times.

"What about our questions?" Yes, the questions. We should definitely go back to the questions. I said the first thing that occurred to me. "Do you, uh, have any hidden talents?"

His eyes looked hooded and sensual. "I think I've already shown you part of my special talent."

Holy crap.

Again with the amused expression. "But I also play piano and am decent at dancing. Not the nightclub kind. Real partner dancing."

"I've never done that before." This entire experience was becoming full of things I'd never done before.

"I would love to show you." Was he talking about the dancing or the other thing? "And you? What talents do you keep hidden from the world?"

He wanted me to think of what talents I had when my mind had turned into a vast Nico-induced wasteland. Only one thing popped into my head.

I pushed against him, and he let me go, stepping aside. I hopped down and went over to the fridge. I hoped he couldn't see how my hands shook while I pulled the door open. The cold air soothed my flushed skin. I thought I had noticed . . . there.

I brought out a container of fresh cherries and popped the top open. I walked over to the opposite side of the island so that we had it between us. "I learned how to do this at the one slumber party I went to in junior high."

Breaking off the stem, I put it into my mouth. He looked fascinated, putting both hands on the counter to lean in my direction. It took longer than I expected it to because it had been so long since I'd last done it. Factoring in Nico's hungry gaze did not help things either.

Finally, I fished the stem out and put it on my palm, holding it out for him. "I can tie them into knots with my tongue."

I felt proud of myself right up until he groaned, shaking his head. "Katerina, do you have any idea what that does to a hot-blooded Latin man?"

"How fortunate for me then that you are Monterran," I said, echoing back his words to me when we first met.

As he placed the phrase I'd just used, he started to laugh and I joined in, the physical moment broken between us, but a new, fragile, emotional one starting in its place.

Despite my inexperience, even I knew that I had been flirting with danger. I put the stem down on the counter. I also knew I couldn't push him too far and expect him to still respect my requirement. It was time for me to go back to my room. By myself. I put the cherries away.

"Okay then. Good night." I got to the door of the kitchen when I heard him say something.

"Next time, choose the gelato instead of ice cream. Gelato is infinitely superior."

Next time. Like there would be a next time of this. I would lie in my bed and starve myself every night before he'd get a repeat of tonight. I would go down into those dungeons and find some manacles and chain myself to my bed before this would happen again. I just nodded, like I agreed.

"Do you need me to help you find your way back?"

"Nope!" I barked. "I'm totally capable of going back to my room." I hated when he looked at me that way—like he totally understood me and knew exactly what I was thinking and he thought it was funny.

Thankfully, he let me go without another word.

I woke up to blinding sun as a short, balding, serious-looking man in a well-tailored suit threw the curtains open. I held my hands in front of my eyes to block the light out. "What's happening?"

"You need to wake up, *signorina*. Your flight to Paris will be leaving soon."

What the what? "Flight to Paris?"

"His Royal Highness is the guest of honor at a charity ball in Paris this evening, and he would like for you and Signorina Beauchamp to accompany him."

"And you are?" More strangeness in the Monterran castle.

The man bowed to me, and I could see the shiny top of his head. "I am Giacomo Rossi, assistant secretary to Her Royal Highness, Queen Aria. I have been sent to assist you while you are staying with us."

Oh yeah. Nico had mentioned something about this guy last night. That probably meant I should get up. But my head felt heavy, and my eyes were burning. "What time is it?"

"Six twenty."

I groaned. "They have one of those in the morning, too?"

"May I get you some coffee? An espresso?"

"I don't drink caffeine, thanks." I didn't like to take in anything that would alter my body's chemistry. Giacomo looked unfazed. Most people looked ready to give birth to kittens when I told them I didn't drink coffee.

"Hot chocolate then?"

"Sure."

"We have a busy schedule today," was his response. "I have taken the liberty of packing a bag for you, *signorina*."

"Please call me Kat." I was already being darlin' and *bella*-ed to death. I didn't need another name. I mean, I understood that Monterrans used endearments at the drop of a hat with people they'd only just met, but it would be nice to be Kat again. "And that was very nice of you, thank you, but I don't really have anything to wear to Paris. Or to a ball."

"I have already purchased several dresses and suitable pants outfits for you and packed them."

That made me sit straight up in bed. "What?"

"I used your current clothing to get the correct sizes. I also purchased matching shoes and some other accessories for your use."

Another girl might have been exuberant about free clothes. But I hated charity. It made me feel small and pathetic. I did not want something for nothing. "I . . . I can't accept it. That's too much."

Giacomo gave me a pointed look. "It's already done. There will be expectations when you are out with the prince."

I didn't care about anyone's expectations and was about to tell him that when he said, "It would be upsetting and offensive to the queen and her family if you refused this gift."

That took the wind out of my sails. How could anyone say no? "I'll leave everything here when I go back to the States."

I got a disapproving face that reminded me of a grumpy Tim Gunn. "I do not think His Highness will have any use for them when you are done. You may take them with you."

He lifted up the tablet he had been carrying and turned it on. "You have approximately ten minutes to shower and dress, and a car will be waiting for you by the west exit. From there we will drive to the airport, and spend an hour and a half in flight until we reach Paris. I have scheduled several designers to come to the suite where you and Signorina Beauchamp will select gowns for this evening. I have also arranged for hair and makeup artists to be there. You will have some free time today to shop or explore the city, if you wish."

Much as I appreciated his attention to detail and planning, I wasn't sure I much liked somebody else making plans for me. Plans that nobody had bothered to run past me first. "Do I have any say in this at all?"

"No, Signorina Kat. I'm afraid you do not. Now you have nine minutes."

I wanted to be stubborn and refuse, but I had promised both Nico and Lemon. If I went back on my word, that would open a door for Nico to go back on his. Not to mention that I always kept my promises. I jumped out of bed and ran to the shower, taking the fastest one I had ever taken. I got out to brush my teeth and saw a bag on the counter. I peered inside. It was a toiletry bag, with almost everything packed except for the stuff I was currently using. I rinsed out my mouth, threw the toothpaste and toothbrush into the bag, followed by my brush once I'd put my hair in a ponytail.

In the closet Giacomo had laid out a pair of nice slacks and a cotton button-up shirt. I pulled out a pair of jeans and a purple sweater and put them on instead, along with a sturdy pair of tennis shoes. I put some extra jeans, shirts, and sweaters into my toiletry bag. My other suitcase was gone. I guessed that Giacomo had it sent down already.

"Kat, darlin'?"

I came back into my room to find Lemon. "Finally." I threw my arms around her.

"What the devil is this for?"

"I'm just happy to see you. I waited hours last night to talk to you." I stopped hugging her. She made me feel real and grounded again.

Lemon's hazel eyes lit up with interest. "I want every single little detail. Let's get down to that car before it leaves without us."

I grabbed my toiletry bag, winter coat, and the to-go cup of hot chocolate Giacomo had left for me on my nightstand. I took a sip. I groaned. I wanted to bathe in this stuff. It was a good thing we were only staying in Monterra for a couple of weeks. Otherwise I was going to get seriously fat.

She started pumping me for information, and I began telling her about the beginning of our tour, what he said, what I said, how he looked, what I did, how I felt.

I saw Giacomo tapping on his tablet, standing next to a giant door at the bottom of the main stairs, and we headed toward him. The door had been opened, and I saw a black stretch limo. "Make sure you sit with me on the plane so we can get to the good stuff," Lemon said. "I don't think we'll have any privacy in the car."

I heard male voices come up behind me. Their words echoed through the front entry hall and down to us. "You know he's only interested in her because she's convenient. She's not even pretty."

"She's nothing but a challenge to him."

I turned to look and the men stopped talking, and two of them smiled at each other. I felt absolutely sick to my stomach. They were talking about me. Me and Nico. And that he only wanted me because I wouldn't let him have me.

"Of all the rude, hateful . . ." Lemon whispered next to me. "Ignore them. They wanted you to overhear them. They deliberately spoke in English to make sure you understood."

"Aren't those his friends?"

"Salvatore is his friend, but that wasn't him talking. Those other two are jerks. I met them last night and disliked them on sight. They're like a couple of foxes in a henhouse. Don't listen."

"But why would they . . ." She didn't let me finish. She hustled me outside and into the waiting limo. I sat on the back seat while Lemon sat kitty-corner to me on the side seat. I started to move so that we could sit together when men began coming in through both doors.

Dante and Rafe greeted me with more cheek kisses, asking me how my day was and wondering if they could do anything for me. I held back tears and just shook my head. Oblivious, they greeted Lemon in the same way and sat next to her, keeping her wrapped up in conversation. She looked over at me with a concerned expression and shrugged apologetically.

Was any of that true? Did they all think I was some stupid little ugly thing throwing myself at Nico?

Salvatore and the two douche bags got into the car and sat on the empty side seat. Dante rushed to make introductions. Davide, the Conte di Lerio, and Francesco, the Barone di Atanni. Francesco was the one talking about me earlier. He had an awful, evil smirk on his face. "They are family friends who also serve on the board of Nico's charity, representing their families."

Davide and Francesco said their hellos, pleasure to meet me sort of thing. Davide at least had the decency to look embarrassed. I could only nod, afraid that I might start crying if I spoke. Lemon gave them the dirtiest, meanest look I had ever seen her give anyone. And I had seen her mad plenty of times.

Nico was the last one to the car, and he apologized to everyone for making us wait. I couldn't believe how much better I felt when he sat next to me. Like sitting next to a roasting fire after a day spent out in the snow.

"Good morning, *bella*." His smile faltered, and he put an arm around my shoulders. "What's wrong? Has something happened?"

Me and my stupid expressive face. I refrained from resting my head on his shoulder. I wanted to fall into his embrace, to let him help me. But I had to stay where I was and stop sending mixed signals. "Nothing. I'm fine."

"Are you certain?" he asked as someone outside the car closed the doors. We pulled out with black SUVs in front of us and behind us.

"Yeah. Totally sure."

"You have only to tell me what dragons need slaying, and I will see to their quick deaths."

That made me laugh in spite of myself, and Nico looked happier too. He took his arm away and pulled out his ringing cell phone. He said, "*Mi scusi,*" to me, and then *"Pronto,"* when he answered the phone.

I looked out the window, ignoring the conversations going on all around me. It was my first look at the castle from the outside, and it was one of those fabulous fairy-tale kinds, all gray stone and tall towers, with slanted roofs covered in thick snow. We passed through a massive outer wall on our way down the hill.

I had my hands at my side, and Nico's hand was next to mine. He used his littlest finger to gently rub the top of my hand. Instead of it being something that got my blood racing, it comforted me and improved my mood. I didn't get a chance to talk to him as he had one phone call after another during the entire trip.

Before long we were on a tarmac, next to a small airplane. A stewardess stood at the top of a set of stairs. I looked over at the airport. "Don't we have to go inside? Get our passports checked?"

"Not when you travel with me, you don't." Nico grinned, putting his phone away. In addition to the people in our car, there was an SUV full of security, and another one that had secretaries or assistants like Giacomo in it.

Everyone moved to the plane, and Nico took my hand to help me up the steep steps. I didn't need his help, but I didn't make him stop either.

Inside there were comfortable-looking cream-colored leather chairs separated by small tables, and some full-length couches made of the same material.

"Wow." A private plane? I'd only ever seen them in movies, and now I was getting to ride in one!

Lemon came and commandeered me away from Nico. "My turn now," she said with a flirtatious smile, and it flooded me with warmth when I realized that Nico hadn't even looked at her or responded. His gaze was instead fixed on mine, until one of his secretaries handed him a stack of papers, directing him to a different area so that they could talk.

Lemon and I buckled in as the very pretty flight attendant asked if she could get anything for us. I said no, and Lemon asked for coffee.

"Okay, this is pretty amazing," I told her.

"You won't believe this, but it has a full bathroom and a bedroom on here, too."

"How do you know that?"

"Because Dante offered to 'show' me the bedroom." She rolled her eyes, and we both laughed.

I saw the two brothers talking to their "family friends."

"What are the twins like?" I asked. "I haven't actually spent any time with them yet."

"Rafe is quieter, more easygoing. Loves to read, but really loves videogames. He's finishing up his degree in gaming design. And Dante . . . well, let's just put it this way. I am wildly attracted to him."

"Which means he's an obnoxious playboy with no real ambition who will break your heart."

Lemon sighed. "You got it. I will be steering clear."

I put my hand on her arm and squeezed. "Good thing you have Salvatore. How's that going?"

"Slowly. Slowly, but surely." She tapped her perfectly manicured nails on the armrest. "But let's talk about your boy, shall we?"

I let out a happy sigh. I picked up where I'd left off in the story, watching Lemon's eyes grow bigger and bigger as I built up to the kiss in the moonlight garden.

"And then?"

"Then he kissed me."

Lemon squealed out loud, and almost everyone on the plane turned to look at us. "Shh," I told her, giggling.

"I'm as excited as a hen on a hot griddle. I can't believe it's finally happened! My little unicorn finally has a dent in her horn!"

"And there's more."

"More?" she shrieked.

I again shushed her and told her about our kitchen rendezvous. As I remembered my conversation with Nico, it struck me how easy it was for me to talk to him. I'd never been able to manage more than a few fumbling words around guys before. But with him, everything just flowed. Lemon was the only other person I'd ever experienced that with, but a large part of our conversations succeeded because of her socialness and ability to carry it one-sided if she needed to.

I finished up the story with mine and Nico's arrangement and the rule I'd put down.

She narrowed her eyes at me. "You're not going to let him kiss you again? Are you crazy?"

"Not according to the court-appointed psychiatrist."

She made a face. "Not funny. You know what I mean."

Lemon knew a lot, but she didn't know everything. Maybe I should tell her and then she'd stop pushing me. An icy fear gripped my spine when I thought of confessing. "I can't. I can't handle being with him."

She took me by the hand then and stayed quiet for a moment. "I know you don't want to talk about it. Heaven knows I've tried to get you to. And I respect that it's private. But if you aren't going to tell me, darlin', you need to tell somebody. You need to stop shutting everyone out. Stop making up reasons to not be with someone. You need to move past whatever it is so that you don't live your whole life in fear."

The attendant returned with Lemon's drink, and I crossed my arms, shaken and upset. I turned to look out the window. Maybe she was right. Maybe it was time to tell someone. It would be hard to tell Lemon, though. Who knew what kind of conclusions she'd already come to? How would she react? Would I still be able to look her in the eye after it was done? Would she tell me how stupid I'd been? I'd spent the last ten years beating myself up. I didn't need my best friend doing it too.

Lemon excused herself to use the restroom, and I looked over the seats to where Nico sat. He was deep in conversation with the men and women surrounding him, looking very serious. I liked having the chance to observe him without him knowing. I was quickly disabused of that notion though when a small half smile appeared, followed up with a knowing look in my direction. I turned away from him.

Insufferable. So annoying.

A small voice asked me then if that was how I really felt about him, or if I was doing exactly what Lemon had accused me of. Making up excuses so I wouldn't have to be real with Nico.

If I was just living in fear.

Chapter 8

I didn't want to discuss the Nico situation any further, and Lemon didn't press me. Instead, she invited the twins to join us. They told us several hysterical stories about trouble they'd gotten into while at boarding school. The mindless laughter was infinitely better than serious introspection.

Dante made googly eyes at Lemon the whole time, but she didn't encourage him at all. Which seemed to only make him try harder.

The plane landed and I freaked out once, right as the tires made contact with the runway. I gripped the armrests and let out a sigh of relief when we started to slow down. When the pilot told us we could disembark, everybody stood up at the same time. I heard Dante offer to take Lemon's carry-on bag, but she refused.

Nico made his way over to me and, smiling, took my hand. I followed behind him to the exit. Where I was pretty sure he started swearing in Italian. He looked over his shoulder at me.

"Stay behind me," he said. He said something in Italian to the security still on the plane. Nico stepped back to allow two men to pass by us. He tugged on my hand to indicate that I should follow him. When we reached the bottom of the stairs, two more men flanked me on either side. We began walking to the car.

I heard the noise before I could understand what was going on. As we stepped off the plane, there were dozens of reporters and photographers. They were all calling out and there were a series of bright, blinding flashes. The cold winter air swirled around us, with snow flurries dancing in and out of the crowd.

We ran to the limo and dove inside. Everybody from the first car ride piled in behind us, plus one man I didn't recognize. We took off so fast my head hit the back of the seat. "What was that?" I asked.

Nico looked furious. "Paparazzi." He said it like it was a bad word. "Johann, I don't understand how they knew we were here. I was very clear in my instruction that our travel plans be kept secret."

A man with a large, pointed nose and small, beady eyes, topped off by a slicked-up comb-over answered. "Not every hole can be plugged. They are a very resourceful group. Perhaps if you'd let go of the *signorina's* hand, they wouldn't have been so interested?"

Johann peered down his nose at me, making me completely uncomfortable. I hadn't even realized that I was still holding Nico's hand, gripping it tightly. I relaxed my hold, but that only made him grab on tighter.

We drove quickly, and Nico kept turning around to see if we were followed. But we managed to make our escape, and he finally relaxed.

Johann started outlining an itinerary for Nico that day. It sounded like one appointment right after the other. It was only eight thirty in the morning, and he already looked exhausted. I wanted to smooth the worry lines in his forehead away.

We pulled up in front of a very old and very beautiful white building. Somebody said the name of the hotel, but it was all French to me.

There were more paparazzi waiting by the entrance. Security jumped into the crowd and did their best to clear a pathway. Everyone got out until it was only Johann, Nico, and me left in the limo.

He gave my hand a squeeze. "Enjoy yourself today, *bella.*"

"Aren't you coming in?" I asked.

"I wish I could spend the day with you, but I have many responsibilities that I must attend to."

Nodding, I said goodbye and left him with Johann in the car. Strangely enough, I didn't want to leave him. I stepped right into the gutter and slush filled my shoes. Lovely. Giacomo appeared at my side to help me through all the crazy people with cameras. I didn't think they realized that I was American, because not one of them yelled anything in English.

Sometimes it was nice to be oblivious.

A doorman let us inside the hotel. The lobby was done up in shades of red and gold, with a huge chandelier hanging down what seemed every five feet or so. They had decorated for the holidays, and there were large wreaths with ribbons that matched the interior of the lobby, as well as several elegant Christmas trees. We didn't have to check in, and were instead led to an elevator separate from the others. One of the bodyguards used a keycard before he could press the button. We went all the way to the top floor.

Francesco, Salvatore, and Davide were shown to their rooms, and the rest of us walked to the end of the hall. "The Presidential Suite," Giacomo announced as he opened the two double doors. A valet followed him in, pushing a trundle that held all of our bags.

Dante and Rafe went in like we weren't walking into the most luxurious, gorgeous hotel room ever. A large front entryway led us into a living room, decorated with modern furniture. A heavily ornate fireplace dominated one entire wall. More chandeliers. A huge dining table that seated twenty off of a small kitchen. And I saw four bedrooms, grouped in twos on either side of the living room. The windows facing out of the living room were floor-to-ceiling and seemed to overlook all of Paris. "That's the Eiffel Tower!" I said, pointing out the window. But nobody seemed excited about it but me.

"If you need anything else, you have only to call me," Giacomo said as he handed all of us our own keycards. "All of the staff is staying on this floor, so we should be readily accessible. The designers' teams should be here shortly."

The twins went to claim two of the bedrooms. That left two, so I supposed that Lemon and I would be sharing. We opened the doors of the two empty rooms. One had a huge bed, bigger than a king. The other had two beds. "This is us!" Lemon said. She went back and grabbed her suitcase, pulled out the handle, and rolled her luggage in. It was a pretty room, decorated in pale violets, dark purples, and silver.

I flopped backward onto one of the beds. Not as nice as the bed at the palace, but still better than every bed I'd had growing up. We started exploring. I looked at the fancy leather-bound folder full of information about the hotel, read over the room service menus, and then went into the bathroom when Lemon called for me. The mosaic-tiled shower was big enough for twenty people and had more showerheads and gadgets than a car wash.

"Look at that tub!" Lemon exclaimed, clapping her hands together with glee. Lemon adored a good bath, and I knew she'd make use of that jetted tub before we left.

"Breakfast!" one of the brothers called. We came out of the room and the dining room table had a large assortment of breads and pastries. "Try this one," Rafe said to me. "It's called *pain au chocolat*."

I took what looked like a croissant from his hand and bit into it. There was melted chocolate inside! How had I lived my whole life and never had chocolate inside of bread before? "Are you serious right now?"

Rafe looked confused and adjusted his glasses. "Serious about what?"

Lemon laughed. "That means she likes it. A lot."

"Oh, we've gone past liking. I am ready to marry this thing."

Dante came out of his room, reminding Rafe about their first appointment of the day. They left and promised to see us later.

Before I had a chance to go back and jump on the bed like I wanted to, there was a knock on the front door. Lemon answered it and let in Giacomo, who was followed by several severely skinny French women dressed all in black, who were pushing racks of clothes and carrying suitcases. They set the racks in the middle of the living room and then started propping up portable tables. They opened their suitcases and took out the contents, arranging them on the tables.

"Some of these gowns have been pulled directly from the rack, some will be couture originals," Giacomo said. "Any of them will do well for tonight."

This was Lemon's grown-up equivalent of a kid in a candy store. I noticed her rack had more dresses than mine, and she started flipping through them. "I'm so excited, I'm shaking. But that could also be from all the coffee I've been drinking today."

I halfheartedly looked through them as well. All different kinds of styles and colors. How was I going to choose? I had no love for fashion. But when I found it, I knew.

This dress was The One.

With reverent hands I lifted the hanger off of the rack. The dress was strapless, the palest pink, and the entire bodice and full, flouncy, floor-length skirt were covered in sparkly crystals.

"Oh."

By this point Lemon had already disrobed and tried on three different dresses, laying the ones she didn't want over the back of a chair. Where a pissed-off-looking Frenchwoman was putting them back on hangers while glaring at Lemon.

Lemon caught sight of me holding The Dress. "Did you find one you liked?"

"I think so." There was a tag attached to the side. I lifted it up and my eyes went wide. "Lemon, this dress is frakking *thirty thousand* euros."

"So?"

"So I can't wear a dress worth more than my student loans." What if I ripped it? Or stained it? Both of which were highly distinct possibilities. "I can't afford this."

"You don't have to buy it. These designers are lending us these dresses because you'll be pictured wearing it while you're with Nico. Those pictures will go in a bunch of magazines. The designer gets publicity, and you get to look gorgeous. Win-win."

I found it pretty unlikely that anyone would want to take my picture. With a downcast heart, I put the dress back. "I can't wear it."

Lemon got that determined look in her eyes. She came over and took the dress off the rack. "Yes, you can. For once in your life, you will wear the dress and go to the ball and dance with the prince. And if you won't, I will make you."

Was this third grade? "Make me?"

"Yes, make you. You've lived a hard enough life. I won't let you go on doing things I know you'll regret later. You deserve at least one night of fun. Try this on. Now."

Lacking Lemon's self-confidence, I went into our shared room and closed the door. Before I even stepped into the dress I knew. It was perfect. The sheer, soft lining felt amazing against my skin. I had worried it might be too short because I was so tall, but the hem went all the way to the floor. Like it had been made for me.

I came out of the room holding the bodice, because I couldn't reach the zipper. Lemon had a delighted expression in her eyes and told me to turn around so that she could zip it up. "You look amazeballs."

I went back into our bathroom where we had a full-length mirror. I twisted from side to side and puffed the skirt out. I even did a couple of twirls to see the skirt flare out. I caught myself smiling in my reflection. "You're sure this is okay?"

"Trust me," Lemon said. "It goes perfectly with my master plan."

Before I could ask her whether the plan she was referencing was the one to help market Monterra and Nico to the world, or the plan to get me a boyfriend, she had left.

I came out into the living room, and Giacomo stopped what he was doing. He wore an expression of pride. "You look *bellissima*, Signorina Kat." I thanked him.

Several of the women came over and started poking and prodding me. I gave Lemon a questioning look. "They're going to tailor it so that thing fits you like a glove." Once they'd finished, they unzipped me and had me step out of the dress. I hurried back to our room to get redressed, not wanting to stand around in my underwear.

When I came back out Lemon stood in a strapless, deep red, mermaid-style dress. Flounces shot out just above her knee, and it was belted in the middle with what looked like a belt made out of a bunch of cubic zirconia. "What do you think?"

"You look sort of perfect," I said. "But I think you could show up in a flour sack and every guy there would still want to be with you."

"Not every guy," Lemon teased. I rolled my eyes. Could we go five minutes without a Nico mention?

After they finished with getting her measurements, we were directed over to the table. There were undergarments, shoes, and jewelry. Lemon picked up a black, lacy strapless bra and sexy matching panties.

"I thought you were doing the virgin thing with Salvatore."

"This isn't for him. This is for me. It makes me feel pretty and confident." She put her hand on my arm. "And it's okay to want to feel pretty, Kat."

As I stood there in front of the table, I got an ache in the pit of my stomach. I knew how right she was. We had discussed it many times in the past. I had avoided anything to make myself look pretty. I never worried about my hair. I never wore makeup. Part of that was laziness, but another part was that I hadn't wanted to be attractive to anyone. I didn't want someone to pursue me.

I picked up a sheer white strapless bra. But maybe for just this one night, it would be okay.

After we'd selected everything, and thanked Giacomo for his advice and for arranging the whole thing, we were set loose on the city. Nico's security escorted us downstairs through a back entrance where they had a cab waiting for us. Lemon turned on her shopping homing beacon, and we arrived at what the cabdriver called the Triangle d'Or. Designer shops ran up and down the street.

"I need to get some presents for my parents. And we should definitely buy some gifts for the royal family. Christmas is only two days away."

I frowned. "Do you think they're going to include us in their Christmas?"

"They've included us in everything else so far. I can't imagine they'll banish us to a tower while they celebrate. We have to buy them gifts. If nothing else, to thank them for their hospitality." Lemon put both of her hands against Chanel's display window, fogging up the glass. I was close to asking her if she and the window needed a few minutes alone.

"I don't have any money to pay for presents." I chewed on my upper lip, worried.

"This is on me."

"No, Lemon."

That made her leave her window alone. "Katerina MacTaggart! You let me do this. Or, so help me, I am calling my mother."

My shoulders sagged. "Only if you let me pay you back once I get a job."

She actually stamped her foot. "Stop being so proud. You are *ruining* it for everyone who wants to do something for you. Do you know what it feels like to have stuff constantly thrown back in your face? You want to dedicate your life to helping children. What would happen if every time you tried to help a kid they said, 'No way,' or 'I don't want your help'?"

"That's totally different."

The cold air turned her angry breaths into puffs of smoke. She reminded me of a little dragon. "It's exactly the same."

She was right. I had never thought of it that way. All these years I had dragged my feet, so afraid of giving in to charity, of being seen as less than. All these years that I had fought to maintain my pride. I thought I was just being self-reliant. What I was being was a pain in the butt. And what excuse did I have? As she'd just pointed out, I wanted to spend my time helping others. How much of a hypocrite did it make me that I couldn't accept any help in return?

"Okay," I mumbled.

"What was that?"

"I said okay," I repeated in a louder tone. "You're right, I was wrong."

Lemon blinked a few times. "Do you think we can get that etched on a plaque while we're here?"

I laughed and linked my arm through hers. "Let's go do some damage to your daddy's bank account."

Chapter 9

After Lemon bought out half of Paris for herself and her mother, we ate at an adorable bistro. Once we'd filled our stomachs, we started shopping specifically for presents for the royals. An Elsa doll for Serafina, and a home mani-pedi set for Chiara. Lemon said she'd noticed the queen seemed to like wearing violet, so we picked her up a cashmere scarf in that color. I found a small framed Marilyn Monroe picture with Lemon's favorite quote about women who tried to be equal with men. I bought it with the few dollars I had left in my checking account and slid it into my purse.

My thoughts kept drifting to Nico as we shopped, which I found disconcerting. I darted into a rare bookstore, and Lemon followed me in. I asked if they had any books by Tolkien or Fitzgerald. The man showed me several that were inside cases, some first editions, others autographed. All were priced in the tens of thousands. I tried not to choke. "Do you have something not quite as expensive?"

The shopkeeper brought me out an old-looking copy of *The Great Gatsby*. I ran my fingers over the green leather binding. It was decorated with golden art deco symbols around the edges. "This one is five hundred," he said.

That number made my stomach drop, and Lemon looked at me questioningly. "He's Nico's favorite author."

Lemon slapped her credit card down on the counter. "Then we'll take it."

My instinct was to protest, but I refrained.

Agreeing that we would buy the rest of the presents when we were back in Monterra, we decided to do a little sightseeing. We stopped by the Eiffel Tower and the Arc de Triomphe, taking tons of pictures. Worn out, we found another cab to take us back to the hotel.

We drove in silence, and I wondered what Nico was doing right then. I felt an unfamiliar pang, a hollowness in my chest.

Her phone buzzed, and Lemon pulled it out of her purse. "Serafina and Chiara say hello. Chiara says to make sure we take pictures once we're all dressed up and send them to her."

I smiled. "Tell them I say hi and I'll see them soon."

She texted for a minute and then put the phone back in her purse. "How are you doing?"

I looked at my wrapped wrist. "I'm fine." The swelling was gone, and I didn't notice the ache at all anymore. My ankle felt totally healed. Even so, Giacomo had recommended ballet flats rather than heels for the evening, and I was quick to agree. I hated heels. They always hurt my feet.

"I was actually speaking on an emotional level. You just seemed a little sad."

"I was just thinking about Nico. I think—" I paused, recognizing the gravity of what I was about to say. "I think I missed him today." Which seemed stupid considering the fact that I had only met him a few days ago. And had only really talked to him for less than twenty-four hours.

She looked way too happy.

"I mean, how am I supposed to write about him if I don't get to spend any time with him?"

"Somebody's got a crush, somebody's got a crush," she started in a singsong voice.

I pushed against her shoulder. "If you start singing about us sitting in a tree, I will punch you."

"Ow. Love seems to bring out your violent side."

"Stop it. We don't love each other. We're not even in like. Right now, he's just a friend." A friend who made me feel shivery, fluttery, giggly, and like a boy-crazed fourteen-year-old girl every time I saw him, but still just a friend.

"I'm sorry, I can't help but tease you. This is too much fun. I finally found you a guy. We only had to travel halfway around the world, and he only had to be a prince to be good enough for you."

I wanted to give her a stinging retort, but we pulled up to the front of the hotel. Where a horde of paparazzi awaited us. "Should we tell the driver to go round back?"

"Too late now," Lemon said as the driver got out of the cab. He went to the back of his car to get our packages and bags from the trunk. Lemon and I both exited out the same door. I ignored the reporters and the lights until I realized they were talking to us in English.

Not only that, but they were calling us by name.

There were too many of them yelling too loudly to understand what they were saying, so we grabbed our things and let the doorman usher us inside.

My heart pounded frantically, and cold fear clawed its way up to settle in my chest. "How do they know who we are?"

"I have no idea." She looked as frazzled as I felt. It was completely disconcerting having total strangers screaming out your name.

We got in the elevator and up to our room. We agreed to tell someone what had just happened, but as soon as we walked inside the room, total chaos reigned.

There had to be like fifty people in the suite. Tuxedos had been brought in for the princes. Secretaries and stylists ran all over the place. People came over and collected all of our bags, and I only had a moment to wonder where they were taking all our stuff.

Then I didn't care. Because Nico was there. My heart leapt in response.

As if he sensed me, he stopped in the middle of his conversation and turned to look at me across the room. I waggled my fingers at him, and he winked at me. My whole being suddenly felt lighter. I started walking toward him, but Giacomo hustled me into my bedroom. I saw two director's chairs had been set up, along with tables full of makeup products and hair styling instruments.

I was told to sit, and people were hovering over me like vultures, staring at me as they discussed my face and hair situation amongst themselves in French. I reached out for Giacomo. "Please tell them not to slather it on."

Lemon sat next to me in the other chair. "I'm sure they can see that you don't need much with that sickening pore-free skin of yours. But let them put on whatever they want to put on."

"Why?" My hair started going in five different directions, being rolled and brushed.

"Because you'll need the war paint. You're about to go into battle."

"With who?"

"With every woman at that ball who will be ready to claw your eyes out for showing up with the prince. You don't want even a single hair out of place. You'll need the confidence."

I narrowed my eyes at her. "But you'll be there with him too."

"Darlin', we both know he's not going to give me even a lick of attention."

We were done up and twisted around and pulled and tugged until we were finally deemed ready. I thought it was sort of sad that it took an entire team of people to get us to an acceptable level.

As they gathered up their things, Lemon and I went into our bathroom to finish getting dressed. "Don't look in the mirror until we're all done," she said. We turned our backs to the mirrors behind us. She helped me zip up, and then I helped her.

"Ready?"

We turned and I was shocked. We looked flawless. I looked maybe, even, a little pretty. They'd turned Lemon's short blonde bob into a bunch of loose curls, and I had a sleek but delicate chignon. "They gave me fake eyelashes!" I laughed, leaning my face in to get a better look at what they'd done.

"Nico is going to die when he sees you." Lemon hugged me.

I hugged her back. "Poor Dante. His heart is going to give out."

"You mean Salvatore."

I didn't actually mean Salvatore. He didn't follow Lemon around like Dante did. I just smiled at her in response.

We went back out into our room, and it had been emptied out. We put on our shoes and the jewelry we'd chosen earlier. I had big cubic zirconia earrings and a matching bracelet. Lemon had a necklace with a massive red gem and dangly earrings.

"Ready?"

A flock of hummingbirds started beating their wings in my stomach. My hands felt clammy and my spine weak, but I nodded. Lemon went out first, and I followed closely behind. Dante immediately claimed her attention, flattering her and kissing both of her cheeks. She laughed. Rafe told me I was beautiful and kissed my cheeks. Both men wore black tuxedos with tails, a white vest, and a white bow tie. They had a red sash with a pale yellow border that they wore under their coats. Like beauty queens. It made me smile.

Nico stood near the fireplace, just staring at me. He was dressed like his brothers, but infinitely more handsome. I walked over to him shyly, my dress rustling and swishing with each step. I wondered what he thought. Something intense flashed in his sparkling light blue eyes. He didn't say anything. Did he not like it? He swallowed once, twice, and cleared his throat. Then he finally said in a low voice, "I'm afraid you've rendered me speechless. You are breathtaking."

I pulled in a shaky breath, my heart beating a million times a minute. No one had ever said anything like that to me. Ever.

Would it be weird if I swooned at his feet?

"Aren't we the luckiest girls in the world to go to a ball with you handsome men?" Lemon cooed, slipping her arms through Dante's and Rafe's.

"On the contrary, it is our privilege to be accompanying the two of you," Dante responded gallantly, although he only had eyes for Lemon.

"Picture time!" she called out. She took out her cell phone from her little matching red clutch. "Nico, Kat, stand together. No, not like that. Put your arm around her. Like a prom picture."

Funnily enough, I was pretty sure that neither Nico nor I had gone to prom. But as his strong arm stole around my waist, I fought the urge to melt against him. I ignored the fire that flamed up everywhere his body touched mine.

I swear, I was going to develop some kind of breathing condition if I didn't stop losing control of that function every time I got near him.

"Say cheese!" Lemon called out. We cheesed.

"One more!" she said. I saw her expression. She knew exactly what this was doing to me. I curled my hands up into fists, narrowing my eyes at her. So after I killed her and got that shaman to resurrect her, I was going to convert her to whatever faith believed in reincarnation so that I could kill her once again. She had the audacity to laugh.

Rafe took Lemon's phone and directed Dante and Lemon to stand together.

I looked up at Nico and he looked down at me. We stayed put, locked in each other's arms. His eyes focused in on my lips, and I had to resist the overpowering urge to go up ever so slightly on tippy-toe to reach him.

You don't want to kiss him, remember? How could you want something desperately, and then not want it just as much? I was too screwed up for my own good.

Finally, I couldn't stand it and had to let go. But I didn't go far.

Nico let out a large sigh and pushed some fallen strands of hair off his forehead, which drew my attention to his bright red scar. Without thinking, I reached up to touch it, and he let out a low hiss.

"Your poor forehead," I said.

He lightly took my still-bandaged wrist, pressing a kiss to the bare flesh of my palm. I gasped as my skin sizzled. "Your poor wrist," he said, before letting my arm go.

"Think the press will ask you about it?" I put my hands behind my back so that he wouldn't see them shaking.

He didn't seem to hear me, studying me intently. His gaze felt tangible, like he was still touching me even though we stood apart.

Which caused a nervous reaction inside me, and I babbled, "I guess I could just tell them that I hit you with my left hook and you were down for the count."

"I think it would take more than a punch from you to knock me out." Nico looked playful and insulted at the same time. "It would probably have to involve some kind of Taser gun or pepper spray."

Suddenly I couldn't breathe. The edges of the room went fuzzy, and I was back there. Back with him. With the acrid smell of pepper spray making my eyes water and my throat burn. My lungs constricted, and I couldn't catch my breath.

I felt both of his hands on my shoulders, snapping me out of that memory. "What is it, Katerina? What did I say?"

"Nothing," I reassured him. "I'm fine." I was safe. Safe, safe, safe. His eyes were full of concern. I took a couple of big breaths and pasted on a fake smile. "Shouldn't we be going?"

He looked like he wanted to say something, but instead put my hand on his arm. He gathered everyone together, and we went down in the lobby, waiting for the cars to pull up. The paparazzi's cameras flashed through the big plate glass windows.

"Can't we go out the back again?" I asked, pressing closer to Nico's side.

"They're unavoidable tonight, I'm afraid. We will want them to take our picture because of the press it will bring for the event and the charity."

"Is it always like this for you?"

"Only when I go outside of Monterra. There we have anti-paparazzi laws. We want it to be a safe, comfortable place for anyone who chooses to travel there."

80

I imagined it would certainly make his homeland more appealing to celebrities and royals who didn't want their every move photographed. Which would trickle down to regular tourists, who would visit in hopes of catching a glimpse of famous people in the wild. I wondered why other countries didn't do the same.

Johann came over and asked to confer with Nico. Nico excused himself and stepped away. Lemon sidled up next to me. "Isn't this all exciting?"

Exciting was not the word I would have chosen. I slipped my bracelet off of my wrist and twirled it back and forth with my fingers. The big gems caught the light as I whirled it. "I guess."

"I can hardly wait to put those pictures up on Facebook. There isn't a sister at Zeta Beta Gamma who won't be seething with envy." She looked down at my hands. "Be careful there, darlin'. That's worth a lot of money."

I stopped mid-flicker to look at Lemon. "What do you mean?"

"You were worried about how much your dress cost. That bracelet is worth two of your dresses."

"I thought this was costume jewelry." My voice was barely even a whisper.

"Why on earth would they give us costume jewelry? This is the real deal. You've got at least twenty carats in diamonds on your ears."

Great. Now I would spend the rest of the evening checking my earlobes every thirty seconds to make sure I still had those suckers in. I slid the bracelet back on, double-checking the clasp. Another thing to worry about. It sickened me to think about the fact that just one little sliver of my jewelry tonight could solve all of my financial problems.

Someone from security came in, holding the door open. This apparently was the signal for us to get in the cars. Nico came back to claim me, again slipping my hand onto the crook of his arm.

"Stay close to me," he instructed, putting his hand on top of mine.

Always.

I didn't even question where that had come from. I was clearly losing my mind.

Chapter 10

If I had thought the paparazzi at the hotel were bad, it was nothing compared to the teeming throng outside of the Intercontinental Grand Hotel. A wide red carpet ran from the street up to the hotel, and there were beautiful, well-dressed people taking pictures up and down its length.

Lemon was in her element. She climbed out with the twins and posed for picture after picture.

"Ready for our first official royal date?" Nico asked me.

I shook my head. "I don't want to deal with all that." I remembered that stifling, suffocating feeling I'd had earlier with the group outside of the hotel. This one seemed worse.

He looked disappointed, but directed Giacomo to stay with me and called over Lorenz, one of the security guards. They had a quick conversation in Italian. Nico gave me one last smile and got out of the limo. The paparazzi went nuts. Like teenage girls at a boy band concert.

The driver pulled slightly forward, and Giacomo, Lorenz, and I got out of the limo. "Do we go inside?" I asked.

"We will stay here until His Highness makes his way through the press line." I wondered if that's what Nico had told them to do.

It was cold out in the winter night, even though heaters had been set up along the red carpet to warm it. I shivered and ran my hands up and down my arms, trying to warm myself. I watched Nico charm and smile, but the smile didn't quite reach his eyes. I wished I could hear what he was saying.

On the opposite side of the press line stood a crowd of onlookers who called out to people arriving. While watching the frenzy of the crowd, I saw a little girl, about eight or nine years old, crying. She had on a princess costume.

Was she lost? Alone? I stepped off the carpet and into the group, pushing my way through. As I got closer I saw that she was holding hands with a woman who must have been her mother.

"Is everything all right?" I asked. The little girl just buried her face against her mother's leg.

The woman started speaking to me in French.

"Do you speak English? *Anglais?*"

She shook her head no. I turned and almost bumped into Lorenz, human Alp. "Can you get Giacomo?" I asked.

He nodded and spoke into his wrist. Like he was in a James Bond movie. A few seconds later Giacomo arrived. "Do you speak French?"

He looked confused. "Of course."

"Can you please ask her what's wrong with her daughter?" It hurt my heart to see a child cry.

He asked, and the mother explained. Turned out the woman's name was Sandrine, her daughter's Amelie. Her daughter was obsessed with fairy tales and had asked to come out tonight to see a real-life prince or princess, but the crowd was making it impossible for her to see anything.

"Would you please ask her if she'd like to meet a real prince?"

He gave me another strange look, but translated. The girl started sniffling, wiping her tears away. I heard her say, "*Oui.*"

"Please tell Nico that Kat needs him." Lorenz hesitated. I knew Nico was busy. I knew tonight was important to him. But somehow I also knew that if I needed him, he would come. "Please."

Lorenz relayed the message, and my instinct proved correct. Two bodyguards cleared a path for him, and Nico was there. "This little girl came to see you tonight and hasn't been able to make her way through the crowd, so I thought I should arrange an introduction. This is Princess Amelie, and her mother, Sandrine."

Nico turned to the child and bowed deeply to her. Then he crouched down so that he was at eye level with Amelie. He started speaking softly to her, and her face lit up. She got embarrassed and snuggled in closer to her mother.

"The prince just introduced himself and told her it was his honor to make the acquaintance of a princess. He also asked if she would like to take a picture with him." Giacomo continued to translate for me.

Amelie nodded, and her mother took out her phone.

Nico held out both arms to Amelie, and like any woman would, she went right into his arms. He picked her up, holding her on one side. She wrapped her arms around his neck and looked absolutely thrilled. Sandrine took a few pictures.

Then he turned to look at me and held out his free hand. Just like Amelie, I walked right into his embrace. He put his arm around my waist and said, "Smile."

I'd never much liked taking pictures, but it was different with him there.

Nico spoke again to Sandrine, putting Amelie back on the ground where she rushed back to her mother. We said our *au revoir*s, and Sandrine stopped, putting her hand on my arm. "*Merci*," she said. I could see unshed tears glittering in her eyes.

"You're welcome," I said, feeling a bit choked up myself.

The little girl chattered away happily at her mother as they left. Nico put his arm around my waist again, pulling me close to his side. Would I ever get used to the way that made me feel? I needed to be stronger than my hormones. Which might be difficult because it turned out that my hormones were superheroes, able to conquer my common sense and need for self-protection in a single bound.

He had a brilliant smile on his face. A real one. It made my toes curl. "We have a ball to attend, *bella*."

Nico still had some press to speak with, so Lorenz and Giacomo took me inside. We passed through a luxurious lobby into the Salon Opera room.

My eyes went straight to the high ceiling that soared overhead. The entire room was shaped like a dome, and there were statues, round windows, and columns all along the walls. Everything was ornate and elaborately detailed. I'd never seen anything like it. A chandelier as big as a car dominated the center of the room. There was a hardwood dance floor, and on a stage beyond that an entire orchestra performed. The rest of the ballroom had large tables set up with expensive-looking place settings that reminded me very much of dinner with the royal family.

Lemon ran up to me, her smile bright, and she squealed. "How gorgeous is this? Let's go find where we're sitting."

Every table had a name card next to each setting. We started looking for our names and ended up at the largest table nearest to the dance floor. I saw HRH Prince Dominic in the center, and then my name next to his just to the right. My stupid heart skipped a beat. Lemon, predictably, was seated with his brothers, with Salvatore right across from her. "Maybe I should switch the cards out," she whispered. I told her not to. There was probably like some ball police who would kick her out if she did. Personally, I was afraid to touch anything.

A tiny little woman balancing on six-inch heels came up to us. She had honey-blonde hair and dark blue eyes, with a perfect little elfin face. I wondered how she could breathe in her blue formfitting gown. One wrong move and her ample, and obviously fake, chest was going to escape. "You are the ones who arrived with Nico?"

She had a refined British accent, but all I could think about was how tall she really was. She barely came up to my shoulder even with those heels on. Lemon confirmed that we were, and the woman said, "I am Lady Claire Sutherland, an old friend of Nico's from school."

I immediately hated her. My hate surprised me in both its quickness and intensity. She hadn't said or done anything to make me feel that way. In fact, she seemed very friendly. But something inside me reacted violently to her and the possessive way she said Nico's name.

It was up to Lemon to make our introductions because I was gritting my teeth together. A waiter walked by with a tray of champagne, and Claire grabbed two flutes. "Care for a drink?"

"I don't drink."

"Oh." She handed the spare to Lemon, and the waiter walked away. "I'm sure we can send over to the bar and have them get you a fizzy drink."

I felt like a child. But maybe she wasn't being passive-aggressively mean. Maybe she was just being nice and my inexplicable hatred was coloring my reaction.

"Is this your first European ball?" When Lemon said yes, Claire smiled. It looked more like a smirk to me. "Besides the dancing, the best part is the chance to talk to so many interesting people. And there are so many fascinating people here tonight! Like over there." She pointed through the crowd to an older gentleman wearing a colorful dashiki. "That's Ambassador Mndaweni of South Africa. He just presented at the most brilliant conference on eradicating violence against children. I can introduce you."

I wasn't always so great at meeting new people, but Claire grabbed me by the arm and barreled her way through the crowd before I could object. He did sound interesting, and I always liked talking to people who were as dedicated to children as I was.

She made the introductions, and the ambassador smiled and held out his hand to greet me and then Lemon. "Oh, I've just seen someone I must say hello to," Claire said. "If you'll excuse me." She leaned in close to my ear and said, "Be sure to ask him about his wife."

"Are you American students?" he asked with a blinding white smile.

"Yes," was my brilliant reply.

"You are visiting Paris?"

"Monterra, actually," Lemon interjected. "We're here with some friends who invited us. It's our first time here."

"Wonderful. How are you finding the city?"

"It's beautiful," I said. "How is your wife enjoying it?"

The ambassador stilled, and his face went slack. "My wife and children were brutalized and murdered two years ago by insurgents."

My mouth fell open in horror. "I'm . . . I'm so sorry . . ."

"Please excuse me," he said and walked away.

My heart dropped into my stomach. I felt sick. Like I wanted to sit right there on the floor and put my head between my knees. "That did not just happen," I finally said. "She told me to ask about his wife."

Lemon led me over to a table and had me sit down on the velvet-cushioned chair. "You didn't know."

"I didn't know," I agreed. But that was the point. I was letting my guard down with Nico. Missing him. Wanting to be near him. But this ball, that conversation, proved that I didn't belong in this world. I had no idea who any of these people were or how to interact with them. Nico and I had nothing in common. His world was so foreign from mine. I didn't wear dresses that cost more than a car or hang out in ballrooms with the world's elite.

"She set me up."

"That Claire is obviously a horrible person. I've seen leeches that suck less. Somebody needs to hand that garden gnome a stepladder so she can get over herself."

That put a bit of a smile on my face.

"My mother always says stick to the weather and everybody's health."

I didn't need the advice because I was never talking to someone I didn't know ever again.

"I know you don't normally drink, but tonight might be a good time to start."

"No." I shook my head. I didn't want to, and I needed all my wits about me. I saw Lady Claire Sutherland across the ballroom, and she gave me a pointed smirk. I had a feeling this wasn't over.

I should have trusted my gut.

Although, that was the same gut that wanted me to jump up on Nico and plant kisses all over his face, so it wasn't totally trustworthy.

"Come on," Lemon said. "I'm going to put you someplace safe, and then I'm going to get a drink with some bite." We went back to where our name cards were, and she told me to sit in my seat. "I'll be right back."

I wished I had something to occupy my hands besides my little pink clutch, which only had a keycard and lipstick inside. I set it on the table. I wanted to look for Nico, wondered if he'd made it inside yet. I could tell him what had happened and let him make me feel better. I knew he would. Or maybe he wouldn't react the way I imagined he would. Maybe he'd be mortified by my blunder. What if I'd just started some kind of international incident?

So instead I settled for listening to the orchestra and tried not to play my encounter with the ambassador on one endless loop in my mind.

A skinny man with enormous ears and bright red hair sat in Nico's seat, startling me. "Kat MacTaggart, I presume?" He had a thick brogue.

I blinked. "Do I know you?"

"Not yet. But I'm about to become your best mate."

He reached inside his tuxedo and pulled out an envelope and a phone. "The name's Seamus O'Brien. I work for the *Daily Sun* as their royalty correspondent."

He looked at me expectantly, like I should know what that was. I'd never heard of it or him. If he were a reporter, shouldn't he be outside with everybody else?

"My sources tell me you're staying with Prince Dominic in his palace. Is that correct?"

How could anyone know that? "I don't really see how that's any of your business."

"Because I have an opportunity for you." He looked left to right and then handed me the envelope. "Open it."

Inside was a stack of cash. I took in a sharp breath. "What's this?"

"Five thousand American dollars. Consider it a down payment. I will give you fifty thousand dollars in cash total if you use this phone"—he held it aloft—"and get me pictures of the entire Monterran royal family inside their home. The king's been a recluse for years now, and a picture of him post-accident is worth quite a bit."

Fifty thousand dollars? That was a lot of money. A lot. I could pay off all my student loan debt and start fresh. Buy a car. Get some professional clothes for my new job. Afford food.

Not only that, but every time I had to move a kid to a new family or group home, I hated how little they actually owned. I could buy them clothes. Toys. Books. Stuffed animals. Things that would make the transition just a bit more bearable. The possibilities raced through my head.

But how could I do that to Nico's family? He hated the paparazzi. And his family had been nothing but kind to me. "I don't think so." I held the envelope out to him. He took it back from me.

"What's the harm? It's only pictures, and you'd be a lot richer. Prince Dominic is outside right now getting his picture taken by every newspaper in the world. It goes with the position. They expect it." He must have seen something on my face that told him exactly what I thought of his proposition, because he picked up my clutch and stuffed the envelope and phone inside it.

"I will be in Monterra in a few days with the rest of the money. Just think about it. Nobody has to know. I promise to keep you out of it completely. It'll be our secret."

"Wait a second . . ."

He buttoned my clutch back up and put it down on the table. "I'll be in touch."

Seamus O'Brien disappeared back into the crowd before I could stop him.

Fifty thousand dollars. Fifty thousand dollars. *Fifty thousand dollars.*

In cash. I expelled a shaky breath.

And it was just some pictures, right? How much harm could there be in that?

Chapter 11

Lemon returned, sipping on something amber-colored. She handed me a soda, which I put on the table. Next to my clutch. Which made my heart lurch. I should tell her what had happened.

But before I could, there was a bell calling everyone to dinner. I watched the orchestra pack up their instruments. Our table filled up quickly, with Lady Claire Sutherland seated next to Salvatore and Francesco. Right where I could see her. She gave me another smirk, and I suppressed my shakiness. I didn't know if I could deal with her witchery and a guilty conscience.

Which only got worse when Nico arrived and sat next to me. "*Buonasera*." Usually, I loved it when he spoke Italian to me, but I could barely look him in the eye.

I wondered if I had a flashing neon sign on my forehead that said, "I considered selling you out."

He set his napkin on his lap, and the dinner service started. Conversation flowed all around the table, but my attention was fixated on everything that had just happened. Nico kept trying to talk to me, but every time he did, someone else claimed his attention. I could see frustration in the set of his mouth. His very beautiful mouth.

As one course passed into the next, I realized I hadn't really enjoyed any of it. It all tasted like sawdust in my mouth.

If I felt this bad and I hadn't done anything yet, then I obviously couldn't take any pictures and I couldn't take any money.

I resolved to keep an eye out for Seamus and return both the phone and the money. He shouldn't be that hard to find with that hair.

But despite trying to covertly observe the ballroom, I didn't see the reporter anywhere.

I might not have tasted it, but I could still put the food away. It had been hours since our lunch, and I was hungry. Claire leaned across the table at me, and her boobs came up to her chin. I wondered if she could use those things as flotation devices. "If you're still hungry, Kat, we can contact the kitchen and ask them to bring you out another serving."

She was all concern and sickly sweet smiles, but the implication was clear. She was delicate and hadn't touched her food; I was a giant cow who ate too much.

"We can certainly get you more if you'd like," Nico said to me. He put his arm around the back of my chair. Then he leaned in to whisper, "You know how much I like watching you eat."

His breath tickled my ear, and a shiver ran up my spine. "I'm good." I glared at Claire triumphantly. She sat back, angry, and stared at me.

Waiters went back and forth, clearing plates and setting new ones. I hoped I could find Seamus before the evening ended. I reached out for my goblet of water and took a big gulp.

Where something burned its way down my throat. I coughed and sputtered, having already swallowed a quarter of the glass. "What is this?"

Lemon reached across Rafe and grabbed the goblet out of my hand. She took a sip and grimaced. "This is straight vodka." She looked at Nico. "Kat doesn't drink."

He got a murderous expression on his face. He immediately demanded that the head of the waitstaff be brought over to explain how this had happened.

I saw Claire's reaction. I knew exactly how this had happened. Lemon wasn't far behind. "Did you do this to her, Claire?"

"The proper way to address me is Lady Claire," she said with a serene face. "And what a horrible thing to accuse someone of. I've never had anyone dare accuse me of something like this."

"Well, bless your heart." Which was Lemon-speak for inviting someone to get to know themselves in the biblical sense.

But I noticed Claire didn't deny it. She leaned in to Francesco, the guy who had been saying rude things about me that morning, and whispered in his ear. He whispered back to her and she laughed, looking at me as she did so. It was high school all over again and I was sitting by myself in the lunchroom while the cool kids laughed at me.

I was starting to develop a deep loathing for anyone who called themselves Nico's family friend.

Nico didn't get a satisfactory explanation, only that there had seemed to be some kind of confusion and the drink had been brought to me by mistake. The staff apologized to him and me repeatedly. I didn't believe it for one second. I had told her I didn't drink, and she was obviously out to get me. But it seemed like such a stupid and childish thing to do. What was her objective?

Dessert and coffee were served, and the orchestra returned to the stage. They warmed up and then began playing classical music again. Nico stood up from his chair and smiled down at me. "Would you do me the honor of this dance?"

There was no one else on the dance floor. Everyone would be staring at us. And I'd already told him that I had no idea how to do old-timey dancing.

"I can't. I don't know how," I reminded him. He started to say something, but then Lady Claire stood up. "I'll dance with you, Nico."

When she stood up, so did all the men at the table. Nico didn't have much of a choice as he led her out onto the floor, giving me an apologetic look as he went. Once he and that little troll started to dance, other couples joined in.

I scrunched up my napkin in my lap. I had never wanted to do somebody else actual bodily harm, but I was willing to make an exception.

"Ignore that horrible, evil Smurf," Lemon said as she sat next to me. She waved Dante off, and he went to find another partner.

"I feel light-headed." Could I get drunk from one small drink of vodka? I also felt a stabbing, throbbing jealousy.

"You'll be fine. Did you see how quick she jumped up? She practically fell out of her dress. 'I'll dance with you, Nico,'" Lemon said, imitating the harpy's voice. "If I have to roll my eyes one more time tonight, I'm going to make myself dizzy."

"Are you going to dance?"

"I was waiting for Salvatore to ask me, but he's dancing with someone else." She sounded grumpy.

"You know how to dance like that?"

"Darlin', I was a debutante."

Right. I'd forgotten. "Dante wanted to dance with you."

She elegantly raised one shoulder, as if it didn't matter. "He's sweet, but right now he's nothing more than a distraction."

I watched Nico and Claire dance. I swear she was sticking her chest out on purpose, fluttering her fake lashes at him. Was that all I was to him? A distraction?

The dance ended and the couples clapped. Nico made a beeline for me, causing my heart to go into an arrhythmia.

"Now you must dance with me," he said, holding out his hand. "I promise to teach you every step."

No excuse came to mind, so I stood up and followed. Nico took me over to a spot away from all the prying eyes. "This is a waltz. It has a one-two-three step pattern. We're going to make a box with our feet. Put this hand on my shoulder, and your right goes in my left." His right hand went around my waist. "Once you understand the steps, I will use my hands to show you which direction we're going to go. I step forward, and your leg goes back. Over to the side, and then back on the opposite foot. Then we start over."

It took a few tries before I got the hang of it, but Nico was infinitely patient as I stepped on his feet and crashed into him. We were both laughing as we worked it out. But we got it, and I was dancing. Really dancing.

He used his right hand to draw me in closer so that there was barely any space between us.

"I have been waiting all evening to have you to myself," he murmured into my ear. The butterflies in my stomach that had set up residence the second he touched me took flight and lodged themselves in my throat.

As he twirled me to the left, I saw Lady Claire Sutherland staring daggers at me from our table. "Did you ever feel like someone was out to get you?"

He pulled his head back to look me in the eye. "Yes. But I have an entire team of people whose only job is to imagine the worst-case scenario and prepare me accordingly. My paranoia is not my fault."

I laughed again, feeling better than I had all night. The song ended, and immediately a slower, softer one began. Nico pulled me even closer to him, barely moving his feet. His hand splayed against my back, pressing me in. He pulled our hands in, resting my hand right above his heart. I put my head on his shoulder and closed my eyes. This kind of dancing I understood.

Being here with him like this did something to me I didn't quite understand. I felt happy. Settled. Like everything would work out.

He made me feel safe.

There was no way I could ever betray him by taking pictures of him or his family.

Halfway through the song, Johann was there, interrupting. "My apologies, Your Highness, but the Russian grand duke and duchess would like to speak to you personally before making their contribution."

Nico apologized to me and walked me back to our table. He promised to return as soon as he could. I thought I'd take this chance to get to the ladies' room.

I'd only made it a few steps when Claire-the-tart stopped me, digging her talon nails into my upper arm. "Ow. What is wrong with you? Let go of me!"

I tried to shake her off, but she just dug in. "You seem a little slow, so I thought we should have a conversation. Nico is mine. Our families have planned our marriage since we were infants. He's having his fun now. You're just the latest in a long line of many. But you will go away and I will still be here because he's a prince. He needs to marry somebody of quality. Not some pathetic, social climbing commoner like you."

"You think you have an arranged marriage? Do you know what century this is?" Nico was not the sort of man who would flirt with me if he were truly engaged. She had to be bluffing.

That only seemed to make her angrier. "We have an understanding. You're nothing but a passing fancy."

I yanked my arm away. "For someone with an 'understanding,' you seem awfully threatened by me, given all your stupid little pranks."

"I don't know what you're talking about."

I leaned in close, towering over her. She backed up a step. "I think you know exactly what I'm talking about, *Claire*. And Nico sees right through you. Even if your fake boobs are obscuring the view."

She gasped and turned a wicked shade of purple. Tossing my head, I went into the bathroom and locked myself inside a stall. I had no idea whether or not what I'd said was true, but I hoped it was. I hoped Nico was smart enough to see her for what she was.

I hoped he wouldn't be forced to marry someone that evil.

When I returned, it was to see Nico standing by the table, holding my purse in his hands. A wave of sheer panic washed over me, and I walked back on unsteady legs.

"I found this on the floor," he said, handing it back to me. The fact that he was smiling meant he hadn't looked inside, as my frenzied imagination feared he would. I put the purse back on the table, not wanting to check the contents while he watched me.

"Can I ask you something?"

"Anything."

"Are you engaged to Lady Claire?" It chapped my hide to have to use the word *lady*, because she was the least ladylike person I'd ever had the misfortune of meeting.

He laughed. "Not even a little."

"No arranged marriage?"

"No arranged marriage." Ha. I knew it. She was a liar, liar with her too-tight ball gown on fire.

"Good."

"Now that that's settled, I've come to dance with you."

We danced again, with Nico showing me all different types of dances. So often he had to step away to speak or dance with someone, all in the name of his charity. But every chance he got, we were back on the dance floor together, where we danced and I laughed harder and more often than I had in a very long time. And while we danced we talked. It wasn't like a nightclub where we'd have to scream at each other to be heard—the music here was just loud enough to dance to, but also allowed conversations to be easily heard. Talking to him was easy, natural. Comfortable. Which was funny considering that everything else about him set me on edge.

His brothers would fill in, and it surprised me how much I enjoyed being with them. Rafe tried to teach me a complicated dance, which I could never quite get because it seemed like the steps kept changing. He finally admitted that he was making the whole thing up on the spot and wanted to see how long I'd be a good sport about it. I smacked him on the shoulder while we both laughed.

Nico didn't dance with Hobbit Claire for the rest of the night. Which made me a lot happier than it should have.

Finally things started winding down, and it was time for us to leave. Back through the press line with Nico holding my hand, into the limo, and back to the hotel.

Since we were in a group, our goodnights were to everyone at once. I felt Nico's gaze linger on me as Lemon and I returned to our room.

She reported on her progress with Salvatore, which actually seemed to go somewhere tonight. He'd asked her to dance several times, and she told me every detail while we undressed, washed our faces, and took down our hair.

Her phone dinged, and she picked it up. "I set up a Google alert." Lemon started clicking links. "Look, pictures!" There on some tabloid site were pictures of all of us. Although I hadn't realized it at the time, when Nico and I were talking to Amelie dozens of pictures had been taken. It upset me—it had been such a private moment that I didn't want to share it with the world.

They had my name and my college, but that was about it. No mention of my mother or my upbringing, which caused a dart of relief to shoot through me. "Scroll down to the comments."

Which I never should have done, because there was comment after comment speculating about me. People claimed to know me and to have the real scoop, while they spouted off a bunch of lies. I was called every name imaginable, and every part of my appearance was criticized. "I have never seen people so desperate to seem like an expert on a subject they know absolutely nothing about."

"So, this is your first time on the Internet, then? Forget about it. They don't matter." She shut off her phone and climbed into her bed. I did the same.

Once we'd lain down, Lemon passed out pretty quickly. I forced myself to not think about the comments on that website. I tried to sleep, but I kept recalling the awful things people had said. So instead I chose to relive the night and the memories of dancing with Nico in my head over and over again.

I marveled at how different I'd felt in these last twenty-four hours. How so much of my fear had just . . . dissipated. I was still scared of my feelings and still didn't want things to go further than they had, but there was just something about Nico that made me feel less afraid.

Turning over, I noticed that it was early in the morning. And I was, predictably enough, starving. Remembering the kitchenette next to the living room, I hoped that it was stocked like the royal kitchen had been.

I pushed off my covers, moving slowly so as to not wake Lemon. I tiptoed over to the door, eased it open, and closed it behind me again. The room was dark, with moonlight filtering in through the large glass windows. I walked quietly to the kitchen and opened up the mini-fridge. Score! Gelato in the tiny freezer.

"Again?"

I let out a yelp and nearly dropped my food. Nico stood against the window, watching me.

"You scared me to death!"

"*Scusa.*" Sometimes I swore he spoke Italian but thought he was speaking English.

I came into the living room with my spoon and sat down on one of the couches. "What is it they say? We have to stop meeting like this."

"I have no objection at all to meeting you like this." His silky smooth voice gave me goose bumps, but I ignored them. He sat down on the couch across from me, watching me. I noticed he was shirtless. Again. Did this guy ever wear clothes?

"More insomnia?" I asked. He nodded and looked back toward the windows. I followed his gaze and saw the snow falling thick and fast, piling up on our balcony.

"I was wondering whether we'd made enough money for the foundation tonight. I worried that we hadn't."

"What is the name of your foundation? What does it do?" I popped open my gelato and took a bite. Good gravy. He'd been right. Gelato was like a thousand times better than ice cream. I wondered if I could just eat this three times a day instead of regular food.

"The Fiorelli Foundation for a Cure. We're set up to fund leukemia and other childhood cancer research, and to provide financial aid to families dealing with it."

Was it wrong that I liked him even more now that I knew his charity was specifically for kids? "Fiorelli? Is that your last name?"

100

His lips quirked up at the corners. "Technically I don't have one, but yes, the extended members of my family use the name Fiorelli. Our earliest ancestors were Fiorellis."

It shouldn't have made me this happy just knowing his last name.

"I was also thinking about you."

My spoon was halfway to my mouth; I paused and put it back down. "Me?" I actually squeaked. Like a crazy mouse. Like Serafina's crazy tooth mouse.

"Does it upset you to know that I think about you?"

Upset me? No. Make my stomach bottom out and my heart beat about twenty times faster than normal? Yes.

"Why?"

"I feel as if you're a puzzle I'm trying to figure out. As if I'm just one step behind understanding what you're thinking." He shifted on the couch and leaned forward, resting his elbows on his knees. "Like this morning you seemed so sad. But you wouldn't tell me why."

"'Cause your friend Francesco's a douche. He said you're only interested in me because I was convenient. And that I wasn't pretty."

Even in the pale moonlight, I could see the anger flash in his eyes. "He said that to you?"

"He said it near me."

Nico got up and stalked toward the door. I jumped up to follow him.

"Whoa, where do you think you're going?"

He stopped. "I'm going to go get him out of bed and—what is it you Americans say for fighting? Kick him?"

"You mean kick his butt?"

"It will be more punching of his face, but yes, I'm going to kick his butt. No one is allowed to insult you."

Part of me was giddy at having someone who would literally fight for my honor, but I didn't want him to get into an actual fight. I put both of my hands on Nico's shoulders. His bare, very muscular shoulders. "Please don't. He's not worth it. I'm fine. As long as it isn't true."

He grabbed my upper arms, forcing me to look into his eyes. "You know that you are beautiful, don't you? Especially like this?"

I laughed. "Like this? In my PJs? What was it you said to me tonight when I was all done up?" I pretended to remember, even though every word was etched on my heart. "You said I was breathtaking. You've never said that to me before when I look normal."

"Every time I see you, you take my breath away. When you dressed up I could finally say it to you without sounding ridiculous."

"Oh," was my breathy, masterful reply.

"You are a true, natural beauty." He loosened his grip and somehow managed to pull me even closer to him at the same time.

"Okay then."

"What are you scared of?"

"S-scared? I'm not scared," I said, while sounding exactly like a scared, silly girl.

He was doing that touching thing again where he stroked and petted and soothed and made my bones feel like Jell-O. "You are. Tell me why."

"Because I'm a unicorn." I hadn't meant to admit it, but his fingertips must have exuded some kind of truth serum.

"A unicorn?"

"That's what Lemon's sorority sisters call me." I took a deep breath. I'd been terrified of what a man would do when he uncovered my secret, but Nico didn't strike me as the run-away-screaming type. Still, my heart pounded loudly in protest at what I was about to confess.

"Because you don't often see a twenty-four-year-old virgin in the wild. I'm like a mythological creature."

Chapter 12

A look I couldn't identify crossed his features. "Last night, was that your first kiss?"

Had it only been last night? It felt like it had happened weeks ago. "Uh-huh."

A look of sheer male pride settled on his features. "I'm glad it was with me."

I'd never, ever admit this to him, but so was I.

"Come." He took me by the hand and led me back to the couch. Where my gelato had spilled.

"Oh, frak!" I said and went to grab some dishtowels.

Nico stopped me. "You watch *Battlestar Galactica*?"

"Yeah. I love that show."

"Me too. I have all the seasons on DVD. Perhaps we could watch it together sometime."

Just earlier I'd been telling myself that we didn't have anything in common. Used it as an excuse to keep him at arm's length. And here he was saying that my favorite show was one of his favorites, too. I didn't know how to feel about that.

Dishtowels and stain forgotten, we moved over to the couch he'd been sitting on. "You need to explain. I want to understand."

I was busy watching his fingers run across the top of my hand. "Explain what?"

"Why you are a unicorn. I can't believe it's for lack of opportunity."

"You might be surprised. But you're right, that's not exactly why."

He pulled me into him, resting my head on his shoulder. He ran his fingers through my hair. "Tell me."

Lemon didn't even know. For years I'd felt like I needed to keep the secret hidden, that if I took it out and held it up for everyone to see, it would destroy me. I was embarrassed. Ashamed. For so long I'd been weighed down, burdened, and I realized I was tired. Tired of running, tired of hiding, tired of pretending. Tired of keeping everyone at bay. Tired of keeping everything buried.

Keeping a secret was exhausting.

"Calling something by its name is the only way to gain power over it," he murmured into the top of my head. "There is nothing you could say that would change my opinion of you, *bella*."

The secret roared to life inside me, trying to claw its way out. The truth wanted to be set free. And I wanted to be accepted fully for who I was and what had happened to me. The need to tell burned as a compulsion, and I felt the words rising up inside me. I wanted Nico to see me. To understand.

"My mother is a crystal meth addict." It was strange to finally say that out loud. "She has been since I was little. So was my dad. But he got caught and sent to prison. So it was just me and my mom. I had to take care of myself really early on. I could cook for myself by the time I was six. She had a never-ending stream of boyfriends and a never-ending supply of drugs. Looking back, I don't know how she didn't overdose. Do you know how hard it is to watch someone you love slowly killing herself?"

"I might have some idea." His arm tightened around me. "Keep going."

I let out a sigh filled with regret and sadness. "When I was fourteen, more than anything I wanted to be like everyone else. I obviously didn't have the right clothes or the right hairstyle. It was all I could do to survive. But there was this party." My voice cracked and I paused. "I wanted to go. So I took some of my mom's makeup and I did my hair and I went. And the cutest, most popular boy in school, a senior, saw me. He started talking to me and told me I was pretty. He told me to come upstairs so we could talk. I was so naïve. I had no idea what that meant. But I went. And he wanted to . . . he tried to . . ."

My heart beat so loudly I wanted to cover my own ears. I screwed my eyes shut. "He had me pinned underneath him and I couldn't move. I felt like I couldn't breathe. He was so much bigger and stronger. But he was drunk, and I remembered the pepper spray on my keychain from some Take Back the Night seminar at school. I sprayed it in his face before anything could really happen. I was so stupid. I shouldn't have gone. I felt so violated and scared, but like I deserved it for being so dumb."

"You didn't deserve it. No woman deserves it. It was not your fault."

"I haven't told you the best part. When I got home, my mom was passed out, but her new boyfriend started talking to me. I got a bad feeling and walked away from him, but he followed. He kept telling me I looked so grown-up and pretty with all of my mom's makeup on, and he groped me and then tried to kiss me. I pushed him away and ran to the bathroom. It was the only room we had with a lock. He started yelling at me to open the door and then rammed it with his shoulder, like he was trying to knock it down. I remember crying, screaming for my mom, and putting all my weight against the door to keep him from coming in. I knew what he would do to me if he got through, and I was terrified. I've never felt so helpless."

I choked back a sob. I had promised myself a long time ago that I would never cry over that situation again. I refused to start now. Nico's arms tightened around me again.

"He finally passed out, and that was it for me. I knew I couldn't stay there. I crept out and packed a bag and I left. I haven't seen my mother since."

"Where did you go?"

"The first night I stayed in a park. I moved around to some friends' couches. I slept outside when I had to. I even slept under a bridge once. And that was the night I promised myself that I wouldn't waste my life and turn out like my mom. I wouldn't be a teen mother. I would wait until marriage, no matter what. I would never drink or do drugs. Eventually I got found out and a social worker brought me to a group home. She saved my life and helped me get on the right track. That was when I vowed to become a social worker and promised myself that I would help kids in the same situation that I'd been in. I would get a scholarship. Go to college. Get my master's degree. Fortunately, being homeless makes it a lot easier to get a scholarship." I hoped he didn't hear the catch in my voice.

He reached under my chin with his fingers and slowly turned my head so that I was looking at him. "Do you have any idea how much I admire you?" he said in a low voice.

"Bet you say that to all the formerly homeless girls."

"I don't think I've ever said that to anyone before. You are an exceptional person." He caressed the side of my face.

My breath grew thin. "You have a way with words."

"Words are important. Words are the way you decide if you like someone, if you will trust them. I would prefer to woo you with kisses, but since I cannot, I will take the challenge of wooing you with my words."

That look in his eyes had apparently caused my entire nervous system to short out because nothing was working the way it was supposed to.

I was completely and totally wooed.

But that one word, challenge, stuck in my brain. "Is that what this is? My unicornhood is a challenge?"

"I want to kiss you. I want to more than kiss you. But I want those things to show you how I feel about the rest of you." He put his hand on the side of my head. "I am captivated by your beautiful, quick mind. One that never fails to say what you're thinking and never fails to surprise me."

He moved his hand down to my collarbone, and a shiver danced over my skin. "I am mesmerized by your sweet, loving heart. I see what a loyal friend you are. How my sisters already adore you. Your kindness to total strangers."

He lifted his hand and moved it down to my waist, pulling me closer. "I am intrigued by your soul. The sadness there. The determination. The artistry. The realness of you. I am surprised at how much I want to help you and take care of you. To make things better for you."

He planted a soft kiss on the top of my head. "I am attracted to all of you, Katerina MacTaggart. Not just the outside of you."

Nico looked at me again, and I knew right then if he tried to kiss me I would let him. He studied my face and exhaled deeply. "Let's get you to sleep. We have another early flight."

I felt exposed and vulnerable, and I guess I wanted some reassurance from him. Putting me to bed wasn't it.

He helped me off the couch and walked me to my door. He took both of my hands and we stood there in silence for a few minutes before he finally spoke. "I am going to earn your trust. I'm not a patient man. That's something my parents and Johann can attest to. I very often find myself in trouble because I am not willing to wait as a prince should wait. But with you, for you, I will wait. I will be patient. Because I will show you that there are men who can keep their word. I will be a man you can trust."

My throat felt thick, like I might start crying. "I've never known a trustworthy man."

"Then I will be the first."

I was enthralled. Totally and completely deep in his thrall.

And he was making me feel all the feels.

"Good night." I thought he might kiss my hand or my cheek, but he let my hands go and walked over to his door.

I didn't want him to leave. "You don't want to tuck me in?"

"You and I both know that wouldn't be a very good idea." He gave me a parting smile, closed his door behind me, and left me no choice but to go to bed too.

I couldn't believe how much better I felt. Like I'd been living under a rock like Patrick Starfish and someone had finally lifted it off of me. I felt cleansed. Reborn.

And something had shifted between us tonight. Something I couldn't explain or quantify. But it changed me and it changed us. I realized that the fear had vanished. It had been coiled up inside me like a sleeping dragon for so long that I barely knew how to live without it.

I knew that Nico and I would probably grow closer. That there could possibly be an actual relationship between us. I hadn't forgotten that I was leaving in a week and a half. Maybe that made it better. Maybe it would be, like Lemon suggested, a fling. A chance to date someone I knew I couldn't have a future with. To just enjoy the time we had while we had it.

I would just have to make sure that I didn't let things get serious. I didn't need the heartbreak.

Maybe I should stick to that no-kissing rule. That would keep some distance between us. On the other hand, after tonight, there was a definite possibility that I might let him kiss me again.

I climbed into bed, feeling a lightness inside me. It took me a second to realize that what I was feeling was hope.

The last thing I heard before drifting off was Lemon chuckling and saying, "You sly dog, you."

Another early day. "If the morning had a face, I would punch it."

"That's adulthood," Lemon told me. "If you're not tired, you're not doing it right."

"It's enough to make me consider drinking coffee."

"I have some if you want it," Lemon offered, holding her cup out to me. It smelled foul. I passed.

I threw some clothes on and didn't do anything with my hair. Including brushing it. Too sleepy. Fortunately, my suitcase and bag were already packed. I suspected Giacomo was responsible, and this time I was only a little creeped out that he'd been sneaking around our room without us knowing it. I was getting a little too comfortable with this royal lifestyle thing.

I did make sure I had my clutch stowed in my purse. While Lemon was in the bathroom, I opened the clutch to make sure the phone and money were still there. They were.

Nico was on his way out the door when I emerged out of my bedroom. He stopped, brushed past his advisors, and came over to kiss me on both cheeks. "*Buongiorno, bella.* How did you sleep?"

Everyone was staring at us. I felt super self-conscious. "I was kinda hoping I'd wake up this morning and find out the world had canceled today and we could all go back to sleep."

He let out a short laugh. Over his shoulder I could see Johann impatiently tapping his foot and pointedly looking at his watch. "Looks like you need to go," I told him.

"I will see you soon," he said. His light blue eyes were filled with promises that I didn't fully grasp, and then he was gone.

It wasn't until after we went down to the back entrance, climbed into the limo, and headed toward the airport that Rafe mentioned Nico had to stay behind for a few hours. My heart sank with a melancholic twinge.

Which was so stupid. I would see him again. I didn't need to feel sad that we'd be apart for a few hours. I'd somehow managed to spend the last twenty-four years without him.

Davide and Francesco weren't in the car with us. When I asked about it, Dante and Rafe exchanged glances. "Nico said they could find their own way home."

He did that for me. Whether he was just mad and punishing them, or trying to spare me the hassle of having to see them again, he did it for me.

I was touched by the way he always seemed to think of me and what I might want or need. But I didn't understand it. It was both strange and sweet.

When we boarded, I tried to find two empty seats so that I could catch a quick catnap. (Or a Kat nap. Ha-ha.) The flight attendant stopped me. "Signorina MacTaggart?" I nodded. She smiled and said, "His Highness thought you might be more comfortable lying down in the bedroom."

Here he was, still being sweet and considerate by proxy. I couldn't say no to the offer. The room was dark, as all the shades had been drawn. I took my shoes off and sat down on the bed. This was Nico's bed. Did he ever sleep here? I decided I wouldn't get under the covers because that was too weird. But when I lay down, I knew he had been there. The pillows smelled like him. I smiled. And promptly passed out.

The attendant woke me up right before we started our descent. Lemon asked about my schedule while I was putting my seatbelt on. I was having a hard time connecting the two parts. My head felt woozy. "Schedule?"

"Didn't they give you one?" Lemon held her phone up. "Maybe they didn't because I have meetings and you don't."

The belt finally clicked into place. "For your marketing plans?"

"It's going really well. I can hardly wait to read what you write about your time with Nico." She waggled her eyebrows suggestively at me, and I laughed.

"I hope you're not disappointed. It is cool though that they're including you in the planning with all these important people."

She ran a hand over her perfect platinum blonde bob. She paid a very nice man a lot of money to keep it that shade. "Well of course they included me, darlin'. You know everything's better with a twist of Lemon." She smiled at me over her phone. "Looks like I'll have some free time tomorrow if you want to finish up our Christmas shopping."

"Fine by me."

We returned to the palace, and when I stepped inside, I stopped in surprise. Everything had changed. The entire interior had been transformed for the holiday—long, thick strands of green garland that were broken up by velvet red ribbons had been wrapped around columns and doorways. There were fake Christmas trees with twinkling white lights every few feet, next to the suits of armor. I smiled when I noticed someone had wrapped ribbons around the neck of the helmets on the armor. Here in the giant entry hall clear glass ornaments had been hung at varying lengths, like an artistic interpretation of snowflakes.

Festive didn't even begin to cover it. Christmas had exploded in the castle.

Lemon told me she'd see me later as Giacomo hustled me up to my room. Apparently I was to have a meeting with a seamstress. Before I could ask why, Serafina had launched herself on me. "Oof," I said as I held on to her.

"I missed you!" she said in a desperate voice.

I lifted her up onto my hip. "What have you been up to?"

"Nothing. It's been so *boring* without you." Like I was solely responsible for her entertainment. Like she didn't have a life before I came to the palace. I tried not to laugh. I liked her a lot. She was fun.

Giacomo introduced me to Liliana, one of the three full-time seamstresses on staff. She had laid out a variety of fabrics on my bed. I put Serafina down, and she climbed up on the bed to rub the different materials against her cheek.

"What's this for?"

"You will need a cocktail dress for the day after Christmas, and then one for the ball on New Year's Eve," he said.

Another ball? And why did I need a dress for the day after Christmas?

"I need a new dress," Serafina told Liliana. "So that I can match with Kat."

"I just finished two new dresses for you," Liliana responded.

"But I *need* another one." Serafina said it the same way a dialysis patient might say, "But I *need* a new kidney."

"Which color would you like?" Giacomo asked.

"Pick purple! Pick purple!" Serafina exclaimed as she bounced up and down.

"Purple's fine," I said.

"Do you have any preference for style or fabric?" Giacomo asked me in a serious tone.

"Um, just something pretty?"

111

He blinked twice, slowly. "Something pretty. I believe Liliana can manage that. But the ball on New Year's Eve is a costume ball. Do you have an idea of what you would like to wear?"

"I know!" Serafina looked like she was about to burst. "Be Elsa!"

I shrugged. "Okay, sure. I'll be Elsa." A costume ball on New Year's Eve? I had come to accept that weird things were a regular occurrence in this household, and it was easier to just go along with it.

Liliana put me up on this little stand, and then she took all my measurements. It was a slightly disconcerting experience. Serafina told me everything that she had done in the last twenty-four hours since I had abandoned her.

When Liliana finished, she gathered up all her things and left with Giacomo. They had their heads bent closely together as they spoke in rapid Italian. They were probably despairing over my fashion cluelessness.

I put my purse in the top drawer of my nightstand. I wanted it close by just in case. In case of what, I didn't know. But I would sleep easier knowing it was nearby.

I collapsed on the bed next to Serafina. "What should we do now?"

She thought for a moment before saying, "Do you want to meet my father?"

Chapter 13

I didn't know anything about their father, only what that reporter in Paris had mentioned. That he had been in an accident. I admit, my curiosity got the better of me.

"Sure," I told her.

My bedroom door was flung open, and there stood Chiara, chest heaving. "Did. You. Take. My. Phone?"

"I didn't!" Serafina sounded so indignant. For some reason it reminded me of her brothers, which made me smile.

"You're lying," Chiara hissed through clenched teeth. "I know you took it! You always take it!"

"I didn't this time!"

Which was exposed as a total lie a few seconds later when the phone fell out of Serafina's pocket.

"I knew it!" Chiara dove onto the bed to grab it.

"I'm telling!" Serafina howled back, trying to get it away from her sister.

They started screaming at each other in Italian, and I thought it high time I intervened. "Guys, stop! Give that to me!" I pried the phone out of both of their hands and stood up. "Is this Chiara's phone?"

Serafina didn't answer. She just looked at me sullenly.

I handed the phone to Chiara, and she clasped it to her chest like Gollum with his ring. I was going to tell Serafina to apologize, but stopped. She wasn't my kid. They could sort this out themselves.

Distraction always worked well in situations like these. "Come on, what were we going to do? Visit your dad?"

That seemed to snap Serafina out of her funk. "Let's go!"

She took me through a part of their private apartments that I hadn't been in yet. "Have you seen our Christmas tree?"

"I've seen a lot of Christmas trees today."

"No, *our* Christmas tree."

She brought me into a room that seemed unlike the others. This was a lived-in room. Full of modern and antique furniture, decorated in greens and creams, but I could tell this was where the family gathered to spend time together. There was a giant flat screen with video game consoles and controllers. Large, overstuffed, comfortable-looking couches dotted the room. I saw dolls and a dollhouse alongside one wall.

And in the corner of one room, the largest Christmas tree I'd ever seen. Like Rockefeller Center big. Unlike the other pristine trees I'd seen in the palace, it had both white and multicolored lights. There were no delicate, elegant, matching ornaments here. Just a huge hodgepodge of all different types of ornaments and clumps of tinsel.

"Every year we get a new ornament with our name and the year on it."

I touched one of the ornaments and turned it over. Nico's, from when he was a year old. It was hard to imagine him as a baby. "It must be nice to have traditions like that." I had no traditions. Nothing to tie me to a place or a family. Nothing I was a part of.

"We have *lots* of traditions," she said, taking me by the hand. I decided to leave my self-pity party behind.

She led me to a pair of large wooden doors and pushed them open. I heard the queen's voice before I saw her. The king was lying in a hospital bed, and the queen sat to his left, reading a book to him. She stopped and closed the book when we entered.

He had black hair shot through with silver, and brown eyes that he fixed on me as soon as we walked in. He looked skinny and a bit deflated. He had Nico's nose and the same strong jawline.

"Papa, this is my new best friend, Kat."

Serafina climbed onto the bed and nestled into her father's shoulder. He turned his head to kiss the top of her scalp.

"It is a pleasure to finally meet you," the king said, turning his attention back to me. His accent was more pronounced than his children's. "I have heard a great deal about you."

Was that good or bad? And what should I say back? Usually I would be like, "Yeah, me too," but I'd heard hardly anything about him since I'd arrived.

"Please, have a seat." I took an empty chair on the right side of his bed, across from the queen. She gave me a serene and sweet smile. I nodded at her and smiled back.

"Aria? Would you give us a moment?"

The queen stood up, putting the book on the nightstand next to his bed. She told Serafina to come with her, and the little girl kissed her father's cheek before leaving with her mother.

I had to admit, I was more than a little freaked out. What did the king want? As I watched the queen leave, my eyes settled on a large, black, motorized wheelchair. I looked back at him, wondering.

"I am quadriplegic," the king said. "My body has a difficult time leaving this bed, but my mind still can. My wife spends a great deal of time every day reading to me. I know she has other responsibilities, but she insists. I know she must tire of always reading to me."

"I'm so sorry," was all I could think to say.

"I've had a few years to adjust."

"Does the wheelchair not work?"

That surprised him. "It works very well. Why?"

"Oh. I was just wondering why you would stay in here if you had a wheelchair." I had seen the elevators. The rooms were all enormous. He could maneuver easily. "Don't get me wrong, this is a very nice room, but if it were me, I'd hate to be stuck."

Maybe he didn't want to be pushed around everywhere. "Is it self-operated?"

The king didn't respond. I raised my eyebrows in alarm. Had I offended him somehow? I didn't mean to. Typical me though, saying out loud whatever thought crossed through my brain.

The uncomfortable silence stretched between us as he studied me. When he finally spoke, I nearly jumped out of my skin, I'd been so anxious. "So you are the young woman my son has spoken about so often."

I just nodded. I couldn't tell if that was a good thing or bad thing. My heart did a happy skip at the idea that Nico talked to his dad about me, but what if the king didn't want me around Nico? Maybe he was going to tell me to stay away from him. That would seriously suck. I finally felt comfortable enough to spend time with him, and now his dad was going to forbid me from doing that?

He continued to look at me. Irritated, I thought about offering to show him my teeth while he considered my worthiness, but I kept my crazy at bay. Right now I was just jumping to conclusions. I had no idea what he was thinking.

"You must be careful with him," he finally said. "He has been betrayed by women who were interested in only fame and fortune."

I immediately thought of Lady Claire Sutherland.

"I don't care about that stuff."

The king looked thoughtful. "You must promise me that you will be gentle with his heart."

I had no intention of handling any of Nico's body parts, including his heart. Whatever there was between us, it wouldn't last. It would be light, breezy, fun. No hearts would be harmed in the making of our film. No one would get hurt.

But I couldn't say no to a king. He still had that dungeon downstairs. So I smiled and said, "I promise."

A man dressed in white scrubs entered the room, reading a clipboard. He stopped short when he saw me and said something in Italian.

"No, please come in, Dr. Franco. Signorina MacTaggart was just leaving."

I knew a dismissal when I heard one. I was more than happy to scurry out. Before I had a chance to think about what the king had said to me, what he wanted me to do, and what it might mean, Serafina appeared out of nowhere and grabbed my arm.

"My mother has some beauty ladies here today. Let's get a pedicure. "

That sounded wonderful. And just what I needed. "You are one awesome kid, you know that?"

"I really do."

Chiara and the queen joined us, and we all got our fingernails and toenails done. In between the laughing, talking, and teasing, I thought about the king and his wheelchair. Was he embarrassed to use it? Was it too painful a reminder of his life before? He seemed like a proud man. I couldn't imagine it would be easy to let other people move him from his bed to his wheelchair.

We had an informal lunch together, just the four of us. I watched as the queen spoke so lovingly to her girls. I wondered what my life would have been like if my mother had loved me more than she loved getting high.

The girls took me to their rooms to show them off. Despite being in a medieval castle, they were very normal girl rooms. Lots of pink and purple and hearts and boy band posters and stuffed animals. Chiara had a collection of pictures on a bulletin board ripped from fashion magazines. She told me that she wanted to design clothes someday and showed me some of her sketches. She had talent. I didn't know about the fashion part, but she could definitely draw. Much better than I ever could. My art consisted solely of stick figures.

After spending the entire afternoon together, the girls talked me into watching *Frozen*. We agreed to watch the movie in my room. I wanted to start writing down some notes about the time I'd spent with Nico. Not that I needed to, since every moment with him felt like someone had branded them onto my brain. And just thinking of him, pathetically enough, gave me the warm fuzzies.

On our way there, Serafina stopped short. "We should have a slumber party!"

"Yes, a slumber party!" Chiara said. "We could do each other's hair and have facials!"

I was kind of looking forward to getting some sleep tonight, so I didn't find that idea too appealing.

"I don't know," I said. They looked so disappointed.

"It isn't fair," Serafina said in a wobbly voice. "You spent all day yesterday playing with Nico. I want to play with you too."

I tried to suppress the images of the kind of playing Nico and I had been doing. Her lower lip stuck out, and her mouth was trembling. I couldn't resist once she turned those puppy dog eyes on me. She was definitely hitting below the belt.

"Okay. Why not?"

Chiara offered to order dinner for us to have in my room. I couldn't imagine a life where room service was part of my daily upbringing. The girls promised to meet me back in my room so that they could get their pajamas on.

I changed into a soft black T-shirt and plaid flannel pajama bottoms and climbed onto my bed. Lemon had left me a note saying she had more meetings and then plans with Salvatore for that evening, which she punctuated with several exclamation marks and smiley faces.

Serafina ran into the room wearing a nightgown that had Olaf the snowman on the front, and Chiara arrived shortly after in blue silk pajamas. She had a laptop with her that she left on the floor next to the bed. I made a mental note not to step on it.

"Can I do your hair?" Chiara asked me.

"Sure."

She started brushing while Serafina jumped on my bed. The two activities did not go well together. I was getting my head yanked all over the place.

"Have you ever been in love?" Chiara asked me as she started what felt like a French braid.

"Kat loves Nico," Serafina said in between jumps.

"I do not love Nico," I hurried to correct her. That was the absolute last thing I needed—for his little sister to run off and tell him that I loved him.

His teasing would be merciless and unending, I was sure.

"Everyone loves Nico," she replied.

"Why do you ask?" I said to Chiara, desperate to change the subject.

"There's this boy at my boarding school. Ethan. He's tall and has blond hair and dreamy hazel eyes. He's on the rugby team. I think I might be in love with him, but I don't think he likes me back."

Somebody needed to explain to the princess that a crush was not love. Something good for me to keep in mind as well.

"How old are you exactly?" I asked.

"Fourteen." I had a momentary pang as I realized she was the same age I was the night I'd left home. How different our lives were that her big concern was whether a boy liked her or not and mine at that age had been where I would sleep for the night.

"Well, why wouldn't he like you? You're gorgeous and royalty."

Chiara finished up my hair and came to sit in front of me. She crossed her legs and pulled them up to her chest, wrapping her arms around them. "I don't know. I don't know what to do. What to say to him, how to act."

I was so the last person in the world to give her advice on how to get a guy.

"If he doesn't like you then he's a . . . I don't know the word in English . . . *come si dice* . . . ?" Serafina asked.

"A moron?" I offered helpfully.

"*Si*," Serafina agreed. "A moron."

"He's not a moron," Chiara said in a defensive tone. "Just . . . quiet. And sweet."

"Why don't you just tell him he's your boyfriend? That's what I did with Giovanni. I told him he was my boyfriend, and he agreed."

If only life could really be that simple. I tried to imagine myself informing Nico that he was now my boyfriend and didn't have a choice in the matter.

Problem was, I imagined he might agree the same way little Giovanni had.

"The best advice I can give you is to just be yourself." Had I actually just said something so clichéd? Too bad Lemon wasn't there. She probably had a book on how to get a boy to like you.

Chiara let out a moan at what I said and threw herself backward so that she was sprawled out on the bed.

"Mamma says she's very melodramastic," Serafina told me in a stage whisper.

"I am not melodramatic!" Chiara hit the bed with her hands and feet at the same time to punctuate her statement.

"How about we start the movie?" I suggested.

Serafina got the movie going while I grabbed the notepad and pen I'd left on my nightstand. I meant to write about Nico, but I kept doodling hearts and clouds in the column.

I was only seconds away from writing "Mrs. Kat Fiorelli" all over the page. Pathetic. I set my pen down on the bed in disgust.

Just because I was hanging out with a fourteen-year-old girl did not mean I needed to start acting like one.

We were on our third viewing of the movie. Chiara had fallen asleep on the far side of the bed, but Serafina was still barely awake, insisting that we had to finish it. She had cuddled herself against me so that I couldn't move.

There was a knock on my door. "Come in," I called out softly, not wanting to wake up Chiara.

The door slowly opened and there stood Nico. I think my heart swelled up two more sizes. I was so unbelievably happy to see him. Like in a puppy-dogs-wrapped-up-in-rainbows-frolicking-on-marshmallow-clouds kind of way.

His tie had been loosened, and he looked worn out. My feet itched with the urge to jump up out of the bed and run to him. I wanted to comfort him. Hug him. He looked like he'd had a hard day. The urge to be next to him, with him, both confused and surprised me.

"Stay out, Nico," Serafina instructed him sleepily. "You're not invited. Girls only."

"I won't come in, I promise," Nico said, standing at the threshold. "How many times today have you watched this movie?"

I held up three fingers.

"You must be a saint."

"That's me, Saint Kat. Patron saint of midnight snacks and skiing accidents."

He let out a soft laugh.

"Nico, cover your ears!" Serafina told him.

He willingly obliged, putting his hands over his ears with a mischievous glint in his eye.

"Don't tell him about your Elsa costume for the ball," she said. "It should be a surprise."

I didn't think Nico cared what my costume would be, or get why Serafina was concerned about him finding out. I told her I wouldn't, and she finally closed her eyes. I paused the movie, and knew she was asleep when she didn't whine for me to turn it back on.

Nico took his hands away from his ears. "Have my sisters spent the evening telling you all of my secrets?"

"Yep, now I know all about that love child and the gambling problem."

121

He laughed again and I wanted to wrap myself up in his laughter. Which was a weird thing to want to do. But in my defense, I was very tired.

"You are my first stop. I came by to see if I you were available tomorrow afternoon."

"Let me check my schedule." I sat there for a second. "Yep, totally clear."

A brilliant smile. "Excellent. Then I will see you tomorrow afternoon."

I didn't want him to leave. I wanted to talk to him. Hold him.

"I missed you today," he said low and simply, right before he shut the door.

His first stop. Before his parents or his siblings or his advisors or his secretaries. I was his first stop.

And he missed me. I'd missed him, but my insides were turning into goo at the idea that he had missed me.

I needed to stop watching fairy tales because I was starting to believe that I was living in one.

Chapter 14

There was basically no way I was going into the kitchen. But it was my regularly scheduled feeding time.

I wanted to sleep, but now the hunger and the Nico imaginings were keeping me awake. Which wasn't helped by Chiara's snoring or Serafina's teeth-grinding.

That's when I thought I heard a soft knock on my door. Was it Nico?

My heart started pounding again as I eased myself from the bed, trying my hardest to not wake up the princesses. I ran a hand over my out-of-control hair, contemplating a quick run into the bathroom to do some damage control.

But Nico liked the way I looked. Even when I was a mess.

I decided though that I would not let him in. I would make him stay out in the hallway. Where it was safe for both of us.

When I opened the door, there was no one there. The hallway was empty. I looked down and saw a tray. A tray that had a bowl of chocolate gelato, a spoon, and a little vase with moonflowers.

He did it again. Giving me all the feels. He had to be the most considerate, thoughtful man alive.

I brought the tray in and demolished the gelato at my desk, grinning like an idiot the entire time.

Things like this did not happen to girls like me. But it was happening. And it was kind of, I don't know, glorious.

Full and finally sleepy, I went back to my bed and stubbed my toes on something. "Ow!" I hopped on one foot for a second, grabbing my hurt toes. The pain ebbed and I got down on my hands and knees to look under the bed to see what I had kicked. It was Chiara's laptop.

I pulled it out and after I verified that the girls were still asleep, turned it on. Fortunately there was no password and it started right up.

I hadn't been on the Internet since I'd arrived in Monterra. I opened a web browser.

I typed in "Prince Dominic Monterra" into the search box.

There were hundreds of thousands of hits. A lot about his charities, some about him being Europe's most eligible bachelor, all the parties, balls, and premieres he showed up at. I clicked on the "Images" link. An entire screen full of drop-dead gorgeous pictures of Nico. So not only was he beautiful, but photogenic too? Gag. Well, not really gag. More woo-hoo.

But I couldn't fully woo-hoo because all the pictures of him were with one over-the-top beautiful woman after another. Models, royals, celebrities, all clinging to his arm like he was the greatest thing since sliced bread. Which he obviously was, but I felt strangely possessive of him.

I clicked on the "Web" link and started reading some of the titles of the articles. One was called "My Night with the Prince." I hovered the mouse cursor over the link, tempted beyond belief to click it.

It reminded me of what the king had said to me earlier. How women had used Nico. Probably to get paid for articles just like this one. His privacy had been violated all over the place.

My gaze flickered over to the drawer in my nightstand. And here I'd contemplated doing the exact same thing to him by taking pictures. I couldn't be that person. I wouldn't. The reporter had said he would be back in touch with me. I would wait until he was, and then I'd return the phone and the money.

If I were being honest, I could admit it made me just a little sick to give up that much cash. But then I imagined Nico's face when he found out what I had done. That was worse.

He wanted me to trust him. Maybe I needed to be a person he could trust, too.

I shut the laptop and put it back on the floor. I wouldn't read any articles or tell-alls about him. I didn't want someone else's words in my head. I didn't want them running through my mind every time I talked to him.

There wouldn't be any other voice but mine as far as he was concerned.

Nico didn't judge me for my past. I wouldn't judge him for his.

I snuggled into my bed, pulling the covers up to my ears. It didn't matter what Nico had done with any of those other women.

Because I was pretty sure I was the only one getting moonflowers and gelato.

I awoke early the next morning because Serafina was prying one of my eyelids open. "It's time to get up!"

I growled and turned over, hoping she'd go away. She just came over to the other side and started shaking my arm. "Wake up, Kat."

Had no one in this family ever heard of sleeping in?

"Why won't she wake up?"

"She's not a morning person." I heard Lemon's voice and opened one eye to glare at her.

"I'd be a morning person if it didn't start so early in the day." In my defense, sometimes I got up early all on my own. Like at the crack of noon.

"Come on, we're going shopping. There's a lot going on today."

It was Christmas Eve. We would have to finish shopping because we were running out of time. Which meant I would have to get out of bed. Which I didn't want to do.

"Can I come? Can I come?" Serafina was jumping on my bed again.

"Sure," Lemon said. "We already bought your present. You'll need to ask your mother first."

"You got me a present?" she asked in a chipmunk-on-crack voice. "What is it?"

"You'll have to wait until tomorrow," Lemon said. "Now go ask permission and get dressed. We have to leave soon." Serafina tore out of the room, yelling something in Italian down the hallway.

"That goes for you too," Lemon said. "Up and at 'em."

I groaned but knew I had no choice. I wondered where Chiara had gone off to, but I was too tired to ask. I did the bare minimum to get ready, making sure I had warm clothes on because I could see the snow falling outside of every window. We were going to have a white Christmas.

By the time I pulled my boots on, Serafina was bundled up in similar attire and waiting on my bed with an excited grin. A woman I didn't recognize was brushing Serafina's hair and putting it into a complicated braid. "Mamma said I can go!"

Lemon looked up from her smartphone. "So let's go."

I started when I noticed Giacomo standing near the door. I went over to see what he wanted. "Good morning. I understand that you are going shopping."

I nodded.

"His Highness would like you to use this." He handed me a black and gold credit card. Lemon came over to peer at the card. It looked like it had an actual diamond in the center. "His Highness does not want you to concern yourself with finances while you are here. There is no limit on that particular card."

"My daddy has been trying for years to get one of those," Lemon breathed. HRH Prince Dominic II. I ran my fingers over his raised name.

Wow. But no way. I handed it back to Giacomo. "Tell Nico I said thanks, but we've got this covered."

Giacomo looked utterly befuddled. "I don't understand."

"I know. But it's okay. Nico will get it. See ya later, Giacomo."

Serafina grabbed for my hand, and the three of us walked down the hallway. I could see Nico at the very end of the hallway, walking with Johann toward us.

I felt the moment he saw me, because his grin sent shimmery sparkles all over my skin. His smile was dangerous—joy, excitement, and a definite invitation to trouble.

We were about to meet in the middle, and I started to walk off to the side so as to not interrupt him. But the next thing I knew, Nico had picked me up and was swinging me around. I instinctively wrapped my arms around his neck. He put me down away from everyone else. He had my heart up in my throat, thumping loudly. His face was just a fraction away from mine, making my stomach do cartwheels. His minty breath mingled with mine, and I leaned in toward him, holding on to him tighter. His glacier-blue eyes were full of mischief.

"My apologies, *bella*. I thought you were someone else. To think that I nearly kissed you." He was *teasing* me. "I didn't mean to sweep you off your feet."

He let me go, and I was surprised that I managed to stay vertical as I wanted to collapse into a heap. "I wasn't swept," I completely lied. "You think that's the first time that's happened to me today?"

Nico laughed as he kissed my hand (again with the hand kissing!) and told me to enjoy my day, that he would see me soon for our date. At least, I think that's what he said. My hearing wasn't functioning all that well. Or my brain.

Everything was focused on that almost kiss.

I snapped back into reality when I heard Serafina announce, "I told you Kat loves Nico."

"I do not," I said through gritted teeth. I hated how I responded to him, how I felt so out of control. Like all my promises and boundaries just got tossed out the window. How easily I would give in if he pushed. And how he knew it.

"Cream, circus lions, chocolate mousse, you . . ." Lemon said as we continued down the hallway.

"What?"

"Oh, don't mind me. I was just listing things that are whipped."

"I am not whipped! It's not like his kisses are earth-shattering or something. It's no big deal."

Lemon scooted away from me, to the opposite wall.

"What are you doing?"

"I don't want to be standing next to you when God strikes you down for lying."

We had breakfast in town (sadly, no bread with chocolate inside) and commenced shopping. I noticed Lorenz and another guard staying a few steps behind us. Lemon utilized them as bag carriers, which they did without complaint.

I bought Giacomo a red and gold silk Italian tie and a matching pocket square. Royal family colors. I thought he would like it.

We had a hard time picking something out for Violetta. I didn't know hardly anything about her, and had only briefly met her at that one dinner. Serafina was no help. She said Violetta spent most of her time in her room and was very grumpy. Lemon and I settled on some headbands and sparkly hairpins.

The twins were easy—two Xbox gift cards. Lemon wisely decided not to get Salvatore a gift. The way she spoke about him, I could tell, as she would say, the bloom was off the rose. She was already losing interest.

But while we were in the electronics stores, I saw it. The perfect gift for the king. I pointed it out to Lemon, and she agreed. We swore Serafina to secrecy, and she promised not to tell.

Finally finished, we got into the town car to return to the palace. And I didn't know what I was more excited about—seeing everyone opening their presents tomorrow morning or getting to spend the afternoon with Nico.

Lemon offered to wrap everything, and I agreed. She was the kind of person to match up the seams, place the tape underneath the seam so that it didn't show, and put on a beautiful, curly ribbon. I was the kind of person who would twist it up in Sunday comics and tape it until it stayed put.

Giacomo and lunch were waiting in my room when I got back, and I scarfed down the sandwich and soup. I asked where I was headed to next, but Giacomo would only tell me to dress warmly and for the outdoors. Then I spent a much longer time getting ready than I should have. I contemplated the makeup question. I kind of wanted to put some on. Maybe some mascara. But then Nico would know it was for him, and I would feel stupid. But on the other hand, as I reminded myself, it was okay to want to feel pretty. So I settled for some sunscreen and lip-gloss.

A knock at the door. I told my heart to calm down. I opened it and Nico stood there dressed much as he had been the day we'd first met. "Oh frak, we're not going skiing are we?"

His eyes twinkled. "No skiing, I promise."

I saw Salvatore and Lemon holding hands, standing behind him. "Double date?" I clarified. He nodded.

I was strangely disappointed. We hadn't really been on an actual date alone yet. We'd managed to squeeze some alone time in along the way, but I had been looking forward to having him to myself today. So I put on a smile and followed along.

We didn't have a driver today. Nico said he would be driving the black SUV waiting for us. I went to get into the front passenger seat, and he practically pulled a *Dukes of Hazzard* move to get across the front of the car and to my door. He opened it for me. "I could have opened that," I informed him. "I'm not helpless."

"I didn't say you couldn't. I'm being chivalrous."

Apparently he never got the memo about chivalry being dead. Was it possible to both like and dislike something at the same time? To like being pampered and spoiled, but worried about the implication that I needed him to take care of me?

Instead of arguing, I climbed into the car. Lemon and Salvatore sat in the back.

"Where are we going?" I asked.

"That's a surprise. But it is one of my favorite places," Nico said.

During the drive the guys asked us about our classes, Lemon's sorority, what an American university was like.

"Do you have a football team?" Nico asked.

"We don't have a football team. We're not big enough for that. We do have a soccer team, though."

"That's a real football team."

"Not where I'm from."

"Where you're from it is not football either. The ball never touches anyone's feet in American football."

"Sure it does. At kickoff and the point after touchdown. Football. Your thing is soccer."

It was like I had stabbed his puppy and insulted his European pride. Fortunately, we had arrived at our destination. Nico pulled the car off the road and into a not cleared parking lot. The snow had abated since that morning, and the sun was bright above us. I jumped out of the car before he tried to open that for me too. He cocked his head to one side and gave me a disappointed look. I shrugged back.

Nico and Salvatore pulled some backpacks out of the trunk of the car, passing them out. "Water and some other hiking supplies," he told me.

"We're going hiking? Over there?" Lemon asked in dismay. Lemon's idea of exercising was lifting her feet while I vacuumed. "Look at that grass. It's tall enough to go duck hunting with a rake."

"Do you like hiking?" Nico asked me.

"I love hiking. I used to try to spend as much time outdoors as I could because I didn't want to be at home." That made him look sad. "Growing up near the mountains and forests, I don't know. I just liked exploring." I tried to sound upbeat.

"Good." He smiled. "I like it too."

One more thing we had in common. Light and breezy, I reminded myself. Keep it light and breezy.

Because if we didn't stop the in common stuff soon, we were going to end up in serious trouble.

We stopped to let Lemon catch her breath. She sat on top of a boulder, not caring about the snow. By this point Salvatore was carrying her backpack. He handed her a water bottle, and she chugged it down.

"Are you all right?" I asked her. "You look pale and sweaty."

"Southern girls don't sweat. We glisten."

"You're glistening a lot."

"When I pictured my death, there were never this many rocks and trees involved. I've been telling myself for the last twenty minutes that there's a Louboutin sale at the end, but I'm not buying the lie."

"Maybe we should go back," I said to Nico.

"No, y'all go on. Salvatore can take me back to the car and we can wait for y'all there." Salvatore didn't look too enthused about the idea until Lemon raised one eyebrow at him suggestively, and then he was all too eager to head back.

"Have fun," Lemon whispered to me as I readjusted my backpack straps. I started to suspect that this had all been a scam on her part to get me alone with Nico, because she looked just fine walking back to the car.

I mean, I wanted to be alone with him. I just didn't want to be conned into it.

Chapter 15

"We're nearly there," Nico told me as he helped me climb up and over a big rock. "I used to have a much more direct route, but I promised my mother not to use it."

"Why?"

He didn't let go of my hand once I'd cleared the obstacle. Even through our gloves I could feel the heat of his hand.

"You met my father?"

"I did."

"He was in a boating accident a few years ago. My mother is terrified the same thing will happen to all of us. So she asked us to stop doing anything that had any risk involved. Rock climbing was my favorite hobby. I used to climb up that face there to get to the top—you can still see some of the cams in the rock. But a promise is a promise. I gave away all my gear." I could hear in his voice how much he missed it, and the whole thing struck me as unbelievably sad.

"You always do what you say, don't you?"

He gave me a little frown, like I'd confused him. "Of course."

I could rely on him. He wouldn't let me down. He wasn't like other men. I saw that when I looked at him, when I stood with him like this. There was something that felt like security. Strength. Confidence. He was safe. I felt safe.

I liked that more than I should. A heavy, warm glow started up in my heart and spread throughout my limbs.

We finally reached the top of the hill, and he walked me over to the edge. There was a rock carved into the shape of a bench. It overlooked the entire capital city of Imperia. I could see the castle in the distance, perched up on its own hill. Snow blanketed the valley floor, twinkling and sparkling in the afternoon sun. Forests of bright green pine trees filled the landscape. Behind us, I could hear a waterfall falling, crashing into rocks below.

"Everything here is like living in a postcard."

We stood in silence at the edge of the world, holding hands. The moment felt so romantic. "This is like, the perfect spot for a proposal. You should bring your future princess here."

While I wanted to smack myself around for the verbal stupidness spewing from my mouth, I was stopped by Nico's expression. "I have no intention of getting married."

"Ever?" It surprised me how important his answer to that question was.

He shrugged. "When I marry, my father plans to abdicate and make me king. I want to delay that as long as is humanly possible."

I didn't understand why it felt like a thousand tiny daggers were stabbing me in the heart over and over again. I went over to the stone bench, cleared a spot off, and sat down. I felt heavy and uneasy.

There was no future here. Not that in a million years I ever thought it really possible that I'd end up married to Nico, but there had at least been a possibility of it. A chance, however small, at a future. And now he was telling me that there never would be one. My throat felt thick.

Which shouldn't upset me. *Light and breezy, remember?* But it felt like something had just died.

I cleared my throat. "I can understand that. It seems like you have a pretty sweet single life. Traveling the world, doing whatever you want, going to parties and balls."

He sat down next to me and took my hand again. "That's not what a king does. My father still takes care of as many administrative things as he can, and I do the rest. I had scheduled much of the next two weeks as a holiday, but even then you can see that I am still constantly busy. It is fortunate that you came into my life when I could spend time with you."

"You only like me because I didn't want to go out with you." I was feeling contrary. Like I wanted to pick a fight.

He pinned me down with his intense gaze. "That's why I was intrigued by you. But that is not why I like you. And you know it."

I did know it. He'd spelled it out pretty clearly in Paris. I was just being obstinate. I let out a loud, annoyed sigh.

"Are you looking forward to the Christmas festivities?" he asked. He was always good at the changing the subject tactic if things started to go wonky between us. I decided to allow it because I had no real reason to be upset.

"I've never really liked Christmas. My mother was either gone or passed out."

"You've never had even one happy Christmas?"

I paused, remembering. "I did have one. Sort of. I was nine years old. My dad had just gotten out of prison, finally sober, and he took me to his parents' house for the holiday. It was the first and only time I remember meeting my grandparents. I don't think they liked me too much. Anyway, my dad had just started a new job, and he bought me a present. A Holiday Barbie. She was so beautiful—she had a blue velvet dress with silver lace all over it. She was the Millennium Princess. She was the prettiest thing I had ever owned. I didn't even want to take her out of the box. I was happy to just sit and look at her. It reminded me that someone loved me."

Nico squeezed my hand. "And then one day I came home from school and my mom had pawned it. I cried for days. A few weeks later, ironically enough, my dad got hit by a drunk driver and died. So, no, not a lot of happy Christmas memories."

He wrapped both of his arms around me then, putting his cheek on top of my head. "I am so sorry, *cuore mio*."

I nestled into him and took all the comfort he wanted to offer me. Even if we didn't have a future, and this couldn't go anywhere, I decided to take what I could while I could.

"Now I feel guilty that my memories are all full of family, love, and laughter. I wish I could share those feelings with you so that you would know what it was like."

"Me too."

"I will just have to show you over the next few days. Starting right now." He stood up, brushing snow off his pants. I got that dizzy, sweet feeling when he pulled me up and then in close to him so that we were pressed together. He wrapped his arms around my waist. "Will you let me show you what it's like to enjoy Christmas?"

I was starting to feel a bit like a light bulb with my moods—on again, off again. I had been upset about the no future thing, but now I felt myself responding to him and wanting to keep that smile on his face.

"Okay."

As he led me down the hill I realized something significant. I wanted more. I wanted things to progress.

Even if we weren't going to be in a relationship, I was going to kiss him again.

And soon.

Lemon tried asking me what was wrong, but I brushed her off instead of confiding in her. I didn't want to talk about it. I already knew how stupid it was to be upset about something that would have absolutely no effect on me and my future at all. Nico's choice to not marry had nothing to do with me, right?

Right?

Giacomo told me that we would be having a special Christmas Eve feast where seven different types of fish would be the main course. It was supposed to be like a fasting or purifying meal before a holy day, but he said over time people had lost that religious part of it, but still kept the tradition.

Lemon had left his gift on my bed, and I handed it to him. I didn't know if he'd have the next day off, so I wanted to make sure he got it. "For you, from me and Lemon. Merry Christmas."

He held the thin box in his hand and blinked several times. "For me?"

"Yeah. Open it."

He paused again and then finally tugged at the ribbon surrounding the box. He very delicately lifted the tape up, opening it up perfectly without a single rip in the wrapping paper. He lifted the lid and pulled out the tie, holding it up.

"Thank you very much, Signorina Kat."

"You're welcome."

He put the tie back in the box and closed it. He cleared his throat before he spoke again. "You will be expected to wear a cocktail dress. The black or the blue in your closet will suffice. Enjoy your evening."

All stiffness and formality on his way out the door. "Merry Christmas, Giacomo!"

He stuck in his head back in the door and with a slight smile said, "*Buon Natale*, Signorina Kat."

I decided on the blue dress, leaving my hair down and a little bit of makeup. Nico could make fun of me if he wanted to.

But he didn't. When Lemon and I entered the formal dining hall, Nico headed straight for me, looking amazing in a black-tie tuxedo. "Stunning," was all he said before he kissed both of my cheeks.

He offered his arms to Lemon and me, but before she could accept, Dante had whisked her away.

Nico pulled me closer than was necessary and nuzzled my cheek with his nose. Conscious of his family all around us, I stepped back. But not too far.

Queen Aria was seated in her chair by Rafe, which signaled that the rest of us could also sit. Nico helped me into my chair and then helped Serafina, who kept insisting, "I can do it myself! I don't need your help!"

I remembered back to when I wouldn't let Nico open my car door. And realized that I'd had the emotional response of a seven-year-old girl.

The queen had raised her hand to signal for the first course when the dining hall doors opened. Everyone looked toward the doors, curious. And then everyone was on their feet.

It was King Dominic.

Another seat and place setting were added to the table next to Chiara, as the king rolled his way over to his wife. She had tears streaming down her face as he took her former position at the table. She leaned over to kiss her husband. I looked away, feeling that I was intruding on something very personal.

Chiara was also openly weeping, and Serafina was jumping up and down. "Papa's here! Papa's here!"

"Why is everyone staring? Shouldn't we eat?" the king asked, and the servants brought out the first course. The king looked over at me and nodded. I smiled back uneasily. What the frak had that been about? Why did he single me out? Had something I said in his room affected him?

Nico reached for my hand under the table and didn't let go. I had to eat everything left-handed, which took forever.

But it was totally worth it.

During the dinner, the queen read letters from the children expressing their love for their parents. Nico's made me teary-eyed and emotional. I didn't know why, exactly. He explained that it was a tradition for children to write letters to their parents and read them on Christmas Eve. I thought it was beautiful.

After dinner we headed to the family's private drawing room, and in the fireplace, we lit the biggest log I'd ever seen. "*Festa di Ceppo*," Nico whispered in my ear. "We're burning the Yule log to celebrate life and hopes for a prosperous new year. They will keep it burning until New Year's Day."

Then it was to the front door where a horde of servants waited with our boots, coats, gloves, hats, and scarves. There were cars that would drive us to the city center, and we would walk to the cathedral for Midnight Mass.

The king and queen took a separate vehicle that could transport his wheelchair and take them directly to the church. The rest of us piled into a giant limo. Everybody in the car was excited and talking over each other. Nico was a silent, warm anchor at my side.

A giant bonfire lit up the square in the center of town, lighting our way as we climbed out of the car. I could hear bells upon bells, all ringing loudly. There were carolers in the street and vendors out selling their wares. The air smelled of cinnamon, apples, and spice. The snow fell gently around us as we walked together, kicking up flurries. The little Swiss-looking shops with their gingerbread lattices and sloped roofs were decorated with lights and greenery. The people on the street called out to us, and the members of Nico's family smiled and waved. Security prevented anyone from getting too close.

"Look," Nico said, pointing up to the mountain. There was a line of hundreds of torches coming down the mountain. "Skiers carrying the flame down to begin the holiday."

We rounded a corner and there was a massive medieval cathedral. It had tall spires and gorgeous stained glass windows, all softly lit from within. Hymns sung by a choir spilled outside. In front of the church was a live Nativity. With an actual baby and real animals. We stood and listened as a narrator read from the Bible to tell the story of the birth of Christ.

"Just think," Lemon whispered in my ear. "This is where you'll marry Nico someday."

I knew she was teasing, but it made my heart feel heavy to remember that it would never happen.

"Or where you'll marry Dante," I retorted, and she rolled her eyes at me.

"That's about as likely as rain falling upward," she said.

The Nativity reenactment had finished, and we headed inside. The royal family had their own special set of benches in an alcove. The king and queen were already there and waiting for us. Nico made sure that I sat right next to him, with no space between us, and put his arm on the bench behind me. I relaxed, letting the music, warmth, and incense settle around me. I'd never been in a church before.

Serafina sat on my other side. "Are you excited about Santa Claus coming tonight?" I asked her.

"*Babbo Natale* doesn't bring very many presents. *La Befana* brings most of them on Epiphany."

I looked at Nico questioningly. "*La Befana* is a good witch who was visited by the Three Wise Men. They asked her for directions and invited her to come along to find the Christ Child. She declined. She later changed her mind and tried to find the men and the baby, but couldn't. So she is still searching and in the meantime brings good children candy and toys."

Witches? Somebody had mixed up their Halloween and Christmas. "When is Epiphany?"

"January sixth," he replied.

January sixth. I would be gone by then. I would be back in class, working with my kids, doing my thesis.

I would be back home, and this would be over.

Chapter 16

The next morning I expected to be woken up early, and I was not disappointed. Serafina ran up and down the hallway yelling about it being Christmas and for everyone to get up.

I had actually gotten a decent night's sleep. After the church service we had hot chocolate and these enormous doughnuts called *ringli*. Serafina had fallen asleep in the car on the way home, and Nico put her to bed. Which meant he and I didn't get to say good night. Which I was more than a little despondent about.

But now it was Christmas, and I wondered whether I should get changed or not. The royal family tended to dress up for everything. Christmas morning felt more like a pajama situation to me.

Lemon came out of her room the same time I did. We told each other Merry Christmas. I gave her my poorly wrapped present, not wanting to wait. Lemon didn't want to wait either and opened it right there. She squealed when she saw it and said, "You know me so well. I love Marilyn!" She hugged me and then ran back into her room and put the picture on her nightstand. She gathered up the presents for Nico's family and handed me several of them to carry. With our arms full, we followed after Serafina to the family's private drawing room. Everyone was there waiting. Thankfully, they were not in suits and dresses. They were in pajamas. Nico had managed to put a T-shirt on. I didn't know whether to be disappointed or relieved.

The fire burned brightly in the fireplace, and someone had put on Italian Christmas carols. I couldn't tell where the music was coming from. We put our presents under the tree and wished everyone a *Buon Natale*. Nico had a spot next to him on the couch, and he waved me over to sit next to him.

Serafina had a pink Santa hat on that Lemon had given her, and she started passing out the presents. I'd gone to Lemon's house for the last few

Christmases, and having only half the number of people currently present in the room, there were easily five times the presents. I remembered though that for the Monterrans, their major gift giving would happen later.

Christmas morning seemed reserved for gag gifts for the royal family. Chiara had bought Nico a Winnie-the-Pooh tea set, which Serafina begged to borrow. "I will even let you have it," Nico said with a twinkle in his eye as he passed it over to her.

Dante bought Rafe a grow-your-own-girlfriend kit. "I thought you could use the help." Rafe hit him on the shoulder, laughing.

The queen gave the king one of those singing fish, and he chuckled when she opened it for him and it started moving around and singing.

Violetta got a toilet brush and looked thoroughly confused. "What is this?" Which made everyone laugh.

Serafina held up our present for her and asked if she could open it. When Lemon and I told her she could, she tore through that thing like the Tasmanian Devil. "Elsa! I *love* Elsa! Thank you, thank you!" She squeezed the doll to her chest with a look of pure rapture on her face.

Nico squeezed my shoulders and gave me a grin. Chiara loved her beauty supplies, promising to paint all of our toenails. Even Violetta seemed happy about the hair stuff we got her. Which was surprising. The twins thanked us for the gift cards, and the queen opened her scarf and held it up. "Simply lovely, and my favorite color. Thank you."

Serafina handed Nico his present. He picked it up and shook it, holding it to his ear. "Is it a board game?"

"No." I nudged him with my elbow. "Open it."

"Legos?"

"It doesn't make any sound. You know exactly what it is."

"I have a pretty good idea, yes." He grinned. Then he opened it and turned it to see *The Great Gatsby* on the spine. "You remembered," he said, sounding surprised. He showed the book to his family. "Thank you, Lemon," he said over my shoulder. Then he leaned in and with an appreciative look said, "*Grazie, cuore mio.*" Only minor heart palpitations.

Last, there was the present for the king. Serafina handed it to her mother to open. When she got the paper off and they could see the box, I explained. "That's a tablet that has eye tracker software, so you can turn it on and off and turn pages by moving your eyes to the left or the right. And it has speakers so you can download audio versions of books and listen to them."

The whole room fell silent, and I could see unshed tears in the queen's eyes.

"Thank you, Kat and Lemon," the king said quietly.

"Yes," the queen said, her voice cracking. "This was very, very thoughtful of you."

Nico leaned over and kissed me on the top of my head. "My turn!" he said, breaking the mood.

He passed out boxes to all of the women, all similar in size and shape. He handed me mine last. I opened it up and found a long, velvet box. I was scared for a second to open it all the way. I finally did, and there was a ruby shaped like a heart, with a row of diamonds around it. The chain was light and delicate and expensive looking. "Oh, Nico," I said. I looked around and all the women were opening necklaces with different shapes and colors on their pendants.

He looked so pleased with himself. "I can't . . ." I started, but Lemon leaned over Dante and said lowly, "Darlin', when a beautiful man gives you a beautiful necklace, you bat your eyelashes and say thank you."

It was too much. But he looked so excited, and I couldn't disappoint him. "I can't put it on by myself. Can you help?" I handed him the necklace and turned my back to him, pulling my hair up to one side. He slid the necklace on, his fingers on the back of my neck as he clicked it closed. He left his fingers there for a second, and sparkling tingles ran up and down my spine. I dropped my hair and turned to face him. "Thank you," I said as I put my hand over the heart.

"You are very welcome," he said, kissing the back of my free hand.

The gift giving continued for a few more minutes. Lemon and I scored some beauty products (I got some apple-scented lotion that I suspected Nico had a hand in), antique silver frames, and a hand-drawn card from Serafina. The queen stood and told us we all needed to go change to get prepared for the servants' lunch.

I looked at Nico questioningly as people started gathering up their loot to take it back to their rooms. "Every year at Christmas, our entire extended family comes to the palace and we prepare lunch for the servants and their families. It's our day to do for them what they do for us every other day. Can you cook?"

"Does heating up ramen noodles count?"

He laughed. "Not quite what I had in mind."

"I make killer homemade Oreo cookies," I told him. My fourth grade teacher had shared her secret family recipe with me, and it was probably the one thing I made really, really well.

"Then you will be in charge of the homemade Oreo cookies," he said as he helped me to my feet. "Meet us down in the main kitchen," he said, hugging me tightly before reluctantly letting go.

I walked with Lemon and the two younger girls back toward our rooms. My free hand went back to my pendant, touching it again, thinking of what he'd said to me earlier. He'd said it to me yesterday, too. I turned to Chiara and asked, "What does *cuore mio* mean?"

She sighed happily. "It means my heart."

His heart? What? I was close to Muppet flailing arms again.

"I don't know what to do with that," I told Lemon, my tone sounding very panicked.

"I'd tell you what I'd do with it. Enjoy it for everything it's worth."

143

When we arrived in the kitchen, there were like a million people in there. All hugging and kissing and calling to one another. Nico came and found me and took me by the hand. "There's someone I want you to meet. My grandmother."

He led me over to a small woman dressed all in black. I'd spent enough time with Lemon's mom to recognize Chanel when I saw it. "Is she a queen too?"

"No, she is my maternal grandmother. She is Italian and from the House of Savoy, but they were stripped of their lands and titles during World War II." Nico made the introductions in Italian, and I just nodded and smiled politely.

His grandma looked me up and down and said something to Nico that made Dante and Rafe roar with laughter. Nico had pressed his lips together to keep himself from smiling.

"What did she say?" I asked.

"It doesn't matter," Nico said, shaking his head.

I grabbed Dante by his shirtfront as he went to move past us. "Why were you laughing?"

"My *nona* thinks you have excellent childbearing hips," he said, still laughing about it. I let go, and he scampered off.

That just put all sorts of impossible thoughts in my head. Little babies with Nico's black hair and blue eyes, chubby cheeks and soft skin. I felt a physical ache for something that would never be.

Nico led me over to an empty counter. "We'll sort out more introductions later when everything has calmed down. Tell me what you need to make your cookies, and I will get it for you."

I listed off the ingredients, and he told me to wait on the stool next to the counter while he gathered everything up. The kitchen was massive, three times the size of the family's private kitchen. This was where they prepared the food for parties and state dinners. I stopped counting ovens after twelve.

Everywhere I looked there were members of the Fiorelli family. His aunts, uncles, cousins, second cousins, and who knew what else. Nico came back with everything I'd asked for. "I need to find my *Zia* Angelina. She's making the cooking assignments this year."

As he walked through the room, everyone wanted to kiss and hug him (an impulse I understood all too well). He shook hands and got clapped on the back, talking and smiling at everyone as he went.

His family was busy making all sorts of meats and pasta I couldn't identify. They were in the kitchen laughing, fighting, shouting instructions, tasting the food. Warmth washed over me. This was what it felt like. This was what it was to be part of a family.

Did Nico know how lucky he was? Or what I would give to be a part of something like this?

I got to my task making my cookies and the frosting. I was caught up in what I was doing, even humming along mindlessly as someone started singing "Jingle Bells" in Italian. I finished up, frosted them, and put them on a pretty plate. It was probably real china.

Nico grabbed me. "Come help serve." He handed me a plate of what looked like shredded beef. It smelled divine.

In the great hall there were dozens of tables set up full of families. Some of the people I recognized. I saw Giacomo at one table, and he was actually smiling. The tables had been set just as lavishly as they had been for the royal family. There were too many people to serve them individually, so we set the plates down in the center of the tables so that they could help themselves. The Fiorellis were all smiles and compliments. The happiness was overwhelming and pervasive. Like it was seeping into every pore and I couldn't help but feel really happy too.

I noticed Dante and Rafe with giant sacks, distributing gifts to each of the children there. The queen and Nico were passing out presents to the staff members. I leaned against a wall just watching. This was what I wished I could do for the children back home. No kid should go without Christmas. I knew this far too well from personal experience.

Dessert was put out, and I noticed with satisfaction that my cookies went pretty quickly. I also noticed Nico with a handful of them. He brought them and me back into the kitchen where the entire family had assembled to eat their own lunch. I finally got to try a bit of everything, and I was surprised at how well this family could cook.

"Do I get some of those cookies?" I asked Nico.

He shook his head. "Never. They are all mine." Then he proceeded to eat one right after the other, which made me laugh.

"Didn't your mother teach you to share?"

"I share very well, Katerina. You're the one who won't let me share." He said it with a wolfish grin, a small bit of frosting on the corner of his lips. I reached over to wipe it away, and he went very still for a moment, until that mischievous gleam returned to his eyes.

Even in a room surrounded with people, the tension between us sparked and crackled, until it felt like a living thing.

I didn't think I'd be able to hold out for much longer.

"Would you like to come with me this afternoon?" Nico asked, breaking into my thoughts.

"Where?" Because if he said to the ends of the earth, I was pretty sure I was in.

"The hospital. I have some more gifts to deliver."

"I would love that," I told him.

"I need to change," he said, looking down at his jeans and T-shirt, which he looked much better in than he had any right to.

"Time to suit up?" I asked. "Do I have to change, too?"

"You look perfect no matter what you're wearing," he said, giving my hand a squeeze and telling me he would meet me at the car. I returned to my room and brushed my hair, putting it up in a ponytail. I decided since I wasn't a royal, I could wear a sweater and jeans if I wanted to. I grabbed my winter coat.

I stopped by Lemon's room to let her know where I was going. Chiara was there, giving her a pedicure. When I explained where I was headed off to,

Lemon and Chiara exchanged a look. Chiara got a small smile on her face, and Lemon looked way too smug.

"It's for the article," I told her, annoyed.

"Of course it is, darlin'. I didn't say anything. Have fun."

I made it outside before Nico, and a black town car waited for us. A few minutes after I'd climbed in, Nico arrived, kissing me on the cheek. His hair was still damp, and he smelled the way I imagined heaven smelled. "Ready?" he asked. I could only nod.

He explained a little about what we would be doing. Every Christmas the king used to visit the children in the cancer ward in the hospital. Since he could no longer do that, Nico had asked to fill in. He usually went alone because there were activities planned for the extended family that would go throughout the next week, so most of his immediate family would be busy entertaining them.

We arrived with his security, and a man dressed as Father Christmas was waiting for us. He was like Santa, only his coat went down to the floor. We were escorted upstairs to the cancer ward. The sight of all those little bald heads wrenched my heart. I walked behind Father Christmas as he distributed the gifts, not knowing what anyone was saying, but loving the delight and joy on the kids' faces as he spent time with each one, making them feel special. There was truly nothing better in the world than a happy child.

I turned around with a grin, wanting to share the moment with Nico. I saw him talking to some parents, and he handed them a white envelope. The mother started crying after she opened the envelope, and her husband wrapped his arms around her, saying something intent to Nico and shaking his hand. I'd have to find out later what that was about. I watched as he went to each parent in the room, handing all of them envelopes.

After the gifts had been distributed, we stayed and played with the children for a little while. We had a tea party and built block towers and drew pictures and blew bubbles. I couldn't stop smiling at Nico. I loved this. I lived for this stuff.

Hours later, we finally left after a lot of hugs and *grazies*. Nico offered to take me to dinner at a small café that he knew was open on Christmas. When we arrived though, we were the only ones there. I doubted it was typically open on Christmas and wondered how much he'd paid to reserve the whole restaurant for us.

The waitress seemed more than happy to be waiting on us. Maybe a little too happy. She was pretty in that full curves Italian way, her dark hair trailing down her back. I wanted to yank on it and tell her to get away from . . .

From what? My man? My boyfriend? My potential love interest? The guy I was hanging out with?

I was getting totally irrational again. "Back at the hospital, what were those envelopes for?" I hoped to head off my own spiral before I got too out of control.

"Those were for the families to help with their medical expenses and other bills."

"Is this from your charity that we went to the ball for?"

Nico accepted his drink from the waitress and thanked her. "Yes. The foundation is dedicated to not only finding a cure for cancer, but helping to support the families financially."

"Why cancer?"

Nico's eyes went dark. I'd never seen him like that before. "My brother, Luca, was only seven when he died from leukemia. That is why we provide funds for a cure. It was a devastating time in my family's lives. I wouldn't wish that on anyone. So if I can do anything to make things just a little easier . . ."

"I'm so sorry," I said, slipping my hand into his. Luca wasn't my brother, but hearing about his death had a profound effect on me. I had this swell of grief and overwhelming sympathy for Nico. He gripped my hand tightly. "How old were you?"

"I was thirteen. I've never felt so helpless. He was an amazing person. I've never met anyone so loving and kind. So brave at the end. In some ways, you remind me of him. I think he would have liked you."

"It sounds like I would have liked him, too."

Our food arrived, and we fell into silence, eating. I was surprised at how hungry I was. I think all this emotion was burning too many calories or something.

We finished eating, and neither one of us wanted to hang around the café. It was starting to get dark, and Nico offered to go for a walk so that he could show me some of the city. He put my hand on the crook of his arm, and I walked as closely to him as I could. I told myself it was just so that I could stay warm. Yep, a lie.

He pointed out some of his favorite shops and told me stories about the people who ran them. The streets were all empty, with the families in their homes celebrating. It felt like we were the only two people in the whole world.

Rounding a corner, Nico showed me the town square where the winter carnival would begin the next day. He mentioned the kids at the hospital again, saying that since they couldn't come to the carnival, he would send the carnival to them. They would be visited by jugglers, clowns, princesses, and superheroes.

"Sometimes I think you might be a superhero," I told him.

"Not a superhero. Just a humble prince." Which made me laugh.

"You really are wonderful, do you know that?" I think my admission surprised both of us. I couldn't believe I'd said it, and he stopped to stare at me. My heart beat double-time, and I opened my mouth again, wanting to undo what I'd just done. One of my last lines of defense was not letting him know what I really thought about him.

"I do know that, yes," he said with a teasing lilt in his voice.

"Humility is not a strongly ingrained trait in your family, is it?"

"We have the rest of the world to tear us down. Take my sister, Violetta. She struggles sometimes with her weight. Not too long ago the European tabloids were calling her 'Violetta Fatarelli.'"

149

Violetta didn't seem like she had a weight problem. She seemed very normal, very pretty, to me. It went to show that you didn't always know about people's private problems.

"That's so mean."

"I hate tabloids," Nico said under his breath as he began walking away, pulling me along with him. I flashed back to Seamus O'Brien, and my stomach bottomed out. Nico would be furious with me if he knew what I had considered doing. It would ruin everything.

I had to make sure he never, ever knew.

"We should go back home," Nico said, heading toward the car. "It's getting late. Did you want to end our evening?"

I didn't. I shook my head.

"Good. There was something I wanted to show you."

"What did you have in mind?"

He smiled at me. "What I have in mind and what we're going to do are two very different things, *cuore mio*."

Oh, frak.

Chapter 17

Nico led me into the family's private drawing room. "I thought you might enjoy the tree's lights at night."

The Yule log, or its cousin, was still burning in the fireplace. All the lights were off except for those on the tree. He walked over to one of the couches, removing the back pillows and throwing them on the floor. He took off his coat, his tie, undid his cufflinks, and started unbuttoning his shirt.

I was fairly alarmed. Not alarmed enough that I did anything to stop him, but alarmed. "What are you, uh, doing?"

"Getting comfortable." Fortunately (unfortunately?) he had a white undershirt on. He sat down on the couch to take off his shoes, and I did the same. What were we doing? After he'd removed the second one, he looked at the tree. "What is that?"

I looked at the tree. It looked normal (as normal as a five-hundred-foot-tall tree could look) to me. "What are you talking about?"

"Right there. You don't see it?"

"All I see is the tree."

He stood up and went over to the Christmas tree, peering between the branches. He reached in and pulled out a present wrapped in purple wrapping paper with silver snowflakes all over it. He opened the card and read it. "To Kat. Looks like Father Christmas hid an extra present for you."

He walked back with the present and handed it to me. My heart thundered in my chest, and I was glad I was sitting down because my knees felt like melted snow. I took it from him, and he sat down next to me with that "I know something you don't know" look on his face.

"What is it?" I asked.

"How would I know? I'm not Father Christmas." His eyes danced with merriment.

"Is it a board game?" I asked, and he laughed.

"No."

"Legos?"

"Still no. Open it."

I pulled the paper off and started crying. Inside the box was the Millennium Princess Holiday Barbie, just as I remembered her, with her blue velvet dress and tiny tiara.

"You like it?"

For a second I couldn't speak. The tears blinded my eyes and made my voice choke. "This is the best present ever. How did you do this?" I sounded so wobbly and broken.

"eBay. A seller in France had it."

"But I just told you yesterday." I wiped the escaping tears from my cheeks.

"It was not easy to arrange. Make sure to thank Giacomo for his help. He went and retrieved it for me."

My nose was running. Totally embarrassing. I gripped the box tightly, stunned that he had done this. That he had gone to all this trouble to restore something from my childhood that had meant the world to me.

"Thank you," I said, my voice thick. "You can't possibly imagine what this means to me." I put my hand over my mouth, trying to catch my breath.

"I'm glad. You're welcome."

"Why would you do this? I don't understand."

"I had hoped it would make you smile. If I'd known it would make you cry . . ." he teased.

I shook my head. "These are happy tears. I'm just overwhelmed. You're overwhelming."

He looked at me intently, his eyes glittering even in this light. "I don't want to overwhelm you."

"I know." But he still did. I wasn't prepared for this. I didn't have the right thing to say or do.

So I stood up, putting some distance between us so that I could collect my thoughts and myself. I wasn't normally the crying type, and he had reduced me to a puddle of tears with just a doll. I put the Barbie on the small table next to the couch, watching as the Christmas lights reflected off the plastic surface of the box.

No one had ever treated me this way. No one had ever cared about me the way Nico did. How did I thank him? How could I let him know what was in my heart? How he had moved me and made me feel things I didn't know existed?

Nico lay out on the couch, putting one of the pillows behind his head. "Come here."

There was just enough room for me to lie on my side next to him. I stayed put.

"You won't?" I clarified.

"I won't. I promised. I would like to hold you, though."

How could I say no to that after my present? Not to mention the fact that I was all for being held. Especially with the vulnerable way that I was feeling right now.

I lay down, nestling my head on his shoulder. He wrapped his right arm around my shoulders, and I put my right arm across his chest. He put his free hand on top of mine. He rested his head against mine. He took in a deep breath. "Apples," he sighed.

He closed his eyes and five seconds later had passed out. I had no intention of staying there. I decided to stay and enjoy the cuddling for a few minutes, and then I would get up and go to bed.

His breathing was deep and even. I was mesmerized by him. I felt like I only existed to watch him and hold him. His black hair flopped over his forehead, and his wasted-on-a-boy long black lashes rested on his cheekbones. He looked boyish in his sleep, and I could see a glimpse of what he must have looked like when he was little. I smiled. It felt amazing to be with him, like I was warm all over, just by being close to him.

A torrent of emotion flowed through me. This felt good. It felt right. It felt like this was where I had always belonged.

But the last weird emotion I had, right before I accidentally drifted off, was the feeling that I had finally come home.

The sun had just barely started to rise when I woke up. I had a small moment of disorientation, not sure where I was or what was going on. I quickly remembered because Nico had shifted at some point in the night and was lying on his side, facing me. He still had his arms wrapped around me, and our legs were intertwined. I had never been this physically close to someone. My nerves were hyperaware and sensitive at every point where our bodies made contact. And there were a lot of contact points.

Our faces were practically touching. A low, steady thud started in the base of my stomach, and my blood sizzled and snapped.

"I could get used to this," he murmured, his eyes still closed.

"What?" My voice sounded stupid.

He opened his eyes, and his piercing blue gaze turned the thudding into drumming. "Waking up every morning with you in my arms."

"I thought you said you had insomnia."

"I do. Last night was the best night's sleep I've had in I don't know how long." He started tracing patterns on my back with his fingers, running them up and down, making me cold and hot at the same time. "It seems I'll just have to fall asleep with you every night if I ever want to sleep that well again."

"If I was with you every night, we both know there would be no sleeping going on." It was probably one of the boldest things I'd ever said.

He gave me a lazy grin. "That's true."

Then his fingers were in my hair, and I stretched into it like a purring cat, wanting more. I closed my eyes for a second, reveling in the sensations. I tightened my hold on him, without even realizing it. I only knew I wanted to be closer to him.

His fingers stilled, and I opened my eyes to look at him. He was staring at my face. It was more than a little disconcerting. "What are you looking at?"

"I'm counting your freckles."

I put my hands over my nose. "Don't do that."

"Why?"

"I hate my freckles."

"They're adorable." He moved my hands and kissed the bridge of my nose. He was lucky I didn't actually spontaneously combust and set us both on fire. "You're adorable. Beautiful."

I glanced off to the side, not able to endure the intensity of his gaze. I saw my doll on the table and melted all over again. My pulse skittered wildly.

I looked back at him, studying him in return. He hadn't pressured me or made me feel dumb or dumped me or anything that I expected a man to do if I told him I wouldn't kiss him. He had respected me. Spoiled me beyond belief. Wooed me with his words and his actions. Had proved himself reliable and worthy of my trust in every way.

And my affection.

I closed the small distance between us and said, "Thank you for my Barbie."

Then I kissed him.

He pulled back, looking serious. "Does this mean . . . ?" His question trailed off.

"Yes."

He had a very self-satisfied grin. "If I'd known all it would take was buying you a Barbie, I would have bought you the entire company."

"That's not why . . ." I started to protest, but his mouth was moving against mine and there were no more words.

I held my breath, and I could hear my blood rushing in my ears. He tilted his head, angling so that our mouths fit together better. My breath quickened, and I quickly discovered I wasn't the only one affected. I could feel his heartbeat racing under his shirt.

His arms tightened around me, pulling me closer to him. But we couldn't get any closer than we already were.

I wanted to growl because of my frustration. This wasn't like before, when I wanted to kiss him just because I was curious and wanted to understand what the big deal was. I wanted more.

I wanted to know what the stubble on his jaw felt like against my skin (like prickly sandpaper). How his hair would feel underneath my fingers (soft and full). How the muscles in his upper arms would feel (large and solid).

He moved from my lips to my neck, and I leaned my head back as far as I could to give him better access. His mouth moved over my throat, kissing and nipping at me, and it was too much and not enough all at once. My limbs felt heavy and light at the same time.

A warm, strong pressure started to build inside me, and I pulled him back to my lips, where he continued to kiss me like he'd waited his whole life to do just that.

Then a shocking sensation—his fingers had slipped under my sweater and were pressing into the bare skin of my back. I went still, but he didn't seem to notice. Impossibly, my heart beat even faster as I dealt with this new feeling.

I liked it.

I considered doing the same to him, wanting to know what the skin on his torso would feel like against my fingers. His fingertips slowly moved up my side, and I stopped breathing as I waited to see what would happen, what he would do . . .

Then something heavy landed on top of me.

We broke apart to see Serafina scowling at us. "You had a slumber party without me?"

"We did," Nico said, and his voice sounded even and normal. I was panting like a dog who'd just chased down the mailman.

"You're supposed to have slumber parties in your room."

"Hear that, Katerina?" I didn't need to look at him. I could hear the seductive teasing in his voice.

"Can we have another slumber party in your room?" Serafina asked me.

"Yes, can we?" Nico asked.

"We can," I said.

He raised his eyebrows in playful anticipation.

"Serafina and me, I mean." He looked so puppy-dog sad that I laughed. "Nico's not invited," I told her.

She nodded. "Because he's a boy."

"She won't ever invite me to her room, Sera. What should I do?" That set my blood racing again and my heart pounding. He was not playing fair.

She considered this thoughtfully. "Be nicer."

He laughed. "I am very nice to her. As nice as she'll let me be."

"Then you will have to try harder."

He started tickling her, and she giggled and squirmed on top of us. "Stop it, Nico! Mamma is looking for you. All the guards are worried. Johann is screaming at everyone because nobody knows where you are."

Nico rolled his eyes. "Duty calls."

I had to get up first, and then Serafina climbed down. Nico got up and gathered up his clothing. I stood there awkwardly, not sure what to say or do after the Couch Event. He kissed me quickly as he again held me close. "You said I was wonderful," he said in a low, gratified voice.

I did. He was. He promised to see me soon.

I needed to talk to Lemon.

I got my Barbie, and Serafina tagged along behind me, singing a song.

When I had made a promise to myself to wait, nobody had bothered to tell me how amazing everything would feel and how much I would want to keep going. I had thought it would be so easy to draw a line in the sand and tell him to stop. To draw that line and say, "Here, and no further."

I had no idea I'd be the one wanting to move that line all over the place. I'd let him do something that I probably shouldn't have just because it felt *so* good.

It wasn't Nico's fault. It wasn't his promise. And he wasn't doing anything I didn't desperately want him to do.

But it was all too fast and overwhelming. I had to put the brakes on. I was the one who would have to be more careful.

I had vowed that I would wait until marriage. I would keep that vow. I'd never considered all the steps that could happen in between. So I had to keep things in check.

Because keeping my word, doing what I said I would do, was what made me *me*.

I *needed* to keep my promise to myself. I would have to be more vigilant.

Regardless of how much I wanted to rethink the whole thing.

Lemon was waiting for me in my room, on my bed, tapping away on her phone. She looked up when we entered. I noticed that her eyes were red. Had she been crying, or was she just tired? "Somebody owes me an explanation as to why they were gone *all night*. Where have you been?"

"She was kissing Nico. It was gross," Serafina informed her. Lemon's eyes got huge.

"Hey, Serafina, I've been wanting to see your Anna costume. Why don't you run to your room right quick and get it ready for us. Have one of the maids do your hair?"

That got rid of her. Lemon was sly.

She jumped up and hugged me. "Darlin', I am happier than a goat in a Dempsey Dumpster. I want to know everything. *Everything*."

So I told her. All the sordid details I wanted to share. And her eyes got bigger and bigger until I thought they might actually pop out of her head.

"Good heavens, I was only kidding the other night, but you really are going to marry him. I'm going to be a maid of honor for an actual princess."

"What? You need to slow down there. I only kissed him. That's it. Nothing else. This is light and breezy and fun. We're going home in a week. This is not serious. He said it couldn't ever be serious." Our fun conversation had taken a sad turn that was depressing me.

"When did he say that?"

"Yesterday. He told me he wasn't ever getting married."

She waved her hand. "Oh, please. Every man in the world says that, and yet they somehow all still manage to get married."

Lemon didn't get it. She hadn't been there and heard the finality in his voice. He had been serious. But I didn't want to talk about it anymore.

"Why are you dressed up?"

"Turns out there's more family arriving."

I had pulled off my sweater and thrown it on the bed. I stopped to look at her. "How can he possibly have more family?"

"This is more of the extended family. The Fiorellis are related to almost every royal family in Europe. All that intermarrying royals used to do. So we need to dress up to welcome everyone. When Nico told me about the people coming, I thought we should take advantage. I've arranged for a professional photographer to capture everything to go on the website. That TV show is going to give me whatever I ask for and beg me to have Nico on there."

She realized what she'd said a minute too late, probably from the expression on my face. "It won't be a big deal for him, Kat. It will only be pretend. Just to help his country. He won't want them. He has you."

I had forgotten about Nico dating women on reality television. I wasn't sure I could handle that. Or that I liked it. Or that I wouldn't turn into a serial killer and murder every single woman on that show for wanting him.

"No, it's good. It helps me to remember not to get too serious."

"Don't close yourself off to any possibilities. I don't want you to miss out on something great."

But how could I miss out on something that only existed in my mind?

Chapter 18

"How are things going on the Salvatore front?" I asked Lemon as we walked down the hall toward the stairs.

"They're not," she sighed, sounding disappointed. "He's full of himself. The kind of guy who thinks the sun comes up just to hear him crow."

"So, he's already hooking up with someone else?" I clarified.

"Well, of course. I am attracted to him. How could he not be a man whore? Besides, he didn't want to look at pictures of my dogs. Said he didn't like dogs. You know that I don't trust a man who doesn't like dogs. He doesn't understand true loyalty and would probably hide behind you in a bar fight."

"Yeah, personally, when I'm picking my friends, I like the ones who don't make me cry myself to sleep."

I gave her a pointed look, but I didn't press the issue because one, it was over, and two, she'd make the same stupid mistake with some other guy in the near future and there was no point in lecturing her. "Did you tell him what a douchebag he is?"

"Of course not. My momma raised me right. I would never say it to his face—I just tell you behind his back. It's called manners."

We reached the top of the stairs. Below us there was a sea of people in the front hall, laughing and greeting one another. Servants ran back and forth, carrying luggage and coats. I saw Nico just as he saw me, and he waved me down.

I was glad I'd dressed up as everyone in the hall had on a suit or dress. "I want you to meet one of my best friends," he told me, taking me by the hand and weaving his way through the crowd.

He stopped in front of a tall young man with blond hair and blue eyes. I recognized him, but couldn't quite place him.

"Katerina MacTaggart, may I introduce you to His Royal Highness, Prince Alexander of England? Alex, this is Kat."

That was how I knew him. My eyes went wide.

"Pleasure to meet you," the prince said as he took my hand and shook it.

"You too, um, Alexander."

"Alex, please. Only my grandmother calls me Alexander."

That would be his grandmother, the actual queen of England.

I was gobsmacked. I had no idea what to say.

"This is my wife, Caitlin. Caitlin, this is Nico's friend, Kat."

And there stood one of the most beautiful women I'd ever seen. Her makeup was perfect, and her long brown hair looked like she'd just had it blown out. "Nice to meet you," she said, smiling at me.

"I watched your wedding," I said, my mouth slightly agape. "My best friend made me get up at an hour that I wasn't aware existed in the a.m."

"You mean the one where I was upstaged by my sister's bum?" Caitlin winked at me.

I only nodded. Probably had a stupid look on my face.

"How do you know Nico?" she asked.

"That's kind of a long story, but we just met. What about you?"

"Oh, Alex and Nico were at Oxford at the same time and had a lot in common, so they quickly became best mates. That was when Alex and I started dating, so we've all known each other for a long time."

They had a real-life Cinderella story. Caitlin was a commoner. Alex was a prince. The most famous and eligible prince in the entire world. And they'd somehow managed to fall in love and get married and have a baby.

Said baby arrived right then, presumably with his nanny. The woman handed Prince James to Caitlin. "There's Mummy's little boy," she cooed at him, hugging him tight. Their baby was adorable. Big cheeks, bright blue eyes, wispy hair, and a smile that would charm anyone.

"I need to inspect my godson," Nico said, reaching out for the baby. Caitlin handed him over, and Nico held James close, kissing the top of his little downy head.

The sight of handsome, sexy Nico cuddling, loving, and smiling at a baby was too much.

"Oh frak, I think my ovaries just exploded," I accidentally said out loud.

Caitlin laughed. "You and every other woman in here," she joked.

Both men were playing with the baby, talking to him and holding his hands.

"Might I ask what happened to your arm?"

I'd totally forgotten about my bandage. I didn't feel like I needed to wear it any longer, but Dr. Franco had insisted I keep it on for two full weeks to reduce possible swelling. "Nico's been beating me," I said, forgetting who I was talking to.

She stared at me for a moment before she smiled. "Oh, you're joking."

I had just made a totally stupid and inappropriate joke to the future queen of England.

Caitlin looked at me, considering. "I think I'm going to like you very much. Nico has always had exceptional taste, and if he likes you, I know we all will. I'm going to make certain we're seated together tonight at dinner."

"Would you like to hold him?" Nico offered to me.

I held my arms out, and James came willingly. He was babbling and smacking his arm up and down. I loved the smell of babies, their soft hair, their delicate skin. I nuzzled my nose against his cheek, and he smiled at me, grabbing a fistful of my hair.

"He does love hair," Caitlin said apologetically, untangling his hand. I didn't mind, but she took him back.

"Can you imagine having your own children?" Nico asked in an amused way, like the concept of having kids was so far out of the realm of possibility for him. We stood and watched as Alex and Caitlin played with their son. My heart twinged when Alex leaned over to kiss his wife on the forehead, looking at her with so much love that it felt like a tangible thing.

"I used to think no. I didn't want to bring up kids in a world like this."

"You mean, the best it's ever been in human history?"

I nudged him with my elbow. "You know what I mean. But then a friend of mine from college got pregnant, and her baby was due while her husband was stationed in Afghanistan. So I volunteered to be her birthing partner. Which was totally gross, by the way, but when that baby came out and they let me hold her, I decided then and there that I wanted a dozen. Kristi's lucky I didn't kidnap Madison and take her home with me. Because the thought did cross my mind."

Nico had an unreadable expression on his face. "You never cease to surprise me." What had I said now to make him react like that?

"I can show you to your rooms," a servant announced to the royal couple.

"Alex, did you still want to see my plans for the new business center?" Nico asked him.

"Absolutely. Will you be all right?" Alex asked Caitlin.

"We can manage. Go."

The two men walked off, leaving me alone with the princess. "You know they're probably going to go play Xbox or something, right?"

"Of course." She gave me a brilliant smile. "But they don't get to see each other nearly as much as they'd like to, so allowances must be made."

I saw Lemon walking by, and I grabbed her arm, pulling her close. "Lemon, come meet Caitlin."

I'd never seen Lemon speechless before, but it had finally happened. She sort of worshipped Caitlin. After Marilyn Monroe, the princess was her favorite.

"Hello, nice to meet you," Caitlin said, as she balanced James on her hip.

Lemon still just stood there.

164

"Alex always tells everyone to imagine him naked, and it usually breaks the ice," Caitlin said.

"I think imagining your husband naked would only make things worse," Lemon said, and the princess laughed.

Then Caitlin's expression changed, her eyes narrowing and her mouth set. "I didn't know she would be here."

I followed her line of vision and saw Lady Claire Sutherland, again teetering on six-inch heels. The *Titanic* hit the iceberg and started to sink in my stomach.

"Hey," Lemon said, "you think if we catch her we can make her give up her pot of gold?"

"I was thinking we'd end up with a chocolate factory tour."

Realizing that we had been full-on snarking in front of the princess made us both fall silent. "It does make one curious," Caitlin said.

"About what?"

"About whether Dr. Evil's realized that Mini Me escaped."

Then we all laughed, great big whooping sounds that drew the attention of everyone around us.

"I shouldn't have said that in front of anyone else," Caitlin apologized once we'd quieted down.

"I'd like to beat her stupid face in with a shovel, so I think I'm exactly the right person to say it in front of," I told her. "What did she do to you?"

"That plastic, title-digging slag spent all of our university years chasing after both Nico and Alex, and trying to break Alex and me up. But I have to smile and put up with her because his family is friends with her family. Alex knows to steer clear of that one."

"I don't think Nico got the memo," I told her. "She took a crack at me in Paris. I'm not over it."

"Don't worry about her," Lemon said. "We've got her number now. She won't try anything else."

165

"I really should go and get James settled," Caitlin said. "I will see you again this evening, right?"

We agreed to meet up at dinner and for the party afterward. We had to be united in the face of that kind of evil.

"There you go. Living proof," Lemon said once the princess had left.

"Living proof of what?"

"That a prince and a regular person can get married and live happily ever after."

I didn't bother to dignify that statement with a retort.

At dinner, Caitlin had been true to her word and had me seated next to her. Unfortunately for us, Lady Claire was directly across from me, on Nico's right. I hated the idea that I would have to sit across from her all night. I wondered who she'd bribed or threatened to end up there.

Nico helped me with my chair and leaned down to kiss me on the cheek. "You are the most beautiful woman in the room."

That made my pulse flutter. He was obviously wrong, as I was sitting next to Caitlin, but I just smiled up at him. I had worn my new purple cocktail dress and liked the way it swooshed when I moved. I looked up to see Lady Claire giving me a dirty look.

I made a mental note not to leave any of my food or glasses alone tonight. Who knew what she'd try to get me with next.

Caitlin was a master conversationalist, and she asked me question after question about myself without being intrusive. Lady Claire kept trying to get Nico's attention, but he was busy listening to my conversation with the princess. She made me feel so comfortable that it didn't feel like I was making an effort at all. I had this feeling like I really could be friends with her.

Which was pointless because after this week I would never see her again. Except for in magazines and on television.

I saw Lady Claire move her left hand slowly across the table, and she leaned over. To where she had obviously put it on Nico's thigh.

I wished the table wasn't so wide so that I could kick her stubby legs.

But Nico grabbed her wrist and politely, but deliberately, put her hand back on the table. I looked away, so that he wouldn't see me watching. When I looked back, he gave me a million-watt smile.

"He fancies you rotten," Caitlin said to me in a low, conspiratorial voice.

"What makes you say that?"

"He hasn't taken his eyes off of you since he sat down." It was true. Even I couldn't be in denial about the way he was looking at me. It was a glorious, fizzy feeling—too amazing to be contained in just one person. I felt like I should start helping little old ladies cross streets to settle the karmic debt of feeling this way.

"Tell me," she said, putting her napkin on the table. "How do you feel about him?"

"I'm not so good with the feelings. I could get you a sarcastic comment. Or some snark."

She laughed and even her laughter sounded refined.

"I can't wait to tell Alex."

"Why?"

"Back in the day Nico gave him a hard time about falling for me, and as far as I know, Nico's never been serious about anyone. Alex has been biding his time, waiting for some payback. He is going to be relentless in his teasing, I'm sure."

"Is it hard? Being with a prince?"

She looked thoughtful for a moment and then caught her husband's eye. He smiled broadly at her and mouthed, "I love you."

"It isn't always easy. I've had a lot to learn. Still do. There's a lot of protocol and rules. And the paparazzi are more difficult than you can possibly imagine. We waited a long time before we got engaged because Alex wanted to be sure that I could handle all this."

I understood a little bit of it—I'd had a taste in Paris, and I hadn't liked it one bit. I could only imagine how much worse her life was. Based on the magazines I'd seen, reporters never left her alone.

"But I love that man more than life itself. I would walk through fire for him. And that's what I do every day. Walk through fire. In the end it's all worth it because I get to be with him."

The plates were cleared, and the queen announced that there would be music and drinks in the ballroom. The guests stood up, and Alex made his way over to us. "I'm sorry to steal her away, but I've come to collect my beautiful wife. She owes me a dance."

So much adoration and love between them. I wished I could have even a fraction of what they had.

There was no point in considering what Caitlin had said, because our situations were so different. Nico wasn't getting married, and I was leaving.

But as he walked toward me I couldn't help but wonder, would I put up with all of this? Would I walk through fire to be with him?

I had the sneaking suspicion the answer to those questions was yes.

Nico didn't have any responsibilities at this event, so he spent the whole evening glued to my side. We danced and laughed and talked. Sometimes with other people, sometimes just alone.

Lady Claire spent the entire night looking like she might kill me in my sleep. I would have to remember to lock my door.

Hours after most everyone else had gone to bed, Nico offered to escort me to my room. Everything had been packed up, and the staff had all left. We'd sat in a couple of chairs and had talked while the party around us had been undone. I hadn't even noticed. "I don't want this night to end," I told him.

"Neither do I."

But it was late, and I was sure there would be some Fiorelli in my room tomorrow bright and early telling me to get up. "I should get to bed, though."

He held my hand, and I leaned my head against his shoulder, walking slowly. I had no idea how much I loved dancing. I'd never gone to dances at school, or to clubs. It had seemed like a waste of time, and I thought the time would be better spent studying because I didn't want to lose my scholarship. I'd been seriously missing out.

Nico's big, strong hand tightened around mine, and I realized dancing wasn't the only thing I'd been missing out on.

We got to my door, and he turned me so that I was flat against the wall. He put both of his hands on either side of my head. He gave me a lazy smile. "Any ideas for things we could do now?"

"Parcheesi?" Did my voice always sound that high and tight?

"No, thank you." He got closer to me.

"We could watch *Frozen*."

He laughed softly. "I'm certain there is a ring of hell that consists of watching the same movie over and over again."

Then he was kissing me and I forgot everything else. He pressed against me, and I wrapped my arms around him, hanging on for dear life. This man was pure magic with his mouth. I lost all sense of place and time. There was only Nico.

I didn't know how much time had passed before he whispered in my ear, "Invite me in."

That sent a shock coursing through me. I knew what he had in mind.

And the worst part? I wanted to. Desperately.

But I didn't care what my stupid body wanted. I was in charge here, not the other way around. I had a vow to keep. And I was strong enough to do it.

"I will take things as slowly as you want," he murmured across my cheek, trailing small kisses of fire. That made my resolve waver just a little.

"No," I breathed, barely able to mutter that one syllable.

"No?" he repeated, like it amused him.

I knew (well, I didn't know as I'd never "known" anyone ever, but I had a pretty good idea) what would happen if I brought him into my room. *The plan, the promise,* I reminded myself.

He wasn't even kissing me at this point, just running his lips over my skin, like he was inhaling me. I was shaking all over.

"I need things to go slower. Yesterday, right now, it's a little fast."

That made him stop. "You don't like kissing me?"

"That's not the problem. The problem is that I like it too much."

He got one of those male pride smiles.

"The thing is," I continued, trying to calm down my breathing, "I made myself a promise a long time ago that I wouldn't . . . do that kind of stuff until I was married. And if we keep going at this pace, I don't know if I'll be able to keep my promise."

A few moments passed in silence, with Nico studying me. He looked into my eyes, like he was trying to figure something out. "I understand. It's frustrating and I'm not sure I like it, but I understand," he said, sighing as he put his forehead against mine. "But I can still kiss you?"

There was no going back now from that one. It's what happened when you crossed any line with someone—like from not kissing to kissing—it was hard to go back to where you'd been. And then you'd cross that line sooner with the next guy. It was not a situation I was going to fall into, like my mother had.

I put my hands on his head and pulled him back so that I could look at him. "I don't want you to ever stop kissing me," I told him honestly.

He went still at that, his hands not moving. I saw him swallow before he answered. "Careful, *cuore mio*. A man can only take so much."

"Sorry."

"Don't apologize," he said. He took my face in his hands and looked at me like I was the most precious, dear thing in the whole world to him. A feeling I didn't recognize flooded my heart. Like a cross between tenderness and wonder. "Whatever my lady wants, she shall get."

Then he kissed me in a way that literally made my toes curl up in my shoes. I didn't trust myself to stay out here in this hallway with him. So I broke off that magical kiss, told him good night, and slipped inside my room.

I locked the door.

And I didn't know whether that was to keep Lady Claire from smothering me in my sleep or to prevent myself from chasing after Nico and telling him I'd changed my mind.

Chapter 19

As predicted, I had Giacomo in my room early the next morning with a hot chocolate in one hand and an itinerary for the next few days in the other. There were activities sponsored by the family to entertain all the guests—things like horseback riding, spa visits, a hunting expedition, hiking, ice skating, and dinners. He had also blocked out time for me to write, as well as, embarrassingly enough, time to spend with Nico. Giacomo told me he had made certain to coordinate my schedule with Nico's. Nearly every moment of personal time was accounted for. Like, when I should shower and brush my teeth. Thankfully, there were no times blocked out for us to make out. I would have died. I looked up at Giacomo, wondering what he thought about me and the prince. But his serious face revealed nothing of his personal thoughts about the sort of dating thing Nico and I had going on.

My guess would be that he probably disapproved.

Lemon came in to tell me good morning, and we compared schedules. My stuff seemed mostly frivolous, but Lemon's was full of meetings with the head press secretary and his department. There was something called a snow polo match scheduled for that afternoon, and we agreed to meet up then.

I started outlining the time I'd spent with Nico, putting it in chronological order. I decided to leave the personal stuff out, and just emphasize the fun and how awesome he was to hang out with. If Lemon put a picture of him up on the website, I wouldn't have to try too hard to get women to like him.

My nightstand drawer started to buzz. Confused, I opened it. I had forgotten about the phone.

I had a text message.

In Monterra. Will find you at the polo match. Bring the camera.

My stomach clenched tight as a black fear shot through me. I had put this all out of my mind. And now I would see Seamus O'Brien again. I had to get this money and phone back to him without anyone finding out what he wanted me to do.

I would fix this. I would explain and send him on his way.

It would be okay. It had to be.

Lemon and I rode in a car together to the match. I had put the envelope of cash into my inner coat pocket and the phone in my jeans. She told me all about her plans and how well everything was going. She was spending her free time making phone calls to major news outlets and reporters. There was no mention at all of Salvatore.

She did ask me about Nico, and I told her about the recent kissage. She squealed in delight. "I knew you wouldn't be able to hold out."

"Yeah, I didn't exactly stick to my guns for that long."

"You do realize it was a dumb thing to decide to do in the first place, right? When a man with a face like Nico's wants to kiss you, the answer is always yes."

The match was taking place out on Lake Imperia. The temperatures had frozen the lake over, apparently well enough that frakking horses could run around on it. I'd never seen a polo match before, and I had no idea what to expect.

The cold mountain wind made me suck in my breath, filling my lungs with freezing air. I stuck my hands in my pockets and followed behind Lemon, carefully placing my feet in her tiny snow footprints. On the east side of the lake white tents had been set up that were covered on three sides and open in the front to the match. We wandered into an empty one and hoped that nobody would come and kick us out. There were couches and heaters and menus with delicious sounding food, which I immediately started reading.

"Mind if I join you?" Caitlin asked, smiling at us.

"Come in," I invited. Lemon still looked a little starstruck. Caitlin was wearing a furry white coat, a blue sweater, and jeans, with brown knee-high boots. I was bundled up like that kid from *A Christmas Story*, while she still managed to look super put together and refined.

"Where's James?"

"He's with the nanny. It's going to be naptime soon, and I didn't want him out in this cold. And Alex would have kittens if I didn't come see him play. He loves polo."

"Good," I told her. "You can explain what's happening to us."

She explained the rules of the game, saying each player had a specific role to do in offense and defense. She explained what they were, but I started tuning her out. I understood the basics. It was like any other sport with a ball. One team was trying to score a point by getting the ball across the field (or the snow, in this case) to the other team's goal. Like soccer. Or Quidditch.

I asked how the horses could run on the ice. Caitlin said they had special shoes, as well as snow pads that gave them better traction than the humans had. The only worry was getting too much snow stuck in their hooves, so the lake was cleared to prevent that from happening. The horses would also be switched out in intervals so as to not overtire them.

A waiter came to take our order, and I started crowd watching. A minute later I was interrupted by a bright flash. I held my hand up to my face, peering around it to see a photographer taking shots of us. I thought the paparazzi had been outlawed in Monterra. "What the . . .?" I asked.

"This is the official photographer I hired," Lemon explained. "Pictures for the website. You don't mind, do you, Caitlin?"

"No, not at all," she said. We gathered together and took several pictures. I wondered how many of them Lemon was going to get framed and put up on our apartment wall. The photographer finished and went to find another victim.

Which made me think about my little situation. I needed to find Seamus before he found me in the company of the princess. That would just lead to all kind of awkward questions. I hadn't even told Lemon yet. I figured that was mostly because if I didn't talk or think about it, it was like it hadn't happened. Telling her made it more real and scarier.

Our food came, and Lemon finally calmed down enough to have a normal conversation with Caitlin. I listened as the two chatted like they'd known each other their entire lives. I envied their ability to have a conversation with anyone anywhere.

A horn sounded, and the teams trotted out onto the ice. Nico's team consisted of him and his two brothers. They all wore bright red, long-sleeve jerseys, helmets, and sunglasses. They had on tight white pants and black, shiny boots. Nico wore the number three. Alex's team wore blue (which made me understand why his wife had on blue herself), and he was also number three for his team. I didn't know the men he was playing with.

The ponies trotted out, doing a lap around the ice to all the cheering fans. I called out Nico's name as he went by, and he waved to me.

"What is that on Dante's mallet?" Caitlin asked, confused. I looked to where she pointed, and there was something red near the base, next to the hammer part. Then I noticed that Lemon had gone very quiet.

"Lemon?"

"It's a favor."

"A favor? What kind of favor?"

"Not that kind of favor," she said in a quiet, embarrassed voice. "You know how when knights would joust and ladies would give them a favor to wear on their clothes or lance."

"Yes," Caitlin said. "Like a handkerchief or a scarf. Or a ribbon. Usually something with their family's colors."

"Well, I didn't have any of those things in my favorite color. So that's my, uh, you know . . ." Her voice trailed away.

"Your what?" I asked.

"My underwear," Lemon said, blushing furiously, covering her eyes with both of her hands.

Caitlin and I exchanged glances and then howled with laughter. Today's match was being sponsored by a pair of Lemon's red lace underwear. I wondered if anyone else knew.

The referee pulled Nico and Alex aside and had them shake hands, while their horses pranced around, eager to get started. The referee then moved out to the sidelines and blew on his whistle.

A bright red ball was thrown in between the two princes, and the game started. Nico got the first whack, and everyone was riding after the ball.

I put my food down to cheer for the Fiorelli men. Snow polo was a lot more exciting than I thought it would be. My heart was in my throat the whole time, because I was so worried the horses would get hurt or slide and take the players down with them.

But both the horses and the men were in total control. No one slipped. No one ran into each other. No one hit each other with their mallets. I could only imagine the damage I would do if somebody put me on a horse on ice and told me to chase after a big plastic red ball.

The game went back and forth, neither side giving in, until Rafe finally scored a goal and the crowd cheered wildly for him. There were several breaks, called chukkers of all things, like quarters in football where the teams swapped out their horses and took off their helmets to cool off for a minute.

Nico's team scored another goal, and Alex's team scored two in return. There was a small scoreboard counting down the time, and it was getting closer and closer to being over with no winner.

Then Nico burst through Alex's defense, clearly headed toward the goal. I started jumping up and down and calling his name when he gave the ball a final whack, and with only twenty seconds left on the scoreboard, he got another goal!

I thought I might go hoarse from all the screaming and hollering I was doing.

"Poor Alex," Caitlin said, with a twinkle in his eye. "He hates to lose. He'll need some cheering up. I'll see you at dinner?"

When she left I saw that bright red hair belonging to Seamus in the crowd surrounding the lake, even more noticeable against the whiteness of the snow. I told Lemon I'd be right back.

I walked toward Seamus, both relieved that this would soon be over and terrified that I'd get caught before I could get rid of him. My heart pounded louder with every step that I took.

"There you are," Seamus said to me.

"I don't want to do this," I told him. "I can't take your money or take the pictures." I took the camera out and held it out to him.

He didn't take it. He studied me with a disgusted expression. "Fine. I'll double the money. One hundred thousand American dollars."

Before I could respond, Nico was there. Smiling down at me. "Katerina." He noticed who I was with, and my stomach bottomed out when he said, "Mr. O'Brien? What are you doing here?"

"You should ask your girlfriend what I'm doing here."

My veins filled with ice, paralyzing me for a second. My teeth started to chatter and my hands shook. I couldn't breathe. He was going to hate me. Nico would never forgive me.

I had ruined everything.

He looked confused and then angry. "What's happening? Explain yourself," he said to the reporter.

Seamus had a nasty smile on his face. "Just a business transaction. Isn't that right, Kat?"

"I'm calling for security," Nico said, and I had a moment's hope that he might not discover what I had done—that they would throw Seamus out before he could rat me out.

"Before you do that, you really should talk to your girlfriend here. She's on my payroll. I gave her that phone. You should see the pictures she's taken for me."

I hadn't taken any pictures for him, but he sounded so believable it made me more afraid.

"May I see the phone, Kat?" Nico asked, holding out his hand.

He didn't call me Katerina. Despair and terror made me tremble. He always called me Katerina.

But I didn't have anything to hide, so I gave him the phone. He turned it on, and I could see that he was scrolling through something. I didn't know how that was possible since until today, I hadn't taken the phone out of my drawer.

He handed it back to me, and I did not like the expression on his face. It scared me to death.

I looked at the phone, and there was a picture of Nico and his brothers playing video games. I flicked it with my thumb. One of Violetta texting on her phone. Flicked again. Chiara drawing in her sketchpad. Another flick and my heart plummeted. A picture of the king in his bed.

"Nico, I did not take these pictures. I promise you that I did not take these pictures."

"I offered her a hundred thousand dollars to take those pictures," Seamus said, looking way too satisfied with himself. "Does she really seem like the kind of girl who would turn down a hundred thousand dollars?"

What could I say in my own defense? Saying it was only fifty thousand initially and he'd just upped his offer sounded stupid. Mostly because he was right. I was the kind of girl who wouldn't say no to a hundred thousand dollars. I needed it for my tuition. For my future plans. For the kids I loved.

And Nico knew it.

"And before you get too angry with me, she approached me in Paris. She was looking for a way to make a quick dollar. I was happy to oblige."

The hurt, the pain in Nico's eyes was more than I could bear. His face had turned hard, like stone. I grabbed his arm, desperate for him to believe in me.

"Never. I would never do that to you. Or to your family. Seamus came to me, offered me money, and left before I could say no. I'm meeting with him today to give him back his phone and his money." Unshed tears were making my voice thick and my throat raw. I pulled the envelope out of my pocket and handed it to Nico. "I need you to trust me, to believe in me."

"You never said anything about this." Nico's voice was so quiet I could barely hear him.

"I was embarrassed, and I didn't know how to explain." A fearsome desperation clawed its way through me, making it hard for me to think. I looked him in the eyes, even though I wanted to run away and hide. I would stay and face this. I would make him understand.

"You asked me to trust you. And I did. Now I'm asking you for the same thing. I am asking you to trust me. To believe me."

I felt my soul spiral as an unbelievable darkness spread through me. Because Nico just stood there, staring at me. He wasn't saying anything. Why wouldn't he say something? It was like being knifed in the stomach repeatedly, standing there waiting.

"I believe you."

Chapter 20

He said it so quietly that for a minute I thought I had imagined it. That I was so pathetically desperate for him to trust me that I had hallucinated it.

"You believe me?" I had tears at the edge of my words.

He nodded at me and pulled me to him, hugging me tightly. Relief flooded through me as I wrapped my arms around him. That feeling of home returned, but I ignored it and just clung to him. Grateful that I could be in his arms again.

He shoved the envelope into Seamus's chest. "There's your money. I expect you to return to your hotel and leave my country. If you aren't gone in the next hour, I will have my security detail personally escort you out."

"I'll be taking my phone back," the reporter said.

"I don't think so," Nico said. "Count it as the cost of doing 'business.'"

Seamus turned an angry shade of red just before he stomped off. Nico gestured to one of his guards and gave him instructions in Italian. Two guards in black suits with black trench coats followed behind Seamus.

As terrible as this entire encounter had been, I was so glad that Nico had interrupted us. It would have been world-ending if he hadn't. I would have handed that phone over, not knowing that there were pictures on it. I could only imagine the damage that would have done to his family.

And the damage it would have done to us.

I held the phone up, scrolling through the pictures. The thought had crossed my mind that Seamus had set me up and put pictures on the phone in the first place, but these were all recent. I could see the Christmas decorations in the pictures. These had to be taken by someone with access inside the palace. But who would do that?

I let out a laugh when I figured it out. I held the phone up to Nico. "I caught our culprit."

Serafina had taken twenty different selfies. She had stolen my phone and taken all these pictures. She'd stolen everyone else's phones—I don't know why I imagined I would be exempt.

That made Nico smile. I could feel his relief as clearly as my own. "Someone will have to have a talk with her about respecting personal property."

I looked up at him. "I should have told you."

"I should have immediately trusted you. I'm sorry I doubted you."

"I don't blame you. I doubted me and I knew I hadn't done it."

That made him chuckle, and he hugged me again. I saw something move out of the corner of my eye.

Lady Claire. Everything clicked. Why Seamus had lied. Why he tried to make it sound like this was all my idea. I had thought he was just trying to protect himself, but now I knew there was something deeper going on here. How could a paparazzo like Seamus get into the charity ball? How could he be allowed into this event? There was only one way.

If someone who was invited had let him in.

"That horrible little witch," I said.

"Who?" Nico asked.

"Lady Claire did this. Look, I know she's your friend and your families are friends, but she has been trying to set me up since I met her. She introduced me to an ambassador at the ball and told me to say something to him that humiliated me. I told her I didn't drink and she's the one who had them bring me that vodka. She confronted me at the ball, telling me that you guys were engaged and that you were just using me. And now she set me up with that paparazzo to make you turn against me. He said things that were totally untrue, like it being my idea. She's out to get me."

He looked puzzled. Confused.

"I know this sounds crazy. I know she's not like this around you. But I am telling you that she has gone out of her way to sabotage me. Caitlin said

Claire used to do this kind of stuff to her all the time in college. Think about this—how could someone like Seamus O'Brien go to your ball? I know you didn't invite him. How is he here? Somebody had to make sure he got in. And there's only one person I know of who wants to sabotage me."

"Stay here, please," he said as he walked off with long, angry strides.

I wanted to follow him, but he had asked so nicely and I was so relieved that we were okay that I would have been willing to do anything he wanted me to.

Nico was talking to Lady Claire, who was putting on a show of disbelief and pretending to not understand what he was saying. I heard him actually yell. It surprised me. I'd never heard Nico yell before. He looked furious. Like an avenging angel. I could see her pleading with him, putting her hands on his arms, and him jerking back, like he couldn't stand to have her touch him.

A few minutes later he was walking back toward me. Claire, who had been making a show of crying great sobs in front of him, turned off the waterworks and glared at me as he returned.

"She won't be bothering you anymore," Nico promised as he put his arm around my waist. "She'll be leaving soon and won't be bothering any of us ever again."

He kissed me quickly, fiercely, and it was over too soon.

"Now let's go find Alex so I can rub the match in his face."

Alex and Nico went back and forth about the match, arguing in a friendly and joking way, in between bites of food. They were eating like their last meal had been a month ago. Lemon had gone off somewhere with Dante, and Caitlin and I were talking, watching the guys, and laughing at their conversation.

Nico looked over and winked at me before going back to his play fight. The way he looked at me, the way he took care of me, the way he believed in me, all added up to something that I didn't quite comprehend and had never felt before. All these small and big things created a sensation that I only felt when I was with him.

"What are your plans after your holiday?" Caitlin asked me. It was such an innocuous, innocent question, but I felt like she'd just flattened me with a steamroller.

I only had four more days with Nico. Just four more days. Then it was back to real life. I couldn't even think about it.

"Back to school. Finishing up my final semester before I can get my master's degree in social work."

"You know, they have a university here," Caitlin said. "I've heard they even have a king's scholarship that covers tuition. I bet you might have a bit of an in on that one."

I glanced over at Nico to see if he was listening. Wondering if he'd told her about this, or if she'd just come up with it on her own. I realized that Lemon had possibly been involved.

"It's really hard to transfer schools this far along. I would have to take classes over again, and I'm not interested in doing that."

"Oh, well. It's only a few months. Alex and I have certainly had to go through that kind of separation while he was out with the military."

Why did everyone talk about Nico and me as if we were some foregone conclusion? Had he not told anyone else about his plans to not marry? Was I supposed to just hang around him like one of Leonardo DiCaprio's girlfriends? Hoping against hope that he might eventually change his mind someday about marriage, and that I might possibly be the one to change it?

Much as I liked Nico, much as I wanted to be with him, I did not want to waste my life being his accessory.

The winter carnival had begun, and it had completely taken over the capital city. We were scheduled to spend the day there with his family. Nico had already set out early that morning for some ceremony, and we were to meet up with him later. Serafina insisted on staying with Lemon and me. To my amusement, so did Dante. And where Dante went, Rafe wasn't far behind.

The sun was high, the air was cold, and the snow crunched under our feet as we walked through the market. There were Christmas ornaments, musical instruments, homemade soap, hand-carved toys, clothing sewn by hand. Anything you could imagine was for sale. The man at the ornament booth was actually blowing the glass himself, and we stopped to watch him for a little while. I picked up one of his snow globes and was tempted to buy it. He had Nico's castle inside of it. I put it down when I saw the price.

The market was full of people, and the scents of gingerbread and sugar cookies filled the air. The twins bought themselves and Lemon a hot drink called mulled wine, and they got hot apple cider for Serafina and me.

There were musicians on the corners and small groups of singers. I saw a juggler on another corner. One street had been blocked off by a large stage, and there was a group of dancers performing on it.

Aside from all the hustle and bustle, what probably impressed me most was how clean everything was. Pristine. All the little storybook stores and houses were in perfect condition. Like I'd wandered into a pretend place that didn't really exist. I wondered how involved Nico was with keeping his city looking like this.

As if on cue, I felt his arms sliding around my waist, and he planted a kiss on the side of my neck.

"I was just thinking about you," I told him.

"I like occupying your thoughts," he said. I smiled and turned around to kiss him properly, but I had to stop when Serafina started making gagging noises. His brothers laughed, and I knew the exact moment my cheeks went red, because they started laughing harder.

"Come on, y'all. Let's leave them alone," Lemon said to Dante and Rafe, trying to take Serafina with her as well.

"No! I want to stay with Nico and Kat," she protested as she wrapped herself around Nico's leg.

"She can stay with us. Go have fun," I told my friend. She gave me a hug and said she'd see me later. I assumed we would run into them at some point during the carnival. It couldn't be that big.

I was wrong.

Serafina wanted to go to the petting zoo in the main park, and so we headed that way. I gasped when we got there. The entire park was full of ice sculptures.

"Serafina picked the theme this year. Winter Fairyland."

"I wanted *Frozen*, but nobody would let me have it."

There were fairies, trolls, princesses, knights, mermaids, and Disney characters all perfectly formed in ice. They looked like they could come to life at any moment. Blue, pink, and purple lights hit them from behind, and I bet they looked amazing at night.

Near the petting zoo was a kid-sized castle that looked just like the Fiorelli family castle on the outside. They had a free hot chocolate station next to it, and I grabbed one. I took a sip. Not nearly as good as the stuff Giacomo brought me, but still good. They had a cookie-decorating table next to it, and I seriously considered creating something delicious for us to eat, but Serafina had already run into the petting zoo.

The zoo was as overrun by kids as it was by animals. There were reindeer, goats, sheep, white rabbits, guinea pigs, Shetland ponies wearing cardigans, and one very fat and very annoyed miniature donkey.

Beyond the petting zoo I could see a carnival dedicated solely to kids. There were games and rides. I guessed we would be spending some time there next. Nico put his arm around me, and I leaned into him. Even when it was this cold, he still seemed to be radiating heat.

"You do this every year?"

"Every year. It's tradition and has been for generations. It used to be much smaller, but every year we add something to it."

He told me about all the nighttime activities. The Mozart concert by the Monterran Symphony Orchestra. The nightclubs with DJs and famous bands. Bobsledding and ice horse racing. Opera performances. The Vienna Boys Choir singing. An ice hockey game. They even had a bar made solely out of ice. Everybody had to wear special clothing to drink there and could only stay for thirty minutes at a time.

"And then we have the costume ball at the end of the week as the finale."

"Why a costume ball?" Maybe I shouldn't have asked. These were the same people who had a witch delivering presents at Christmas. Why not Halloween costumes too?

"Mainly because my great-great-grandfather wanted to consort publicly and openly with his mistresses without public redress. By wearing masks and costumes, nobody suspected he was up to no good."

"What costume are you wearing?"

His hold on me tightened. "I'm not telling."

"Then neither am I. Guess you'll just have to hope you recognize me."

He looked at me seriously. "I would know you anywhere."

I gulped. "We'll see in a few days."

He grinned and then kissed me gently and softly, and I had to stop him before we lost track of time and space and potentially his sister.

The days went by too quickly. There was a moonlit carriage ride one night, and Nico and I cuddled up on the back bench under a blanket so we could kiss without anyone giving us a hard time.

He took me dancing at nightclubs. To cafés and restaurants. To quaint bookstores. Always sat next to me at dinners with his family. Took me to all the events he could at the carnival like the concerts and the operas. Whenever he had a free moment, he was showing me something else darling and wonderful about Imperia. He was making me like him more and more every time we were together.

And every midnight, there was a tray of moonflowers and gelato waiting for me.

But as much fun as I had, as much as I enjoyed being with him, it was like there was this axe hanging over our heads because our time was quickly coming to an end.

Nico was also careful to never be alone with me. We were always surrounded by other people. He didn't walk me back to my room anymore. And when he did kiss me, it was like there was a wall between us. Like he was holding back. I knew that he did it because I'd asked him to, but I didn't like it. It was a frustrating limbo to be in—we couldn't go forward, and I didn't want to stay stuck.

I finished my article for Lemon. She wanted me to finish before we left so that she could make sure it got uploaded correctly. It was bittersweet writing everything down. I loved the chance to relive those experiences over again, remembering how much I had changed since I'd first come here. How much I enjoyed being with him. How much I wanted to be with him. But it was all tainted by the idea that soon I would be gone and it would be over.

"How many words?" she asked.

"Six thousand, two hundred and forty-three," I told her. "We can call it an even six thousand."

"I'll let the press office know so they can get you your money," she told me.

Six thousand dollars would help with my tuition problems, but it wasn't enough to cover everything. I still had to figure out a way to make up the difference.

And then, before I knew it, it was New Year's Eve and the night of the costume ball. I sat in my chair next to my fireplace in my perfect Elsa costume, sobbing my eyes out as one of the stylists did my hair in a massive side braid.

We would be leaving the next day. The next day! And I would never see Nico again.

"What is it, *signorina*? Should I send for someone?" the woman asked anxiously.

"No," I said, wiping my tears away. "I'll be fine."

And no matter what, I would be. Reality would return tomorrow. I would take this night, this one last night, and I would make it count.

Chapter 21

I had stopped crying long enough for them to finish my makeup. I slipped my feet into my icy blue flats just as Lemon came through the door.

Well, she didn't just walk in. She sort of had to turn sideways in order to fit herself through.

"I was expecting Marilyn Monroe!" I told her.

"Scarlett O'Hara, at your service." She curtsied. She had a white with green flowers antebellum dress on, cinched with a giant velvet green sash, and an amazing number of hoop skirts. She had somehow even gotten the hat with the green ribbon.

"Elsa, huh? Serafina's idea?" I nodded. "I promise not to make any ice queen jokes this evening," she told me as she whipped out a fan, fanning herself with it. "I do believe we have a ball to attend where some handsome princes are waiting for us."

We took a couple of pictures with her phone. I had returned the one Seamus gave me to the drawer, after I took out the SIM card so that he couldn't contact me again.

Entering the ballroom was like entering another world. Unlike the few frat Halloween parties I'd attended in college, no one was trying to see who could be the biggest slut in the skankiest costume. No, the women here were dressed like historical figures and princesses and characters from stories. I didn't have to see anyone's cleavage or their rear end. It was refreshing.

Caitlin found us first. She had dressed up in an elaborate pink and purple kimono and done herself up as a geisha. Lemon and I oohed and aahed over her outfit. "I got it as a gift the last time I was in Japan." She pointed out Alex, who had dressed up like a pirate, including the hook for a hand.

I found Nico all on my own. He was walking across the dance floor toward me, dressed up as Mr. Darcy. My favorite character by my favorite author. He made Colin Firth look like a man in an ape suit. I ordered my knees to keep me upright. He had on black boots that went to his knees, tight light brown pants, a velvet blue coat, and one of those white necktie things they wore.

"Look at him," I told Lemon. "I'm not even good enough for him."

I hadn't meant for that to spill out, but it did. A truth that, until now, I hadn't really acknowledged.

"You are good enough for him," she replied. "He's lucky to be with *you*. And darlin', if I ever had a man look at me the way Nico looks at you, I'd never, ever let him go."

I took Lemon's fan and used it, trying to cool my flush. He stopped before me and bowed. I knew this costume was another thing he had done just for me. Which made me woozy and light-headed. So not fair.

"Good evening, Queen Elsa. May I have this dance?" The orchestra started up, as if they'd been waiting for Nico to ask me. I nodded and he twirled me onto the floor.

We were halfway through our dance, with Nico telling me a story about a time when he was in college and he and Alex had gotten locked out of their dorm room and how they'd climbed the outside trellis to get back in, which had fallen off. He got to the part where both the police and the paparazzi showed up when there was a tap on his shoulder.

There stood Alex. "Pardon the interruption, but I have someone I wanted Kat to meet." He looked suspiciously happy. "Kat, this is Franz von Croy. His family is from Austrian nobility. He's a very distant cousin of Nico's." Franz was tall—not as tall as Nico—but tall. He had pale blond hair and dark brown eyes. He wore some kind of military uniform. He bowed to me, and I smiled back. What was this about?

"Hope you don't mind him cutting in," Alex said, as he maneuvered Nico away from me. That wasn't what I wanted. We only had a few hours left. But Franz held out his arms, and I felt like I didn't really have a choice but to dance with him.

I tried to look for Nico, and finally caught sight of him with a thunderous expression on his face that made my insides twist. He stormed out to one of the balconies. Franz was very nice, if a little boring. I didn't understand what was happening. He asked me several questions about myself, and I really tried to be polite, but I just wanted Nico. Even our dancing was a little awkward. With Nico I could just move the right way, and we always seemed to dance in sync with each other. I stepped on Franz's foot more than once, but he was very gracious about it.

As soon as the song was over, I thanked him and headed straight for the balcony. Nico was sitting on a chair, in the cold, his arms crossed over his chest.

My costume was flimsy, and I started rubbing my arms to keep them warm. "What are you doing out here?"

"Seething."

"Seething? About what?"

His eyes glittered in the low light. "Apparently, I am an extremely jealous person. I didn't know this about myself."

"Who are you jealous of?"

"That pompous fool you were dancing with."

"Franz?"

"On a first-name basis?" He sounded bitter and angry.

"I'm on a first-name basis with everybody. This isn't the nineteenth century. And what exactly do you think is going to happen with him and me?" I was flattered, excited, and felt another emotion I couldn't quite identify. Some kind of female pride, I suspected. I'd spent so much time being jealous of that English tart and here was Nico, feeling the same way. It seemed ridiculous, since I'd barely let Nico kiss me. What did he think I was going do with some guy I'd just met?

"I have imagined quite a few things. Including me going back in there and taking him apart with my bare hands."

That shouldn't have made me so giddy. I should have been appalled. I told myself that I didn't need him to take care of me. That I wasn't anyone's possession. But some instinctual part inside me loved feeling protected and cared for. I didn't even mind that he was possessive of me. Because I'd certainly had my fair share of feeling possessive of him. I came over to him and crouched down next to his chair. He turned to look at me. "I promise, I am totally immune to whatever charms he might have."

"Are you?"

"Yes. He's no you."

It was what he needed to hear, apparently. He pulled me up and onto his lap, where he kissed me senseless. I started shivering, and this time it wasn't from Nico. It was really, really cold.

"Let's get back inside," he suggested, and I agreed.

Nico stuck to me like my shadow. Which I didn't mind. I didn't want to talk to Caitlin and Alex. I didn't even really want to talk to Lemon. Everything was focused solely on him. Every dance was with him. Every conversation with him. I wanted this night to last forever. Because it was the last memory I would have with him.

"My father is here," Nico said, with a touch of wonder to his voice. I turned to see his dad surrounded by people, all wanting to speak with him. The king smiled and nodded at everyone, still regal regardless of his situation.

"He doesn't normally come to stuff like this?"

"Not since the accident."

"Look at him. He's glowing."

"He loves the attention. Feeling needed. Sometimes I worry about that. If I become king, what will he have to live for? What will make him feel needed? So often you hear the stories of men who retire and then die when they don't have a reason to get up every morning. I can't take that from him."

"Your family will always make him feel needed," I said.

"Most of his family will grow up and move away. He needs to be king. *I* need him to be king."

I felt like I was on the verge of something important. But before I could say anything else, Caitlin and Lemon came to take me to the bathroom with them, since some women always had to go in packs.

"You do know what the Franz thing was about, don't you?" Caitlin asked. "Alex was trying to make Nico jealous."

"Tell him he succeeded," I said. "Nico was, in his own words, 'seething.'"

"Oh, that's going to make Alex far too happy. He's waited a long time for Nico to have a relationship that he could torment him about."

They had a commercial bathroom right off the ballroom with stalls and a comfy couch to sit on. I sat there to wait. One of the stall doors opened and Violetta came stumbling out, coughing. I could very clearly see her reflection in the mirror. She was wearing a white toga and had her hair piled up high on her head. Her eyes were glassy, and she was giggling.

"You okay, Violetta?"

She looked at me in the mirror with her eyes just like Nico's. She looked euphoric and sweaty. Her pupils were dilated. I recognized that expression.

She was high.

"Just fine," she replied in a breezy tone, giggling on her way out of the bathroom.

I had to find Nico.

I worked my way through the crowd until I found him, right where I'd left him. "Violetta is high."

"Are you certain?"

"Trust me, I'm certain. I'd even bet that it was crystal meth she was taking." I remembered the story Nico had told me about Violetta's weight problems and how the press had made fun of her. A lot of girls used crystal meth for quick weight loss, while not realizing that the effects were short-term and that your body became accustomed to it so quickly that you'd have to take more and more to maintain that loss.

Then I realized that Nico didn't have the reaction most family members had when they were told someone was doing drugs. He didn't seem surprised. He didn't deny it. He didn't try to rationalize it or explain it away.

Which let me know this was not the first time this had happened.

Nico took me by the hand and went to tell his parents. His father directed the head of security to find Violetta and bring her to something he called an anteroom. He wheeled off with the queen, myself, and Nico following. We went into a small room right off the ballroom, full of couches and benches. Nico and I sat down.

A few minutes later Dante and Rafe came in with their sister. I was glad Chiara and Serafina were in bed and wouldn't be a part of this.

Violetta started asking questions in rapid Italian. Nico translated next to me. "She wants to know what's going on, why she was pulled in here. My father is telling her because she's high again, despite her promising the last time that she would never do drugs again."

She looked furious. The queen looked sad, the king concerned.

"She can't make that kind of promise to any of you. She needs to be in rehab."

Everyone looked shocked when I spoke, as if they'd forgotten I was there. "The drugs have literally altered her brain so that she can't quit without help. I don't know what she was on before, but crystal meth is not something to mess around with. She needs professional help."

"I am not going to rehab," Violetta said, grinding the words out. Her euphoria had turned to aggression. I noticed that she didn't deny doing drugs, or that, as I'd suspected, it was specifically crystal meth.

"You have to stop, *cara mia*. Please. This will kill you. We can't keep going through this." The queen looked devastated. "I can't lose another child."

Violetta actually rolled her eyes. "If I promise to stop, can we please drop this? Nobody wants the embarrassment of me going to rehab. The paparazzi would be all over this."

The queen and king exchanged glances, and I had to say something. Part of my master's degree program had focused specifically on drug addicts because so many of the children in need had addicts in their lives.

"It's better for your family to be embarrassed than for you to wind up dead. It's good that you all love her, but coddling her doesn't help anyone."

"Why are you even here?" she hissed at me. "You are not part of this family."

"You're right, I'm not. But Nico's my friend, and your family has been so loving and kind to me. Which has been great for me, but obviously terrible for you."

"What does that mean?"

"You're a spoiled brat. You have an amazing life that people would kill for, and you're destroying it with drugs. You're like a little girl breaking her toys."

That got her full attention. "Do you think you can speak to me that way?"

"I think I can speak to you however I want. I'm not your family. I don't love you. I don't care if you're angry at me. Somebody needs to tell you the truth. Your family has protected you from the negative consequences of your actions. They've believed your lies and enabled you. It needs to stop."

I stood up and looked at her parents. "If she wants to live her life this way, fine. Let her do it. But cut her off financially. Kick her out of your house. She is a grown-up. If she wants to wreck her life, you don't have to finance it."

"You can't really be listening to her," Violetta said to her parents. "Don't listen to her! Don't send me away! I need you!"

"Don't let her manipulate you. You have to be serious and give her an ultimatum. You have to make decisions and stick to them, no matter what. I know it's unnatural for you to turn your back on your daughter. But this safety net you've given her is actually hurting her. If she kept stabbing herself in the stomach, you wouldn't keep handing her knives, would you? She'll get serious about this when you do."

The entire room was silent, everyone just staring at me. I asked Nico to borrow his phone.

I went into a web browser and did an image search with my mom's name. It pulled up her mug shot.

There had been studies that showed teens were less likely to smoke when you showed them what it would do to their faces. They couldn't care less that their lungs would turn black and that they would die. But they did not want extra lines, wrinkles, and yellow teeth. Their vanity was what kept them from hurting themselves.

I went over to Violetta and stood in front of her, showing her the image on the phone. "This is my mother. She has done crystal meth for the last twenty years or so. Look at her face." My mother had open sores. Her face was drawn and sallow. She was losing her teeth. "This will happen to you."

For the first time, Violetta looked scared. I gave the phone back to Nico, and he looked at the image before turning his phone off.

I addressed the king and queen again. "You should get a family therapist to help you through this. It will make a big difference to everyone. But most of all, she has to go to rehab and she has to do the work to get better. It won't be easy on anyone."

I had to leave then, because this was all feeling too personal and too real. I was worried I might start crying. I didn't want to go back to the ballroom. It seemed like a too happy and too fake place with all of those costumes. A wave of exhaustion slammed into me. I had remained cool and impersonal in there, not taking the bait and not yelling at her. It had worn me out more than I would have imagined. I sat down on a bench next to the anteroom, my entire body sagging.

Time passed, and Nico came out of the room. He stopped short when he saw me. "I was just coming to find you."

"Here I am."

"Violetta agreed to go to a rehab facility. They're taking her right now. Some of my father's secretaries are making the arrangements. How did you know that would work?" he asked, sitting down next to me.

"I didn't. But I know how loving parents are with their druggie kids, and your way obviously hasn't worked. I thought I would try mine."

He closed his hand over mine, holding me. "Thank you. Thank you for helping my sister. For helping all of us." He let out a ragged breath. "You see, I do know what it's like to watch someone I love slowly killing herself."

I put my head on his shoulder and sighed. "Life sucks sometimes, doesn't it?"

He put a finger on my chin and turned my face to look at him. "I was actually thinking that my life right now is pretty wonderful, *cuore mio*."

"Even with what your sister's going through?"

His intensity shocked me. "Even then."

We stayed silent, just looking in each other's eyes. I felt like I could see his soul. I had never felt so connected to anyone before.

"Do you want to go back to the ball?"

"No. Honestly, what I really want is to go to sleep."

He nodded. Then he stood and pulled me to my feet, leading me toward the front hallway and the stairs.

I had probably way overstepped my bounds in that room, but it felt good that I was able to help. Pretty soon I'd be doing this exact same thing on a daily basis. It helped to lessen some of my sadness.

The same sadness that nearly overcame me when I realized that this would be my last night with him, and it was all about to end.

Chapter 22

"It's weird to think that this time tomorrow I'm going to be back in Colorado," I said as we went down the hallway that led to my room.

It was a bit of a desperate ploy to get Nico to DTR. DTR was a phrase that Lemon's sorority sisters had introduced me to. It meant "define the relationship."

I waited for him to say something. Anything. To show me that all of this had mattered to him the way it had mattered to me.

I felt like he cared about me. I thought he was attracted to me and liked being with me. But maybe this was the price of inexperience. I didn't have any past relationships to compare to this one so that I could better understand. I didn't know what he was thinking. This could all be no big deal to him. Just another girl to hang with until she left.

But it wasn't that way for me. There was more here. At the snow polo match, when I thought I was going to lose him forever, I was desperate and terrified. Now I really was losing him. This was it. I couldn't even pretend like he wanted a long-distance relationship. He hadn't said a single word about it, even though we'd spent so much time together. We just kept going along in our little bubble like life would always stay that way.

It wouldn't.

If I had more courage, I might have just asked him where he thought things would go between us. I had tried so hard to keep this casual, but I was losing that fight.

We stopped in front of my door, and he took both of my hands. "What if you didn't have to go?"

"But I do have to go."

"You couldn't stay for even a few more days?"

I wished I could. "I really can't."

He nodded, not quite meeting my eyes. Did he want me to stay? Would he miss me? I wondered if by cutting him off from more physicality, had it changed how he felt about me? Had it made him not like me as much? He'd been so careful recently to keep me at arm's length. This was the first time we'd been alone in days.

We heard a loud commotion coming from the ballroom. They were counting down to midnight.

"There's a myth that says the person you kiss on New Year's Eve sets the tone for the rest of the year," he told me.

"Talk about pressure. What if you're with someone like Lady Claire? Then your whole year would be shot," I replied. "I wonder if Hershey Kisses would be a good substitute. Then your year would be filled with chocolate-y goodness."

He didn't even crack a smile. "Happy New Year, Katerina."

"Happy New Year, Nico."

The bells from the town started to ring, and fireworks exploded outside the castle. Then they started exploding and ringing inside me as Nico kissed me ever so gently, ever so softly, as if he feared I would break.

The end of us felt like a living thing. I wanted to chase it away. I didn't want to face it.

I wanted him to really kiss me.

So I showed him what I wanted. I pressed against him, trying to melt into him. I felt desperate, clinging to him. I kissed him with everything I had, my mouth insistent on his.

It only took Nico a second to realize that I had shifted gears. Then his lips were all urgency and insistence, fierceness and passion.

That wall he'd put up, the one he stayed behind so that he didn't get too out of control, shattered. He wasn't holding back.

He kissed me harder, tangling his fingers in my hair. Everywhere he touched and everywhere he kissed scorched me. Like I was being branded. My heartbeat was out of control, my breathing worse.

His kisses were hungry, his hands impatient. He explored. Tasted. Memorized.

And I gave back as good as I got.

The intoxicating deliciousness of it all consumed me. He kissed me everywhere he could find skin. He lifted me up so that I was flush against him, my curves pressing into his edges. I ran my fingernails along his scalp, and he groaned in response. The sound sent little yummy thrills up my spine. I couldn't kiss him enough. It wasn't enough. I wanted more.

I wanted more than just this.

If this was our last night, I wanted this memory of him.

I pulled back. "Nico . . ."

But he closed the distance between us, his mouth hot on mine, searing me. My entire world had turned into overwhelming sensations, rampant fire, and a drowning need. I could feel his restraint slipping away with each moment, each kiss.

He kissed my cheek, my jaw, my neck, my collarbone. "Nico," I tried again.

"Don't ask me to stop." His voice was rough and hoarse.

"I don't want you to stop," I told him, and he went still. He pulled his head away to look at me.

"What are you saying?"

I let go of him and gently pushed his arms away. We were both breathing hard and staring at each other. My legs finally obeyed me, and then I went over to my door and turned the knob. I stepped inside a few feet and then turned to face him. He had both of his hands on the doorframe.

"Nico, I'm inviting you in."

But he didn't move. I stood there feeling vulnerable and totally out of my depth, needing him to make this okay. My heart hammered in my chest, waiting for him to walk over to me and take me in his arms.

Still he stood. Staring at me. The light from the hallway backlit him, and I couldn't see his face or his eyes.

I nearly walked back to him so that I could take him by the hand. But I didn't. I needed him to close this gap between us, to make me forget everything.

"Do you realize what you're saying?" His voice was low and intense, sending new shivers through me.

"I know exactly what I'm saying."

I waited and waited. He left me standing there. Alone.

My nerves tensed and my breath seemed to solidify in my throat. Did he not want this? Had I misread the entire situation? Time seemed to both speed up and slow down.

When he finally spoke, he startled me. "I want there to be no misunderstanding between us. More than anything in the world, I want to accept your invitation." He stopped talking, unmoving. "But I can't dishonor you and disrespect your values. You would hate me tomorrow for it, and I would hate myself. So I think I should say good night before I lose the ability to walk away from you."

My soul fractured into a million pieces. My blood pounded in my temples, and I was sure I had turned a bright scarlet red, since my cheeks felt like they were on fire. He was saying no. He was rejecting me.

I had offered him all of me, and he said no thanks.

I had never been so embarrassed, so humiliated in my entire life. A dark anguish spread all over me, weighing me down. My limbs felt heavy, like I was moving underwater.

I slowly walked back to the door, looking up at him.

"Say something," he pleaded.

I closed the door in his face. And then I locked it.

"Katerina . . . *cuore mio*, please . . ."

"Go away, Nico. I don't want you here." I hoped he couldn't hear my despair, couldn't hear how hard I was trying not to cry.

I put my forehead against the door, listening. He stood there for several minutes before he finally walked away, taking my heart with him.

I tugged at the zipper, trying to get out of my costume. I nearly ripped it in my frenzy to get it off. I couldn't stand it. I had to get it off.

Finally, I was free. I didn't even bother with pajamas, just crawling into my bed and pulling the covers up over my head.

I could actually taste the mortification. I was not only upset by his reaction, but by what I had done.

How could I have done that?

That wasn't me. Who had I turned in to?

I had to get back home. To my real self. This was all just a fantasy. I needed my studies, my schoolwork, and my kids. I thought of my plans. My degree, my job, my apartment. Those were things I had dreamed of. Planned for. Worked for. Those things were real. They were what I wanted.

I had never felt so disappointed and ashamed. I always kept my word. Always. And now, the most important promise I'd ever made to myself, the one that had mattered the most, I had just been willing to throw out the window.

For what? For a guy who hadn't ever even said how he really felt about me? It wasn't even like I could rationalize it as being in love. We weren't in love.

Were we?

I finally let the tears loose, big angry ones that covered my cheeks and made my eyes burn. Sobs racked my body, and I shook with the intensity of my pain.

I couldn't get over what I'd done. What I'd wanted to do. What I had asked Nico to do. I wanted someone to blame, someone to be my scapegoat. But the only one who'd messed up was me. I didn't need to worry about somebody else, like Lady Claire, screwing up my life. I was doing a pretty good job wrecking it all on my own. I felt like such a fool.

An undesirable, stupid fool.

I must have finally fallen asleep after spending hours running the night through my head over and over again, wishing I could have done things differently. Wishing that I could have retained my dignity and held on to my promises. How sad that Nico had to keep my promise for me! I had never imagined that I could be so weak.

I went to unlock my door and found it opened. My costume was missing from the floor. When I went into my closet, I saw that Giacomo had already packed for me. I opened my suitcase and took out the dresses and all the other clothes they had made for me. I left them on a shelf. I put the Elsa costume on a hanger and left it swinging in the closet. I grabbed some clothes to travel in and put them on. I brought the suitcase out and put it on my bed.

Opening my nightstand, I took out Nico's gifts and the phone. I was angry, but I couldn't leave the Barbie behind. Or the necklace. They meant too much to me. I put them in my suitcase. I picked up the phone and thought about leaving it behind. But someday I might want those memories again. Those pictures. I would take it with me.

There was a knock on my door, and my heart throbbed in my throat. I wasn't ready to see Nico.

"May I come in, Signorina Kat?"

It was Giacomo. I was both relieved and disappointed. "Come in."

"I have this for you." He handed me a heavy, cream-colored envelope that had the royal family's crest on it. It was fringed in red and gold stripes. I opened it up, afraid of what I might find. But it was just a check for six thousand dollars for the article. In the other hand he had my favorite hot chocolate, and I took a sip before setting it down.

"Do you have everything? May I help with any other packing?"

"I'm good." This would be the last time I would see him. The last time Giacomo would take care of things for me. "Hey, thanks for everything." I wanted to hug him, but he didn't seem like the type to do hugs.

"You are most welcome."

I zipped my suitcase up, leaving the envelope on my bed. "I feel like I should tell you how awesome you've been, Giacomo. I never could have survived all this without you."

He adjusted his glasses and straightened his tie. I wondered if I'd embarrassed him. "It has been an honor to serve you, my lady."

I laughed. "I'm no lady, Giacomo. You and I both know that."

He grabbed my hand, which surprised me because he was always so formal with me. "You are one of the truest ladies I have ever known."

I couldn't swallow, and I wanted to cry all over again. I just nodded in response. What could I say to that?

He patted me awkwardly on the arm and walked out.

I sank down on the bed, refusing to cry. I looked at the check again. It was a lot of money.

But it was tainted. I couldn't take it. I didn't need Nico's money. I could figure out my tuition problem on my own. I put the envelope on top of the nightstand.

I got my toiletry bag from the bathroom and didn't bother with any of it. I didn't want to brush my teeth or fix my hair. It would be my carry-on. I made sure I had my ticket and my passport. I didn't want anything to get in my way of leaving this country.

Lemon and I had a train to catch. It would take us to Milan, and from the airport there we would eventually make our way back to Colorado.

I was going home. Home. The word sounded hollow and false in my head. Because my heart felt like I was leaving my home.

There was a noise in the hallway, and I looked to see Serafina standing just behind the doorframe, hiding from me.

"Did you come to say goodbye?"

She nodded and then ran over to me, jumping into my arms. She started crying, soft little sad sobs that tore at my heart. I held her on the bed, rocking her back and forth.

"I don't want you to go," she said.

"I have to go."

She looked up at me. Frak, I had really come to love this kid.

"Will I see you again?"

I didn't want to lie to her. "I don't think so."

Her cries got louder. "But why can't you just stay? Stay and marry Nico? Then someday you would be a queen. Like Elsa. Don't you want to be like Elsa?"

How could I tell a seven-year-old that her brother wasn't going to marry me or anybody else?

I kissed her on the forehead and made soothing sounds. "Don't cry, everything will be all right."

"What if I promise to be good? What if I promise to never steal your phone again? Then will you stay?"

She was absolutely breaking my heart. "Oh, sweetie, you didn't do anything wrong. This has nothing to do with you. This was only a holiday for me, and now it's time for me to go home. I have school and work to get back to."

She just kept crying, and it was all I could do to keep from joining her.

"I am really, really going to miss you," I told her.

"I am really, really going to miss you," she said through her tears. "I wanted you to be my new sister. I like you much better than Violetta."

That made me laugh. I hugged her tightly. I wished I could put her in my suitcase and take her to Colorado with me. Instead I put her in my bed, pulling the covers up around her. I brushed some of the tears from her cheeks. "When you miss me, I want you to watch *Frozen* and think about all the times we watched it together. Can you do that?"

She nodded her head, clutching the blanket.

"Good. Because every time I watch it, I will think of you."

"Promise?" she sniffled.

"I promise." I kissed her again on the cheek, picked up all of my bags, and forced myself out the door. In the hallway I found Chiara. I could not go through this again.

But she didn't cry. She asked me to e-mail her and stay in touch, that she had more sketches that she wanted to show me. I didn't have any intention of talking to any member of Nico's family in the future. So I didn't say yes, but I didn't say no. I just hugged her.

"Please take good care of your family. Especially . . ."

She interrupted me before I could continue. "Nico?"

Even hearing his name hurt my heart. "Serafina. She's a little sad."

"I will." We hugged again and Chiara left. I knocked on Lemon's door, and she took one look at me and dragged me inside. "Tell me everything."

"We don't have time. We need to get to the train so we can get to the airport. What are you doing?"

She had her personal stationery out. "I was writing a thank-you note to the king and queen. They left late last night for some reason, and they took Violetta and the twins with them. Which is probably a good thing because I don't want to have a whole scene with Dante before we leave. You can sign them if you want."

Lemon's mother was huge into thank-you notes and had raised her daughter to be the same way. I picked up the card and, without reading it, signed my name to the bottom. I was glad I didn't have to see anybody else in Nico's family. My farewell tour was wearing me down.

"I also wrote a note to Caitlin. Their flight was early this morning, so you didn't get to say goodbye. You disappeared last night." She had an accusatory tone, but I was in no mood. I signed that card too. Lemon put the cards into the envelopes and sealed them shut. She left them on her bed. She looked around her room, as if she wanted to remember every detail. While I couldn't wait to get out of there.

"We need to go."

"You need to explain yourself."

"Not here. Not in this place."

There was something on my face that let Lemon know I was serious. I grabbed one of her suitcases, and she managed the other three (wearing one and rolling the other two).

"I asked Giacomo to call for a taxi to take us to the train."

I nodded, not trusting myself to speak.

The stairs were no fun with the suitcases. I half-expected to see Nico around every turn. My heart kept jumping and falling when he didn't appear.

I wanted to leave without saying goodbye. I didn't want to see him again, to relive that humiliation from last night.

Outside there was a town car, not a taxi. The driver ran over to help us with the suitcases.

"We were supposed to have a taxi," I said.

"His Highness insisted that I drive you to the airport in Milan."

No way was I letting that happen.

"You can take us to the train station." I took the train to get into Monterra, and I could very well take the train back out. I didn't need Nico's car or his driver.

The driver looked panicked. "No, I can't. I have to take you to the airport."

I sighed. I didn't want to get the poor guy fired. He didn't deserve to lose his job over my stubbornness. I handed over one of my bags. He put our suitcases in the trunk, and Lemon and I climbed into the car. I shut the door behind me.

"Now will you talk?"

"Not yet. I'm not ready yet." I could see the worry in Lemon's eyes. I didn't want to deal with anyone else's emotions right now. I could barely deal with my own.

I closed my eyes. I had never felt so bone-weary and exhausted. I didn't want to think about Nico and why he hadn't come to say goodbye. Not that I wanted to see him again, but it hurt that he didn't want to see me.

I just wanted to sleep.

Lemon woke me up when we got to the airport. We had plenty of time to check in.

But when we stepped into the airport, looking for our airline, I noticed a man with a sign that said "MACTAGGART" and "BEAUCHAMP." No question that it was for Lemon and me.

I was going to ignore it, but then Lemon saw him. "What is that about, do you think?"

Maybe Nico was going to make some grand gesture here in the airport. Surrounded by people so that I wouldn't make a scene or scream at him. I didn't want to find out.

But Lemon was already walking toward the man with the sign. "I'm Lemon Beauchamp."

"Prince Dominic has arranged for a flight for you. His personal jet is waiting."

That was the last straw. I was not flying home in his jet. "Nuh-uh. Not happening."

"Please, Kat. We have three layovers on our way home. It's going to take forever. This will take us directly there. I don't know what happened with Nico, and I'm sorry for whatever it was, but we have school first thing tomorrow. I don't want to be exhausted. Do you?"

I couldn't remember what it felt like to not be exhausted. But there was no fight left in me. No strength to dig in my heels. And I didn't want to spend the entire day sitting in airports. So I gave in.

The man got our luggage and put it on a trolley. He told us to follow him. He took us through a specialized security line, and we walked down a long hallway to go out onto the tarmac.

Standing at the end of the hallway was Nico.

Chapter 23

I felt frozen in place, just staring at him.

He wore a black designer suit with a dark blue tie. He had on a black trench coat that swirled and fluttered around his legs as the winds blew. His face was set and serious. He looked like a cross between a Roman gladiator and a fashion model who had just walked off the runway.

Lemon walked up to him, and they talked. She looked back at me and then headed out to the plane. I watched her get on board, leaving me behind.

I didn't want to talk to him. I didn't want to experience all the emotions I'd gone through last night again. I just wanted to go back to school so that I could put all this behind me and pretend like it had never happened.

He stood waiting, all of his attention focused on me. My stomach twisted and turned, and it was again hard to move.

Maybe I could just ignore him and walk past him. I was so churned up inside, emotions coming so fast and furious, it made me feel like I was drowning. I was afraid talking to him would make that dam burst, and I'd be a crying mess. I didn't want to cry in front of him.

I was level with him and refused to look him in the face. His hand darted out and grabbed my upper arm, making me stop.

"Katerina, please. I want to talk to you about last night." His quiet voice sounded hoarse and sad.

Furious, I snapped my head to look at him. "I am not talking to you about last night. You made your feelings very clear."

"You don't understand . . ."

"No, you don't understand. I was such an idiot. I feel so stupid. And I don't want to feel this way anymore. I'm going home."

"Don't. Please. Stay." He said each word as if they'd been wrenched from inside him.

"Stay? What possible reason can you give me to stay?"

Nico didn't say anything to that, even though part of me desperately hoped he would come up with the answer that would make me forget all of last night and forget my life and just stay and be happy with him.

Just silence. Which made me angry, for some reason. "That's what I thought. I can't stay here in this fairy tale. None of this is real."

His eyes looked blank. "You think what happened between us wasn't real?"

"None of this is real," I repeated, with more conviction than I was feeling.

"What if it was real to me?"

I closed my eyes and inhaled my breath sharply. I couldn't let him sway me. I knew how easily he could. I had to remember what mattered. Hang on to the pain and shame and humiliation from last night.

"You don't do commitment, and I don't do casual. There's no future between us. We had our fun, but now it's time to go back to reality."

I saw him flex his jaw several times, his cheek twitching in response. "Is that really what you think about me?"

"It's what I know. It's what you told me. Remember? What, did you change your mind?"

"Maybe I have."

"Maybe?" I let out a short, bitter laugh. "You want me to give up my life, my whole future, for a maybe? That's not enough. Look at us. We live on two different continents. You're going to be a king, and I'm from a trailer park. It would never work, even if you maybe, might possibly, someday, change your mind."

"I don't want this to be it. I don't want to never see you again. Can I come and visit you?"

My traitorous heart leapt up and said *yes, yes, yes* over and over again. But if I told him he could, if I held on to that hope, what would happen to me when he didn't come? When I was disappointed because he was too busy or had found someone else? And how would I feel if he were in Colorado? Could I ever forget the way he made me feel last night? The anguish, the embarrassment, the complete blow to my self-esteem? I was afraid that every time I looked at him I would remember. It was too much. I needed to protect myself. So I shook my head. "I don't want to see you again. I don't want you to come to Colorado."

My words sounded so false and empty.

We stood for several minutes, studying each other. I saw a storm of dark emotions in his bright blue eyes. Sadness, anger, concern, and finally, acceptance.

"This is your decision? This is what you want?"

"Yes, this is what I want. We both knew this would end. Goodbye, Nico."

He still held on to my arm and I tugged against him, but he didn't release me. I was perilously close to tears. I didn't know if I could hold out for much longer.

"You need to say goodbye and let me go," I told him, my voice breaking slightly.

Leaning in, he gently brushed his lips against mine, and they tingled in response to his very brief kiss. He let go of my arm.

"*Addio, amore mio.*"

I walked away from him without looking back. I climbed the stairs into the jet and sat down across from Lemon. I refused to think about the last time I'd been in this plane, on my way home from Paris.

I sighed. The fact that I had just thought of Nico's palace as *home* was not lost on me.

I resisted the urge to look out the window to see if he was still there by closing the panel. The flight attendant came to check on us as the pilot announced that he was ready to take off.

We sat in silence as the plane taxied to the runway and then lifted up into the sky. When we were in the air and the pilot had turned off the seatbelt light, I asked Lemon, "Do you know what *amore mio* means?"

211

She looked so sympathetic. "I do. It means my love."

His love. I wanted to laugh. Now I was his love. After he made me feel like crap and, as Lemon would say, lower than a bow-legged caterpillar. I wasn't actually his love. Maybe it was another one of those Italian endearments that didn't really mean anything. It was just something to say.

Liar, my heart whispered. *You know he meant it.*

It didn't matter, I argued back. I needed a future. I could never live my life on hopes and dreams. I had to have goals and plans. Things that were concrete. Things that made me feel settled. I needed to go back to what was familiar and just forget all of this had ever happened.

"Now you have to explain," Lemon said. "Tell me everything."

I felt wrung out, like I had nothing left inside me to give. But I knew she would never leave me alone until I told her the story. This time I didn't leave anything out when I recounted everything with Violetta and then what had happened outside of my room, right up to seeing him a few minutes ago. I gave her every bloody, gory, gruesome detail. I spoke in a monotone voice because if I let any emotion creep in, I would never recover.

At some point in my story she had changed seats so that she could sit next to me and put her arm around my shoulders.

After I'd finished up with our encounter on the tarmac, she started shaking her head. "Y'all need to be slapped."

"Why do I need to be slapped?" I asked indignantly.

"Because you've fallen in love with him."

"Don't be ridiculous. No one falls in love with someone they've only known for a couple of weeks. It's insane."

"Says who?"

"Common sense, for one."

She pursed her lips and stared at me. "Oh. You're in the denial stage."

"No, I'm not."

"See?"

If she were anyone else I would have pushed her arm off and walked away.

"Okay, maybe we won't call it denial. Just being selective about the reality you're choosing to accept."

I shook my head. She didn't understand. I couldn't possibly be in love with him.

Could I? My heart started to beat faster.

"You don't love someone you've only known for two weeks," I repeated, as if this would convince both of us.

"Some people take two years and others take two minutes. Two weeks might just be how long it took for the two of you."

I might actually love him. It might be why I took last night so hard. Because I loved him and I wanted to show him physically that I loved him, and so his rejection made me feel like he was rejecting my feelings for him.

My cheeks flushed red, and tears welled up in my eyes. I thought of how happy I was with him. How I lived for the moment when I would get to see him again. How he was always so tender and caring with me. How he'd become the most important person in the world to me.

I did. I did love him. I thought of all those confusing feelings I'd had while I was with him, and I just didn't recognize what they were because I'd never been in love with someone before.

Oh, frak. I loved Nico. I was in love with Nico.

"And you know he loves you."

"He doesn't," I denied. It was all I could do to deal with the new fragile realization that I loved him. I didn't need my world turned any more upside down.

"There are only two reasons a man like Nico would say no to an invitation like that. He's gay, or he's in love with you and told you the truth of why he wouldn't take advantage of you. And darlin', that man is not gay. If he didn't love you, he would have been more than happy to take you to bed."

I didn't have a response to that. Was Lemon right? Had I been making this situation all about me and not truly stopped to think of why he'd said no? I'd been so focused on how I felt and what I wanted that I hadn't even considered *why* Nico had done it.

"Like how you wouldn't take his money for the article. You couldn't take his money because you love him."

That wasn't why I left the money behind. Was it?

I felt like I didn't know myself or my own mind anymore.

"How could someone like Nico love someone like me?" I grasped for an argument to make this not true.

"Because you're fabulous and he's smart enough to see it. What did the man have to do? Write 'I love Kat' on his forehead? Because I don't know how much more obvious he could have been."

"He could have told me," I said. "I asked him to give me a reason to stay, and he didn't answer."

"If he had told you he loved you, would you have really heard him? Would you have accepted it?"

No, I wouldn't have. I would have thought he was trying to assuage a guilty conscience for hurting me. I wouldn't have believed him. It probably would have made me angrier.

Had he somehow known that?

Did everybody else just know me better than I knew myself?

"It doesn't matter. It doesn't matter how I feel about him or how he feels about me. I'm going home. I'm finishing up my final semester, defending my thesis, and graduating. Then I'm becoming a social worker and helping kids. I have a plan."

She looked angry as she pulled her arm away from me. "You and your plans! Life changes. People change. Plans change. What if you could have a life with Nico? What if you became a queen? How many more kids could you help as queen of an entire nation than you ever could as a social worker? The difference is exponential."

I couldn't live my life on what-ifs. I needed what would be.

"Tell the pilot to turn the plane around," she said. "Don't leave things like this with him. If you don't, you will always regret it."

The word *regret* snapped me back to my memories of last night, and I was in that moment again, acting unlike myself, feeling totally rejected. It made me feel irrational. "I'm not throwing away all of my hard work for some guy. I'm getting my degree."

"No one's arguing that. Of course you should get your degree. But take a couple of extra days and work things out with Nico."

I wouldn't do it. I was not that girl. I was not going to be pathetic and throw myself at him in the hopes that he might want to do more than just hang out.

I just shook my head.

Lemon sighed. "You are too stubborn for your own good. Like a mule at feeding time. Just once it would be nice to see you stand and face your problems instead of running away from them."

It seemed like the plane's walls were closing in on me. As if my psyche wanted to prove her correct, I found myself with a desperate need to escape. "I'm going to go take a nap," I told her.

My breaths were hard and uneven. Some part of me knew what she was saying was true. But I couldn't do it. I couldn't turn around and beg him to love me when he'd given me up so easily. He hadn't really tried to stop me. He hadn't come on the plane to spend the next few hours trying to talk me out of it. He'd just stood there while I walked away.

I closed the bedroom door shut. I kicked off my shoes. I looked at the bandage on my left wrist. It had been two weeks. Time to take it off. I slowly unwrapped it, letting it fall on the floor in a pile. I climbed into his bed, and this time I got under the covers. His pillows still smelled like him. I buried my face in his scent and let my tears turn the pillowcase wet.

The flight attendant woke me up, and I stopped by the bathroom before I took my seat. My nose was red, making me look like Rudolph. The whites of my eyes had gone bright pink. I couldn't remember ever crying this hard. Not even the night I left my mother's trailer for good.

I picked up the pillow I had sobbed all over and brought it out with me. Even if it was stealing, I was going to have this piece of him. When I came back into the main part of the cabin, Lemon offered me her hand in a conciliatory gesture. I paused only for a second before I took it, and she squeezed. She was my best friend. She would always be my best friend. She only wanted to help me do what was right for me. I needed to remember that.

When the plane landed, the attendant moved to open the door. I grabbed my bag and pulled out a pair of sunglasses. The Colorado sun seemed brighter than I'd remembered. Maybe it was because of all the crying.

I stepped off the plane and into a flurry of flashbulbs. There were paparazzi everywhere. I froze, not able to understand what was happening.

"This way, Kat!"

"Kat, is it true that you're dating Prince Dominic?"

"Why did he kick you out of the palace, Kat?"

"Is it true that you're pregnant?"

My mouth dropped, and I could only stare. This could not be happening. On the worst day of my life, I did not need a pack of mangy hyenas feeding off of my carcass. I squeezed his pillow tightly against my chest, as if it could protect me.

"Keep walking," Lemon said. We didn't have any security here. There were no guards to clear a path for us or to keep us safe. It was just the two of us. "Don't speak to any of them and keep your head down."

She put her arm around me and we walked through the paparazzi, with flashes going off and them screaming questions in my ear.

"You should have given me my pictures," one Irish voice said to me. I looked up to see Seamus O'Brien flash a camera in my face twenty times in a row. He sneered at me. "I'm about to make your life miserable."

I knew it wouldn't be the last time I saw him.

Lemon and I pushed through until we were inside the airport, and the reporters could no longer follow us.

"What am I going to do?" I asked her, looking back at the line of paparazzi who were still yelling and taking pictures behind the glass.

Lemon handed her bag and her passport to the customs agent. "I'll tell you exactly what you're going to do. From now on you're going to wear the same exact outfit every day. A white T-shirt with jeans and tennis shoes."

"Why?" I asked as the agent took my passport and stamped it. I tried not to look at the Italian stamp we'd received when we first arrived in Milan.

"The paparazzi need different pictures for the magazines. If you always wear the same outfit, it makes the pictures boring and no one can tell what day it is. It makes it seem like it's all from the same set of pictures. Celebrities do it all the time. Also, don't talk to the paparazzi. Don't engage them, don't give them good shots of you. Don't respond to their insults or lies. Eventually they will leave you alone because there won't be anything worth reporting."

We made our way through the airport with our bags, heading to the front of the terminal to catch a taxi back to our apartment. But all of the reporters had moved out front and were waiting for me there.

"I can't do this." I couldn't live this way, under constant scrutiny.

"You can. I will be there every step to help you. Come on."

I had wanted so badly to go back and have everything be normal.

But would anything in my life ever be normal again?

Chapter 24

"What do you mean a clerical error?"

First thing that Monday morning I had made my way to the financial aid office. I had to walk the entire way across campus with the paparazzi taking pictures and shouting their questions. Everyone looked at me as I walked across the quad and through the hallways, and I knew why. I was on every celebrity gossip site, and I had even managed to make both the local television news and newspaper. On the positive side, since I didn't have a phone, I didn't have to deal with all the requests. Somehow they found Lemon's number and bombarded her nonstop. She got so used to saying, "No comment," to every phone call she received that she'd nearly hung up on her mother, who had not been pleased.

The financial aid woman I was speaking to typed a few things into the computer and stared at her monitor. "All I can tell is that we were in error when we said your scholarship had been defunded. It is fully funded, and we have a check waiting for you." She got up out of her seat and walked over to a filing cabinet.

All that stress and worry about my tuition, rent, and ability to eat had been for nothing. Just some kind of clerical error. This seemed surreal.

Especially since, just two weeks ago, this same woman had apologized and told me there was no mistake, the scholarship money had run dry and that she didn't know what to tell me.

She returned with a check and handed it to me. Enough to pay for everything that I would need for the next four months.

I was safe. I would graduate. My life would go on as I'd planned.

This should have made me elated.

It didn't.

After my morning class in Management in Human Services Organizations, I had arranged to meet Lemon for lunch in the student center. Another struggle through the paparazzi. They said the most horrible things to me, trying to get me to react. I kept my head down and my sunglasses on. I missed my mountain Lorenz, who would have shoved everyone out of the way. Giacomo, who would have told me what to say.

But most of all, Nico, who would have protected me from all of this. Which made me both angry and sad.

We sat down together at a table after we got our food, ignoring all the other students who were staring at us and whispering. Pretending like there weren't reporters outside the windows still trying to get my attention.

"You should go to the dean," Lemon told me. "This is unbelievable. He should keep them off campus."

"Maybe I'll go there next," I told her. I had fieldwork that afternoon and needed to prepare some notes for the field seminar scheduled for the end of the week.

If I could just keep busy, if I could just keep my mind on school, I wouldn't think about him.

I dropped my bag onto the table, and the cell phone spilled out. I had unpacked last night when we got home, putting my Barbie and my necklace in the back corner of my closet shelf. I couldn't bear to see them or what they represented.

But the phone I'd dropped in my book bag. I didn't know why. It made me feel better knowing it was there.

Lemon picked it up. "Is this the phone from the paparazzi?"

"Yeah, I disabled the SIM card so it's basically a glorified iPod at this point. I feel bad for keeping it."

"Don't. Consider it payment for services rendered for everything that redheaded snake is putting you through. Why don't we go over to the place across the street and get you a phone number on my family's plan?"

Before I could protest, she held up a hand. "Don't do that Miss Independence thing you do when you're upset and won't let anyone help you. You don't have to carry the weight of the world on your shoulders. You have people who love you. I'll take care of it for now, and you can take the payments over when you get your job. I'm so tired of you not having a phone. When I'm shopping I *need* to be able to take pictures of myself in outfits and text them to you right then to see what you think."

I knew that wasn't why she wanted it for me. I also knew she was trying to make me laugh. But I felt like I didn't have any laughter left inside me. I could only manage a weak smile.

"That sounds good," I told her.

My own cell phone would certainly make my life easier in arranging my appointments, study groups, and talking to my advisor. Lemon promised to keep the number private so that I wouldn't have to deal with any reporters.

She got up to throw her trash away, and I held up the phone, refraining from opening the camera's gallery. I wasn't ready to see his family. Or him. Not yet.

I wondered if I ever would be.

One week went by. Two. Then three. A full month passed. I kept time by the number of paparazzi outside of my apartment. The dean had banned them from campus, but that didn't stop them from camping out on the sidewalk next to my home. I did everything Lemon said. I wore the same clothes every day. Ignored them. Didn't react. Little by little they left, until there was only Seamus O'Brien. And then even he gave up. I had my life back, and it had only taken thirty days of hell.

And whatever idiot said time heals all wounds should be tied up to a railroad track and run over by a train repeatedly. Then we'd see how well time would heal those wounds.

Because time wasn't healing my wounds. I felt like I was the one who had been hit by a train, sleepwalking in constant pain through my life. I smiled when I was supposed to, replied when I was supposed to. Did my schoolwork. Concentrated on finishing up my thesis.

My wounds weren't healing. They were all open and festering.

I missed Nico. I missed him so badly it was an actual physical pain that never went away. I thought about him constantly. He was always the last thing on my mind when I went to bed, and my first thought when I woke up.

If I'd had any doubt about whether or not I was in love with him, that had been erased. I knew it as well as I knew anything. I loved him.

I didn't tell Lemon. She would have done something to make me talk to him if I had. I pretended like I was fine, but when she thought I wasn't looking, she had an expression of worry and concern on her face.

There were a lot of things I'd been doing that I hadn't told Lemon about. Like hanging out with the Italian Club. They met once a week and had lunch together, and spoke Italian the whole time. I had no idea what anyone was saying and I never participated, but it made me feel better to hear his language being spoken.

I started meeting with a counselor in the counseling office. As a student, I could meet with a professional on a weekly basis for free. I thought it might be a good idea given the legion of personal issues I'd managed to accumulate over the years. I really liked Bethany. She felt comfortable and never pushed me farther than I was willing to go. Sometimes we talked about Nico, but I tried to steer clear of all mention of him.

Even with Lemon I'd had to put a moratorium on all mentions of Nico and anything that was Fiorelli-related. I knew she was still deeply involved with them because of her thesis and the work she was doing for them.

Sometimes she broke the ban, like last night when she showed me a video from Chiara and Serafina. Serafina sang "Let it Go" for me, told me she missed me, and wanted to know when I would be back.

My heart ached to see them. I actually ran my finger over the phone screen, as if I could reach out and touch them.

"What do you want me to say?"

"Just tell her I miss her too." Any more than that, and it really would break my heart.

Not that a broken heart was anything new to me. I walked around in a haze, feeling like somebody had taken a piece of me and I couldn't function without it. Like the human version of the Tin Man.

Lemon had even set me up on a blind date, saying I needed to get back out there again. Whatever that meant.

I had only gone so that she wouldn't constantly bug me about it.

Matthew was nice enough, I suppose. He took me to a diner near campus, and I thought I should try. I should make conversation. I should find out about him.

But I didn't care. I didn't want his brown hair and brown eyes. I wanted Nico's black hair and blue eyes. I didn't want Matthew's smiles. I wanted Nico's smiles.

I wanted Nico there to tease me and comfort me and love me. Matthew was a very poor and pale substitute.

I listened to him talk, my food tasting like sawdust in my mouth. Which made me even more sad, because I had always loved the burgers there. Matthew certainly loved talking about himself. He was a boy who cared about boy things. Like PlayStation games and how drunk he planned on getting that weekend.

Nico was a man worrying about the fate of nations and taking care of hundreds of thousands of people. He worried about curing cancer and providing financially for families with sick loved ones.

There was just no comparison. At least Matthew was smart enough to figure it out. When he walked me home, he didn't try to kiss me or say he'd call me. I was relieved.

The one thing that time was doing for me was giving me the opportunity to more objectively analyze that night with Nico.

I had considered writing everything down. In one of my classes we had learned about the technique that was often used with abused children and soldiers with PTSD—by writing down their stories they were better able to psychologically let go.

I couldn't write about Nico. I tried, but I couldn't. I had thought maybe I could write a romance about our situation. But it proved impossible because one, nobody would believe a guy like Nico would be interested in a girl like me, and two, I didn't want to share him with anyone.

Not to mention the lack of an actual happily ever after.

As I remembered that night, making notes, I was better able to put things in perspective. I remembered every word he'd said to me, as clearly as if he were standing in the room and saying it again. I wrote it down in my notebook so that I could study it.

I want there to be no misunderstanding between us. More than anything in the world, I want to accept your invitation. But I can't dishonor you and disrespect your values. You would hate me tomorrow for it, and I would hate myself. So I think I should say good night before I lose the ability to walk away from you.

When my own emotions could be taken out of it, when I could look at his words and really see what he had said, I realized how dumb I had been.

He didn't reject me. He wasn't turning me down. He wanted me. He said he'd wanted me. He wanted me so much he wasn't sure he could walk away. He tried really hard to make sure that I wouldn't freak out the way that I did. He wanted to respect me. He wanted me to keep my promise. He knew me well enough to anticipate the fallout of him coming into my room. And he was right. I would have hated both of us. I wouldn't have been okay with it the next morning, no matter how much I wanted him that night. Not that that was how anyone else would have felt about it, but Nico knew me well enough to predict exactly how I would have felt.

He cared about me and wanted me, and I had walked away. I'd once accused Violetta of acting like a spoiled brat breaking her toys, and that was exactly what I had done. I had ruined everything because I was so caught up in my own drama and immaturity.

But I didn't know how to fix it. I couldn't just call him up and say, "Just kidding! Let's get married, 'kay?"

Because caring about me and wanting me was not the same as loving me. And despite what Lemon thought, despite what I wished for, he'd never said he loved me. He'd never said he wanted to marry me.

Caring about me was not enough. I couldn't be with a guy that I loved who only cared about me.

I was worth more than that.

A few days later, as I sat in a class designed to help parents be reunited with the children that had been taken from them, my phone rang. The number showed up as "Unknown." Only a few people had this number, and they were all in my contact list. I wondered who it was. I told the instructor I was shadowing that I'd be right back.

I stepped out in the hallway, about to click Accept when I noticed a little message under the "Unknown" that said the call was international.

It was Nico.

I knew it. I felt it. He was calling me.

A rapturous joy exploded inside me, quickly followed by an icy panic that gripped my heart. Why was Nico calling me? What did he want?

I stood there, frozen, unable to make a decision. Should I answer? What would it do to me to hear his voice? What would I say to him? So many things had changed since I last saw him. I'd figured out so much. I didn't blame him the way that I had.

My failure to act became my decision. The call flickered away, and my phone sent him to voice mail. I sat watching my phone, praying. *Please leave a voice mail. Please leave a voice mail.*

I almost shouted with glee when my phone dinged and the voice mail icon appeared at the top of the screen.

But then I was too scared to listen.

I put the phone back in my pocket and returned to the class. I didn't hear a single word said the rest of the hour.

Nico called me. Nico called me.

Nico called me.

I wondered how he'd got my number, and I knew Lemon was probably to blame. I finished up my other fieldwork for the day, drifting through the motions. I stood at my bus stop, willing the bus to arrive faster. Once the bus dropped me off, I ran to my apartment. I fumbled badly with my keys, but I finally got inside. I dropped my book bag, shook off my coat, and sat down on the couch. I called my voice mail and put it on speakerphone.

Nico's rich, warm tones came over the line. I smiled and my heart swelled. Until I realized what he had done.

The entire frakking message was in Italian. Italian! This could potentially be the most important voice mail of my entire life, and I didn't understand a single word of it.

I could call him back and ask him what he'd said. But I wasn't ready for that.

I could take this phone over to the Italian Club and they could translate it for me right away.

Or I could get on Google and hit up the translator.

I was worried that if he said anything remotely nice, I would have no shame and I'd put all my credit cards together to come up with enough money to jump on a plane and go back to him.

I reminded myself that there was no future there.

And if Nico had changed his mind, if he wanted a future, he knew where to find me.

Chapter 25

I was working on my thesis, getting it ready. Only one more month to go until I would present. I needed to make sure my PowerPoint presentation was running as smoothly as I wanted it to. Lemon was in her room working. She had been doing a lot of that lately, and it usually meant that she was doing stuff for Nico's family and she was considerate enough to keep me out of it.

I could hear her voice, and I got up and turned the television on so that I wouldn't wonder. Nico had never called me again, and I just couldn't call him. I didn't know what to say. And with every day that had followed in the next two months, I grew more and more despondent. He wasn't going to call me again. He had given up. I really had destroyed us.

I heard the words "On this season's *Marry Me*, this summer twenty-five single women will compete for one lucky bachelor. With one surprising and shocking twist . . . our bachelor is a real-life prince!"

I stood up and walked over to the TV. I had totally forgotten about that stupid reality show that Nico was supposed to be on. I sank onto the couch, watching previews of catty women fighting and sniping at one another. The show promised drama and romance. My heart sank as one beautiful woman after another appeared, all saying how much they loved him. He really would forget all   about   me.   The narrator explained what was coming up and how difficult the decision would be for the prince.

And then at the end, he said, "And introducing our newest bachelor, Prince Dante of Monterra."

I saw Dante's picture on the screen, and my mouth dropped. It was Dante. Dante was doing the show. Not Nico.

I started crying. Loud, ridiculous sobs that drew Lemon out of her room.

"What is it, darlin'?"

I pointed at the television, hiccupping loudly and unable to speak. But the advertisement had changed.

"You don't like adult diapers?" she asked.

I hiccupped/laughed. "No. Dante's doing *Marry Me*. Not Nico." I started crying again.

"Okay, just tell me this. On a scale of one to Adele, how bad is it?"

"Full-on Adele," I told her through my tears. "I miss him, Lemon. You were right. I love him. And I'm so relieved that he's not doing that stupid show that I can't stop crying."

"Dante said Nico's completely miserable. That he's never seen him like this about any girl. The whole family thinks he's in love with you."

"You talk to them about me?"

She nodded.

"Do you ever talk to Nico?" I asked the question tentatively, afraid of her answer.

"I don't, I'm sorry. He's avoiding me the same way you avoid talking about him. Personally, I think y'all are stupid and should just get together and work this out. Now stop crying and get back to work. The end of the semester will be here before you know it."

I went and sat back at the table, knowing my night was now shot. The thesis would have to wait until tomorrow.

My cell phone rang and it surprised me. No one called me at night except for Lemon, and she was in the next room.

I looked at the screen. "Unknown."

This time I eagerly clicked the acceptance button, my heart pounding wildly in my chest. "Hello?"

There was a long pause. "Kitty-Kat?"

It was the last voice I ever expected to hear. "Mom?"

"Yes, it's me."

How did she get this number? Why was she calling me?

"Are you there?"

"I'm still here." A rush of strong emotions fought within me. I wanted to hang up on her. I didn't owe her a thing. I didn't have to talk to her. She had done nothing but make my entire childhood miserable. But some morbid curiosity made me stay on the line.

She let out a big sigh. "I'm sorry for just calling out of the blue, and I know I can never make up for what I've done to you. But I wanted to let you know that I've been in rehab for the last three months, and I am now ninety-three days sober."

"That's great," I said, not sure why she was telling me.

"I'm part of a program that paid for all of my rehab, and they're renting an apartment for me to live in. Part of the reason I could never get clean was I kept being around the same people in the same place. But now I have a new place to live, and they've promised to help me get started in training as a hairdresser. I'm going to have a place to live and a job." She sounded genuinely happy and excited.

"That's great," I said again, not sure what else I should say. I worked with social workers every day. I knew the federal and local government programs and private funding inside and out. I had never heard of one that did what she was describing. It made me a little uneasy.

"I just wanted to let you know that I'm trying to get better. And maybe in a few months when I'm settled in Boulder, you can come visit me?"

There was so much hope in her voice that I couldn't just tell her no. "We'll see," I said. "I'm glad you're getting better."

An awkward silence started, and then she said, "Okay, well, I need to go. You can call me at this number if you ever want to talk."

"Okay," I said.

"Bye," she said and hung up.

I put my phone down on the kitchen table and noticed my hands were shaking. I couldn't believe that had just happened. I literally hadn't spoken to my mother in ten years. I hadn't even known whether or not she was alive. Not only was she alive, but she was happy. And she was off of drugs. The thing I had spent my whole childhood hoping and praying for.

The cynical part of me knew it was unlikely she'd stay that way, reminding me that I couldn't ignore the recidivism rate for addicts. The odds were that she would relapse and go right back to her old way of life. Most addicts had to go through rehab multiple times before they could get better. This was only her first time, as far as I knew.

But there, in the deepest part of me, was a small spark of hope.

It made me turn my laptop on and reconnect to the Wi-Fi. I usually kept off the Internet so that I wouldn't be tempted to look up pictures of Nico and his family. If he was dating Scarlett Johansson or Zoe Saldana, I didn't want to know about it.

Boulder was about forty minutes away by car. I didn't know how long it would take by bus. I logged on to my banking site to see if I would have enough money to make the bus ride over to her and still pay my bills.

My account came up, and it said my balance was over forty thousand dollars.

I sat there with my mouth open, like I was trying to catch flies with it. Had the bank screwed up? I'd heard about this happening to other people, the bank making errors and then taking the money back.

I clicked on my account link, and it brought me to my statement. I scanned through it and there was a deposit from Amazon. For thirty-eight thousand dollars.

That had to be wrong. It had to be. I opened a new browser and went to my Amazon author account. I'd never sold more than three books in a month. The number of books I would have to sell to make up this amount was astronomical.

There was no mistake. I had sold tens of thousands of books. I looked at the dates and opened yet another browser window. I had a suspicion and entered the title of my book, my pen name, and told Google to look for it.

Some images came up. It was Violetta, and it was Fashion Week in Paris. She looked wonderful, her eyes bright and alive. And in her lap was a hard copy of my book, *Once Upon a Time*. There were interviews of her talking about my book, praising it. The book was everywhere. Other celebrities and royals were pictured with it, title side out so that everyone could see. She'd made me that week's fashionable accessory.

Had Nico been behind this? The tears returned, and I picked up my phone, more tempted than ever to call him.

Instead I listened to his message again. I knew it by heart, as I listened to it at least three times a day.

I was ready to see pictures. I was ready to remember. I opened up the camera's gallery and realized that Serafina had stolen the phone again after the snow polo match. There was one of Nico and me laughing. One of us kissing. Another of us at dinner, and him looking at me like he loved me.

I ran into my bedroom and opened my closet. I pulled my necklace off the shelf, putting it around my neck. Once I had clasped it closed, I adjusted the pendant and wrapped my hand around it. I put the Barbie on top of my dresser, where I could see it every day.

I had to fix this. After my thesis was done and presented and defended, I would take some of my book money and go back to Monterra and find a way to fix this. Even if we only ended up friends, and regardless of what I'd said to him in Milan, I didn't want him to stay away from me.

I needed him. I loved him. He had to be in my life in some way.

I focused all of my energy on making sure my thesis was flawless. I practiced my presentation over and over again. I figured the best way to keep myself from being nervous was to be well prepared. I made up my own mock questions, trying to anticipate what the committee might ask. Lemon would quiz me, and I quizzed her as well. I just had to not think about her content as it all related to Nico's family.

My countdown now was not just to finishing my thesis and graduating, but getting to see Nico. He became my reward, my incentive to work my hardest so that I could be with him again.

Two days before my presentation, Lemon and I went clothes shopping. I wanted to spend all of the time I had left preparing, but she convinced me that I needed something professional to wear. I would need a whole new professional wardrobe when I started my job. Fortunately, I now had the money to do something about it.

I did kick myself for leaving those dresses in Monterra. One of them would have worked perfectly for the presentation.

We picked up some pantsuits, skirts, and dresses, along with matching shoes. I even picked out some pretty underwear to give me that extra boost of confidence.

The morning finally arrived, and I sat outside the committee's room, trying to breathe normally. This was it. Everything rested on the next one to two hours.

My advisor, Professor Stevenson, came to the door and invited me in. Her smile was bright against her beautiful mahogany-colored skin. "Remember to stay calm. We're just going to have a conversation. This is a formality."

I nodded. I could do this. I tried to shake off my anxious nerves. It helped that I had probably overprepared. I presented flawlessly and didn't make a single mistake. I answered every question succinctly and knew what I was talking about. After an hour and a half, the committee asked me to step outside.

A few minutes later, Professor Stevenson stuck her head out of the door. She looked serious for a moment, and my stomach dropped down to my feet. Then she smiled. "You defended it successfully."

I ran up to her and hugged her, laughing as I jumped up and down. So unprofessional, but I was too excited.

"Go home and celebrate," she told me. "You've earned it."

This was it. Now I could make plans to see Nico. I had to make a quick stop at the Graduate Studies Office to pick up my graduation packet. It was really going to happen. I would graduate and have everything I ever wanted.

Including, possibly, Nico.

Should I surprise him? I could call Giacomo. I bet Lemon could get me his number. Giacomo would tell me what Nico's schedule was and where I could see him. He'd probably even help me arrange the whole thing.

Or should I just call Nico and explain and then make plans together?

The possibilities seemed fun and endless. I tried to imagine the look on his face when I walked through his door.

I imagined it might be just like mine when I walked into my apartment and found Nico sitting in one of our armchairs.

Chapter 26

I just stood there, blinking repeatedly. Was this real? I was about to walk over and touch him, just to make sure I wasn't hallucinating.

"Did you pass? Did your thesis presentation go well?"

I nearly collapsed to the floor. He was real. I had missed him so much I worried I might actually pass out.

"Yes," I finally managed to speak. He was wearing another suit, and I wondered if he was hot. We didn't have air-conditioning, and while the mornings were still cool, the afternoons had started to have a bit of heat to them.

A million questions ran through my mind. What was he doing here? When did he get here? How did he know about my thesis?

"Can I, uh, get you something?" I didn't know what else to say. "We have, uh, milk, I think. Possibly water."

I was losing my mind.

Nico got up and walked into our tiny kitchen. He opened the fridge and then the freezer. He turned to smile at me. "Gelato?"

I nodded again.

"Perhaps I should get you something. You look like you need a stiff drink."

I needed something. Maybe I was in shock. He might need to take me to the hospital.

Nico grabbed a bottle of water and came over to hand it to me. I noticed he was careful not to touch me. He stepped closer to me and I thought he might kiss me or hug me. I looked up at him in anticipation, hoping.

But he reached his arm over my shoulder to close the door behind me. The door I had left open when I saw him.

He returned to his armchair, and I followed behind him, sitting on my couch. Just staring at him. Frak, he was more beautiful than I'd remembered. How had I been so mean to him? How had I walked away?

"You're wearing my necklace." He sounded hopeful, and my hand flew to the pendant, just as it did a million times a day. I nodded.

He wasn't here to talk about jewelry. And if he wouldn't say why, then I would just have to find out.

"I have some questions for you," I said. I thought maybe I should wait for him to talk and explain himself, but he seemed content to just sit in that chair and look at me.

"Twenty?"

I could hear the smile in his voice. Things had to be okay if he could tease me. "Maybe not twenty, but I need you to answer them honestly."

"All right."

"How did you know about my thesis?"

"Lemon."

I should have known. I put the water bottle on the table. My mouth was dry and my pulse frantic, but water was not going to help.

"Did you fund my scholarship?"

"Yes."

"Did you pay for my mom go to rehab?"

"Yes."

"And get her a new place to live?"

"Yes."

"Did you tell Violetta to carry around my book and talk about it?"

He shifted in the chair, putting his left ankle on top of his right knee. "That was all Violetta's idea. She wanted to thank you for what you had done, and came up with that plan on her own."

"Did you make Dante go on *Marry Me* instead of you?"

"I didn't have to push him hard, but yes."

"Why?"

He looked at me incredulously. "Do you really not know?"

"I wouldn't be asking if I did."

He didn't respond. My heart was practically bursting at the sight of him, desperate for him to say why he was there and how he felt, and he wanted to keep playing this game. That irritated me.

"Well, you need to stop doing that kind of stuff for me."

"No."

No? "Why not?"

"Because I need to know that you are safe and happy. Now it's my turn."

I wasn't sure I wanted to answer the questions Nico might ask. But I just nodded.

"Why did you leave the money?"

"I didn't want it. It didn't feel right."

"Why?"

I considered Lemon's explanation. But instead I said, "I can't explain it. I just couldn't take it."

"Did you think about me at all while we were apart?"

Tears welled up in the corners of my eyes. My throat was thick as I answered, "Every day. Every minute of every day."

He stood up then, looking angry. "Why didn't you answer my message? I waited and waited for you to call back. You know how impatient I am, and I have tried so hard to give you all the space and time you needed, but you just ignored me. For three months, you've ignored me."

"I didn't ignore you. I didn't understand what you had said. The message is in Italian." I took my phone out and played it for him on speakerphone. Nico started firing off a response that I didn't understand.

"You're doing it again. Talking in Italian."

He ran both of his hands through his hair. He looked frustrated. "I tend to do that sometimes when I'm feeling emotional."

Emotional? My heart skipped a beat. If that kept happening, being near him was going to be the death of me.

"Do you want to know what my message said?"

I nodded, and fluttery butterflies started going kamikaze in my stomach.

"I said that I missed you. That I needed you to know how I felt. That I loved you. I do love you. I am in love with you. I told you that I wanted to spend the rest of my life with you. Do you know what it's like to leave a message like that and get no response?" He sounded mad.

I had turned into a statue, just blinking at him. "You love me?" I whispered.

"Of course I love you. And you love me, right?" There was a heartbreaking mixture of hope and vulnerability on his face that turned my insides to mush.

I stood up and walked over to him. His words had given me strength. I made sure he was looking me in the eyes. "I love you so much. I love you more than words. There is no way to express to you just how much I love you."

Then he hugged me, wrapping his arms around me and holding me tightly, like he would never let me go. I threw my arms around his neck, so grateful and glad to be with him again.

"Why didn't you tell me?" He murmured the words into my hair.

"Why didn't you tell me?" I countered. "Everyone knows the man is supposed to say it first."

He pulled his head back to look at me. "Says who?"

I rolled my eyes. "Everybody in the whole world! Have you never watched a romantic movie?"

"I didn't tell you because I was worried about scaring you off. You were so vulnerable and innocent that I was afraid if I told you how I was feeling, you would run away from me." He let out a short laugh. "Look how well that turned out. You ran away anyway. And if I'd told you my true feelings, I never could have kept a distance between us so that I could respect you the way you deserve to be respected." He reached up and brushed some stray hair from the side of my face. "From the moment we met I knew I would fall in love with you."

He placed a soft kiss on the side of my temple, and I sighed with pleasure. My Nico was back. "At the airport, I was so angry. I felt like I was in this alone. That I had fallen in love with you, but you said it wasn't real. I thought you saw me as some plaything to pass the time. That wasn't the first time a woman had treated me that way. I let you go when I shouldn't have. I should have told you. I should have fought for you."

Nico carefully set me down. "So I am going to fight for you now. I know this isn't the perfect moment, but I can't wait any longer."

He pulled a blue velvet box out of his pocket. He got down on one knee, and my heart stopped. Like, actually stopped. I couldn't breathe.

"I've let the situation with my father affect me too much. I let it affect my decisions and what I wanted out of life. I was afraid that if I became king, he wouldn't have a reason to go on. But he and I had a long conversation about that, and I realized that I had to stop being afraid. My life is not easy. I am always busy, always traveling. I have so many responsibilities, and it will only get worse."

"This is a terrible sales pitch," I told him. He nodded.

"I know it isn't fair for me to ask, because you deserve a husband who will always be with you, treating you like the queen that you are. But I have to ask you. Katerina MacTaggart, will you do me the honor of becoming my wife?"

He held the box out to me.

"What's in there?"

He looked confused. "You know exactly what's in there."

"A board game?"

He finally smiled. "No."

"Legos?"

"Not Legos. Look."

He opened it for me, which was good because my hands were shaking so hard there was no way I could have managed it.

Inside was a diamond ring with a gem so big it looked like it had to be fake. But I knew it wasn't. It was an enormous pear cut, surrounded by smaller red rubies that I realized were in the shape of hearts. Which was appropriate, since I was his *cuore mio*. He knelt there, waiting for an answer. Which seemed silly, because what other answer could there be than yes a million times over?

It would mean that I would be queen. I didn't know how to be queen. I knew though that there would be people there to help me every step of the way. People who loved me.

People like Nico.

I couldn't imagine anything better.

"Yes, Your Royal Highness, Prince Dominic of Monterra. I will marry you."

Nico gave me a beautiful grin that made me happier than I could have imagined. He put the ring on me and picked me up, swinging me around in a circle.

He kissed me over and over again, kisses full of joy, excitement, and promises. It made me light-headed.

He set me down and glanced at the bedrooms. "Is an engagement close enough?" he teased as he nuzzled my neck.

I smacked him on the shoulder. "Engaged is not married, mister."

Good thing I'd shut that down, because a second later Lemon came out of her room. That could have been awkward. "Praise the Lord! Finally! Let me see that ring."

I held it out to her, and she let out an appreciative whistle. "I am happier than a calico cat with a bowl full of cream. It is about time y'all worked this out." She hugged me, telling me congratulations. Then she did the same with Nico.

"You'll be my maid of honor, right?"

"Obviously. I'm just trying to figure out how to best tell the world. A press release? No, not enough impact. Morning talk shows? No, we'll go the Alex and Caitlin route. We'll choose one reporter to interview you from the palace. Make it highly exclusive, so that the entire world will be dying to hear more. Love that . . ." She had stopped talking to us a while back.

"Just as long as it's not that Seamus O'Brien," I called after her.

"No paparazzi," she agreed. "Someone substantial. Okay, I have to go make some calls. You two kids have fun. But not too much fun. At least, not before the wedding."

She went into her room and closed the door.

"Feel like celebrating?" Nico asked me.

I really, really did.

We went out the front of the apartment, and on the street just outside there was a row of black SUVs. I saw Lorenz getting out of one of the cars, and Giacomo was right behind him. But before I could say anything, Serafina burst out of another car and came hurtling at me.

She threw herself into my arms. "I'm so excited that you're going to be my sister and I will get to see you every day!"

"How do you know I said yes?" I teased her. "I might have said no."

She gave me a very serious Fiorelli look. "Nobody says no to Nico."

"Ha," I told her. "Shows what you know. I've said no to him plenty of times."

He leaned in and whispered against my skin, making my stomach tighten. "But you won't for much longer."

I hugged Serafina and looked at him. "Is your entire family here?"

"Yes, even my father."

"Your father came?" I was so touched that his father would make this journey. I knew it couldn't have been easy on him.

"Of course he did. You're going to be his daughter. Part of our family forever."

I couldn't believe how wonderful that sounded. My whole life I had wanted a happy family, with parents and brothers and sisters. In addition to already being the best possible future husband in the entire world, without even knowing it, he was making all of my deepest wishes come true.

Violetta came over next and hugged me. "I'm so sorry for how I treated you. I'm very grateful for your help. You were right. I couldn't do it on my own. Thank you for helping me get my life and my family back."

I hugged her in return, which was awkward with Serafina still in my arms.

Chiara was behind her with a massive notebook. She gave me a quick, one-armed hug. "I brought you a bunch of wedding dress material samples. We will have to use a Monterran designer, of course."

I laughed. "We have plenty of time for that, I'm sure."

Next were Dante and Rafe. "Well?" Dante asked. "What did she say?"

"Yes, obviously," was Nico's reply.

Dante crowed and held out his hand. "Fifty euros, please." Grumbling, Rafe took out his wallet and handed him the money. For some reason that made me laugh again. Like I was so full of joy that my soul was looking for every opportunity to let it out.

"It's a good thing I didn't say no. You would have been super embarrassed."

Nico kissed me on my cheek. "I knew you would say yes. That you loved me too."

"You are so cocky," I said, nudging him.

"Not cocky," he corrected me with another kiss. "Just sure of you."

We went over to the car where his parents were. The queen kissed me on both cheeks and told me how happy she would be to have another daughter, and the king smiled at me from his seat and said he was glad Nico had finally come to his senses. That he thought I would make an excellent addition to their family.

I then hugged a bewildered Giacomo, who wished me "much happiness in your future endeavors." Lorenz just gave me a look, so I refrained.

Nico showed me to our car, and all of his siblings insisted on riding with us. There was no room, so I had to sit on Nico's lap. Which neither one of us minded, at all.

"So, do you have any attractive friends you want to introduce us to?" Rafe asked. "I mean, as long as we're here."

I laughed again.

"Chiara was right, you know," Nico whispered against my skin. "We need to start planning our wedding right away. I'm particularly interested in the honeymoon part. I thought we could go skiing."

"That's not funny," I said, as he cracked himself up. "If you don't take me to some tropical beach, this will not end well for you."

"It won't matter where we go," he said as he kissed me. "I don't intend to let you out of the hotel room."

I giggled and wrapped my arms around him, holding him. I could only sit there and smile. There was no other way for me to express how happy I felt in that moment.

"What are you thinking?" Nico asked, as he rubbed his thumb across the top of my hand.

I looked at him, feeling like joy was coming out of every pore. "I was just thinking that sometimes fairy tales really do come true."

Epilogue

All I had to do was remember the right order of his names. This was being televised. I couldn't mess it up.

Even Lemon had been surprised by the media frenzy at the announcement of our engagement. Turned out everyone loved a real-life Cinderella story. The American public had been the most excited, because I was one of them. A normal girl from a poor family. And I was marrying a prince.

Tourism had already increased by 400 percent in the last six months in Monterra. Lemon told me we'd have to have a honeymoon baby to keep those tourism numbers up. I didn't tell her that Nico and I had every intention of having a baby as soon as we could. That was between the two of us.

Lemon wore a fitted red bridesmaid dress, and she was trying not to crush my huge, puffy skirt. We were on our way in a horse-drawn carriage that was layered in gold leaf. Against the snow, it looked amazing. Serafina, Chiara, and Violetta had more age-appropriate dresses that matched Lemon's and sat across from me on the opposite bench. They waved like true princesses to the crowds who cheered at us along our route.

I had insisted on a Christmas wedding. First, because I had always dreamed of a Christmas wedding ever since I was little, and second, because I wanted time to make sure that we were making the right decision and that we really did want to be married. It also gave me enough time to help plan this wedding. The queen had taken over most of the planning, because it was like organizing a military operation.

It had been easier to give up my job and apartment than I thought it would be. I had moved into the palace and had spent the last few months getting lessons in deportment, protocol, and Italian. I had dossiers on important world leaders so that I would never again make a mistake like I had with the ambassador in Paris. There were more lessons in style, makeup, and doing my own hair. I studied constantly. Giacomo was as demanding as any of my college professors had been. I also started working with the lawyers to set up the bylaws for my charitable foundation. I planned to provide funding to government agencies so that they could hire more social workers (as I knew from personal experience they were always stretched too thin and needed more help), provide more training for social workers and foster parents, and I wanted to guarantee that every foster child in the world had at least one toy. Lemon had been right. I was going to help a lot more people as Nico's wife than I ever would have on my own in Colorado. But one of the best parts of being in Monterra these last few months? Every night, whether or not Nico was in town, there had been a tray with moonflowers and gelato outside my door.

Nico hadn't wanted the wedding to be so far out because he worried about our ability to last that long without crossing any lines. It wasn't easy to wait, but we managed. I kept my promise and had retained my unicorn status. Thankfully, we wouldn't have to wait much longer.

We got to the church, and I waved to all the people who were cheering across the street.

The king waited outside the church for me, as he was going to escort me down the aisle. The girls climbed out first, and when I got out, the cheering increased. Lemon handed me my bouquet. I had insisted that the main flower be moonflowers. The florist apparently had a not fun time of gluing the petals to wire to make sure they stayed opened, but I couldn't have anything else. Red roses were woven in between what had become my favorite flower.

I waved again to the crowd, while Giacomo fluttered around me, making sure my dress was perfect. He straightened my veil in the back. I had a long train, which Lemon held for me.

I had asked the Monterran designer to mimic the dress I had worn in Paris. The white satin had an overlay of lace with sparkling Swarovski crystals, so that I looked like I was wearing snow. It was long-sleeved so that I wouldn't freeze. I had insisted on a red velvet sash at my waist, tied in a big bow in the back. I wanted it to match Nico's pendant. The queen had taken me into her vault and invited me to help myself to her jewelry for the wedding, but I wanted to wear something that had meaning to me. This morning Nico had sent over a package with matching earrings and a tiara. He had also bought matching earrings for each of my bridesmaids. I had never felt more beautiful.

I put my hand on his father's wheelchair, and we slowly entered the massive cathedral. A choir sang as I walked down the aisle. I saw so many people I knew and loved. Caitlin waved to me as I passed, and I smiled at her. I noticed she was pregnant again.

My mother sat near Caitlin, but closer to the front. She blew me a kiss. Things weren't necessarily great between us yet, but we had been working on our relationship, and I knew that I couldn't get married without her there. Lemon's parents, Sue Ellen and Montgomery, were there as well, pointing their cell phones at us. I saw the friends I had invited from my graduate program, along with Professor Stevenson, and I got more smiles and waves.

Queen Aria sat in the very front row, and she was crying happy tears. It got me choked up and I had to look away so that I wouldn't ruin all my eye makeup.

Then I saw Nico, and only Nico. He wore a military dress uniform, a bright red coat with black pants and a gold sash. I knew Alex was his best man, and Dante and Rafe his groomsmen. But I didn't notice any of them.

My heart lifted at the sight of him. He was about to become my husband.

As long as I could remember the correct order of his names.

I walked up the steps to stand next to him. "You are so beautiful it hurts to look at you," he told me.

A warm glow encased my heart. "I know the feeling," I whispered back.

"I'm glad you showed up," Nico said with a smile.

"Well, I already had the dress on, so I decided, why not?"

I could tell that delighted him and he wanted to kiss me, but he refrained.

The ceremony was long, and in Italian, English, and Latin. We had practiced the ceremony, so I knew when I was supposed to kneel and what I was supposed to say.

Then it was over. We had made our vows, I had said his name right, and we were married.

Married!

Nico kissed me in front of the whole crowd, and last night I had told him not to be embarrassing as I would have to see all these people again. He kept himself in check, but I knew he was tempted to lean me backward and make a scene.

The priest introduced us as Their Royal Highnesses, Prince Dominic and Princess Katerina of Monterra. I had the title of princess since he was the heir and the crown prince. Soon it would be queen. Queen Katerina. The coronation was scheduled to happen in a few months. Lemon expected there to be crowds of tourists for that as well.

When we exited the cathedral, the crowd went insane. There was a limo waiting for us, and we waved to everyone before getting in.

"Be careful not to crush her skirt," Giacomo told Nico as we climbed in.

We sat together, holding hands, grinning.

"Hello, wife."

"Hello, husband."

He kissed me and I warned him not to mess up my makeup, but he didn't care. And soon neither did I. I could always fix it later.

His kisses were full of love and promises for what would happen later that evening.

It was slow going to the palace, and I was glad the windows were tinted so that the whole world didn't catch me making out with my new husband.

As soon as we arrived at the castle, Nico practically jumped out of the car and picked me up in his arms, surprising me. I laughed as he carried me up the steps and through the open door. He was skipping steps, practically running.

"What are you doing?"

"Hush, wife. I'm carrying you across the threshold."

"What's the rush?" I asked him.

"We have to go out on the main balcony and greet the public. Then we have a dinner and reception to get through. The faster we do that, the faster I will have you all to myself."

"Hmm. What if I turn out to be really bad at it?"

He gave me a quick kiss. "*Impossibilie*. And even if it were possible, I am an excellent teacher."

I didn't doubt it. That made my pulse quicken and my stomach throb. A year ago I would have been terrified at the idea of being intimate with a man. But thanks to the counseling and Nico's love and patience, I had healed. I was ready. I was more than ready. I was looking forward to it just as much as he was.

He put me down so that we could quickly climb the stairs. I could barely keep up in my stupid shoes, and I just kept laughing.

Giacomo was waiting outside the balcony doors, talking on a headset. "Not quite yet, Your Highness."

Nico groaned and looked so frustrated that I laughed again. "I suppose I might as well make use of the time. I have a wedding gift for you."

He pulled out an envelope from inside his pants pocket. I opened it, curious. Inside there was a check for one million euros to the Queen's Charity for Children. "The funding for your children's charity. You will help every child that you want to help."

"Thank you," I said. I kissed him hard, not knowing it was possible to love him even more with each passing minute. He put his arm around my waist, kissing me with everything he had, and we only broke apart because Giacomo cleared his throat.

"I got you a wedding present too. I don't have it with me, but I bought you a bunch of rock climbing equipment so you could start climbing again. I know your mom doesn't want you to take unnecessary risks, but I think we just took the biggest risk of all. What's a little rock climbing?"

"*Grazie, cuore mio*," he said. He smiled and looked like he was going to go in for another kiss, but I put a hand on his chest. I had just heard the crowd, and it gave me an anxious feeling.

I was really doing this. I had really married him, and I was really a princess. I had a wave of insecurity.

"This is kind of overwhelming," I told him.

"We'll get through this. You will always have me by your side to face every obstacle in your way."

"Promise?" I knew he would, but I liked hearing it.

"In case you were distracted, I just made some very serious vows back there, promising just that."

"Speaking of which, I am so not obeying you."

He laughed and planted a kiss on the tip of my nose. "I didn't expect you would."

Giacomo looked at us. "Security has made sure the courtyard is safe. You may now go out onto the balcony."

"Ready to see your people, Princess?"

"Only if we're together."

"Always together."

He kissed the back of my hand as the doors swung open. This time I didn't mind him kissing my hand. The roar of the crowd was deafening as we smiled and waved, and walked out onto the balcony, hand in hand, in our first official appearance as a royal couple.

A royal couple who had every intention of living very, very happily ever after.

As always, I am so grateful that you chose to spend your time in a world I created. I hope you loved Nico and Kat just as much as I do.

Want to hear about upcoming releases? (I think Dante and Lemon deserve their own story, don't you?) Be sure to sign up for my mailing list on my website:

www.sariahwilson.com

You can also like me on Facebook or read a few scattered posts from me on Twitter:

www.facebook.com/sariahwilsonauthor

www.twitter.com/sariahwilson

And if you enjoyed this book, I would be totally and completely grateful if you would leave me a review on sites like Amazon and Goodreads.

Thanks again!

Acknowledgments

First off, a big thank you to everyone who nominated this book in Amazon's Kindle Scout program and helped me get to this point. I so appreciate every last one of you!

Thank you to Amazon and Kindle Press for selecting my book to share with the world. Thank you to Scarlett Rugers for her amazing cover and Julie Coulter Bellon for her help with the book description. Thank you to Ric Peeler for sharing his knowledge about skiing, and special thanks to Lisa Ladle for helping me put in all those Italian words.

I also need to thank my beta readers who encouraged me and helped make the story even better: Charity Byrd, Nancy Michelsen, Scarlet Bushman, Candace Wilson, Sherise Robertson, Kris Anderson, Kathryn Olivier, and Nicole Cooper.

Love and gratitude to my children, who sometimes do their best to derail this whole writing thing, and to my husband Kevin (who formatted this book for print), for being my biggest supporter, for always believing in me, and for showing me the meaning of true love.

About the Author

Sariah Wilson has never jumped out of an airplane, never climbed Mount Everest, and is not a former CIA operative. She has, however, been madly, passionately in love with her soulmate and is a fervent believer in happily-ever-afters—which is why she writes romance. *Royal Date* is her fifth happily-ever-after novel. She grew up in Southern California, graduated from Brigham Young University (go Cougars!) with a semi-useless degree in history, and is the oldest of nine (yes, nine) children. She currently lives with the aforementioned soulmate and their four children in Utah, along with three tiger barb fish, a cat named Tiger, and a recently departed hamster that is buried in the backyard (and has nothing at all to do with tigers).

Her website is www.sariahwilson.com.

Made in the USA
Middletown, DE
18 February 2023

25174452R00154